Rogers spoke again into the silence. "Suppose Khruchenko tells us who or what Parsley is. What are you going to do about it?"

"Nothing. I just want to know."

"Just another puzzle to be solved?"

"Yes. I'm tired of the game, too." Sloane glanced at the shadowy form of the only real friend he had made in his life. "It'll be all right. We've taken every precaution."

"I know."

And they had.

ROBERT A. LISTON

A TOM DOHERTY ASSOCIATES BOOK

To my son Stephen

This is a work of fiction. All the characters and events portrayed in this book are fictional, and any resemblance to real people or incidents is purely coincidental.

THE BRANDYWINE EXCHANGE

Copyright © 1987 by Robert A. Liston

All rights reserved, including the right to reproduce this book or portions thereof in any form.

First printing: June 1987

A TOR BOOK

Published by Tom Doherty Associates, Inc.
49 West 24 Street
New York, N.Y. 10010

ISBN: 0-812-50614-6
CAN. ED.: 0-812-50615-4

PRINTED IN THE UNITED STATES OF AMERICA

0 9 8 7 6 5 4 3 2 1

Acknowledgments

This is a work of fiction, although actual places have been used for locales. In particular there is a Brandywine, Maryland. As far as I know it contains no underground facility such as I describe.

I would like to thank Mrs. Susan Crosby Taliaferro of Baltimore, Maryland. She is peerless at finding solutions to medical problems created by authors. Appreciation goes to Capt. Fred W. Eichinger of the Shelby, Ohio, Police Department, who shared arcane knowledge of weapons. Howard H. Knapp, also of Shelby, "took me to the cleaners," and I thank him. Others who provided information were Mrs. Eleanor R. Seagraves of Washington, D.C., and Mr. David O. Strickland of New York City. My wife, Jean, was as always my best critic, as well as long-suffering with my floor pacing. My daughter, Felicia, helped with the manuscript.

I would like to express a special debt to those persons who provided information about intelligence agencies.

R.A.L.
Shelby, Ohio

ONE

They were supposed to bring him in. Yuri Khruchenko was the highest-ranking official of the Soviet KGB to defect in years. He was to be taken to Washington, where Brandywine would bleed him dry of everything he knew.

They had other ideas. They would ask him a few pointed questions, just to settle an old score. Regardless of what answers he gave, they would kill him. Couldn't be helped. He interfered with their plans.

The vehicle turned off US 5 near the intersection with US 301, then went left on Maryland 381. It slowed for traffic in the village of Brandywine, turned into a small shopping center, and finally pulled into a parking space.

This happened every weekday and frequently on weekends, as now. No one paid any attention. The car was a six-year-old Plymouth Horizon, dark blue in color, with a dented fender on the right front. Unwashed and in need of a tune-up, the two-door was as nondescript as the man who alighted from it. He was middle-aged with a slight paunch, had mouse-colored hair, lackluster eyes, and a straight, rather lipless mouth. He wore a lumpy suit appropriate for the summer season, striped seersucker, gray and white in color. There was nothing noteworthy about him, and that was by careful design.

His name was W. Gordon Adams. The *W* stood for Willis, which he hated. He lived quietly in the Georgetown section of Washington in what he thought of as semibachelorhood. His wife, his second, had a career of her own and seemed almost grateful for his absences. She neither demanded nor offered much to matrimony, but she was good in bed and was an occasional diversion, which he needed. He had been happier in his first marriage, but the demands of his job had killed that. He had a son and daughter, both grown now, but he seldom saw them. They considered their father pleasant enough, but something of a workaholic and, frankly, dull, a typical bureaucrat. He spoke little of his work and although his children believed they knew what he did, they truly did not.

Adams was surely laconic about his job. On the rare occasion, perhaps at a social gathering, when someone asked him what he did, he'd reply, "Government." If someone pursued the matter, he would say, "Pentagon." If bad luck prevailed and he was pressed by someone knowledgeable about the Pentagon, he'd add, "Office of Naval Procurement." That was true and could be checked. Naval Procurement did list him as an employee and paid his salary.

In actuality he was an extremely high-ranking official of the Central Security Agency, head of one of the five intelligence zones into which it divides the world, and thus a member of The Committee. He was therefore one of five men who controlled all the overt and covert intelligence operations of the United States government worldwide.

Adams now strode past the storefronts of the shopping center and entered a one-story brick office building which somewhat resembled a post office. It contained offices for lawyers, accountants, a couple of corporations and minor government agencies—all covers. Inside the front door a man sat at a small reception desk. He wore a Pinkerton uniform. He was a US Marine and armed.

Adams approached him. "Good morning. I have an appointment with Mr. Raybolt."

The Marine glanced at a small device on his desk, watching a green light wink on. It was a voice scanner, and the light signaled that Adams had been recognized. Any unauthorized voice would result in a red light, and the visitor would be turned away. If the person had the misfortune to ask for the nonexistent Mr. Raybolt, he would be followed, investigated and considered a security risk for the rest of his life.

The Marine acknowledged Adams, saying he was expected, then pushed a button, which unlocked an interior door with a buzzing sound. Adams turned right down a hallway, stopping before a heavy, unmarked door, which he unlocked with a key. He entered a small room outfitted as an office. A Marine dressed in civilian clothes sat at a desk. He was there in the unlikely event an unauthorized person entered the room. No one ever had, and Adams considered the Marine to have extremely dull duty.

A second voice print was approved and Adams crossed to his right and used a red card bearing a magnetic imprint to open still another door. This took him into a small storeroom. There were shelves containing reams of paper and other office supplies. He reached under a shelf and slid back a panel to reveal an array of buttons, four of which he pushed, a numerical code. Then he stood patiently as the storeroom became an elevator carrying him two hundred feet underground.

Thus did Adams enter the most secret facility

operated by the Central Security Agency. It was its nerve center, hub of its worldwide communications network, huge, unknown to all but those who worked there. Its banks of computers decoded and stored the most sensitive information. It was from the underground facility at Brandywine, not the visible CSA headquarters at Fort Belvoir, that the agency's top leadership worked.

If the truth were known, Adams hated the place. He was slightly claustrophobic and felt uncomfortable underground. He disliked the pasty pallor of his complexion and longed for the sight of sun, grass, and trees. There was a sterility that bothered him, an absence of background noises and of odors as the air was constantly replaced. The gentle hum of computers and the rattle of teletypes would simply never replace the sounds of the real world, rustling wind, traffic noises, and human voices.

He approached a desk manned by a Marine, passed his hands over a fingerprint analyzer, then accepted a columned ledger to write down his code name and time of arrival. Then, using his red card and pressing buttons on a series of cypher locks, he passed through other detection devices and unlocked doors, finally reaching his office. He conferred briefly with assistants about recent developments, then settled down at his desk to read the overnight messages. Most had been decoded for him, but a few had not, for they were in a code known only to him. These he decoded and pondered, for they dealt with the most sensitive matters throughout the European zone.

In a moment he muttered, "Damn!" He prided himself on not using vulgarity, and this was about as serious an expletive as he could utter. They were not using a safe house in Munich to bring Khruchenko in, but a place of their own choosing, known only to themselves. Free-lancing again. There were procedures, accepted practices to be followed, but these two men would not consider them. "Damn 'em!" They were virtually out of control, and he was powerless to do anything about it. They made him feel like a eunuch.

He sat back in his swivel chair and deliberately reined in his annoyance. He shouldn't have sent them on this Khruchenko thing. They were tired, burned out, embittered, and dangerously knowledgeable about Agency activities. My God, they had somehow survived three years as field operatives, the most dangerous and difficult undercover work the Agency could ask of any person. Everyone they started with was dead. They should be retired—and he intended to see to it. But he had to use them this one last time. Khruchenko would surrender only to these two. It was part of his deal. But wasn't it a simple assignment? Just take Khruchenko and bring him in.

Adams sighed. These two men had become a law unto themselves. They trusted no one. They used their own methods. They had even developed their own code for withholding and transmitting information between themselves. It was a one-time pad and none of the Brandywine computers had been able to break it. Damn 'em! He could only hope they didn't realize how important Khruchenko was. If there was indeed a Soviet mole in the CSA, Khruchenko was the man most likely to identify him. If these two agents loused him up and failed to bring Khruchenko in, he would kill them himself—happily.

At birth they were David Stuart Pritchard and Harry Lamont Brown, but those persons had been declared "missing in action" and no longer existed. Their largely fraudulent US Navy files listed them as Lts. David L. Sloane and Harry NMI Rogers. Those were the names they most frequently went by, although in the last three years they had used scores of aliases. In the CSA they were known by their code names, Wolf and Bear, predators both.

In the deepening dusk of a Saturday evening in late May, they approached a dry-cleaning shop on Wernerstrasse, a busy but unfashionable middle class street a couple of kilometers from downtown Munich. They had selected the shop because it was at the bottom of a curve in Wernerstrasse, and its front windows offered a clear view of the street in both directions. It also offered ample escape routes, a sliding door opening to a loading dock at the rear of the building and a side door reached by a narrow walkway. They passed down this, picked the door lock and entered.

Sloane and Rogers had survived three years in the field by leaving nothing to chance. They now began a methodical inspection of the premises. It was extremely unlikely the place was bugged, but they checked it anyway, with Sloane carrying a small transistor radio. No squeal or hiss anywhere on the dial. They made their way to the front. Still no bug. Sloane turned off the radio and inserted it in the right pocket of his blue windbreaker.

There were two large windows fronting on the street with a glass door in the middle. This they now unlocked. A half dozen feet behind the door and centered in the lobby was a low counter, four feet wide, perhaps twice as long. It bore a cash register and phone. Beside it was a hook for hanging garments picked up by customers. A red neon light in the window cast an eerie glow over the space. Good. They would be able to see but not be seen.

To the right of the lobby, behind a partition, was a small office with desk, chair, filing cabinet and two-seat plastic couch. There was no door. Rogers stepped behind the partition and checked the line of sight, even making the motions of a pistol with his pointed finger and thumb. He nodded to Sloane.

Behind the counter was a wall that shielded the rear of the building from view. In the center behind the cash register was a doorless opening, but it was obstructed by the end of the long, oval conveyor on which the newly cleaned, pressed, and bagged garments were hung. Sloane reached up and pressed a switch, making the conveyor move a few feet. The shop did a nice business and the conveyor was full. Good.

Entry to the rear was gained by pushing past the conveyor. This Sloane and Rogers now did. It was a generous space but very cluttered with the conveyor, portable racks for hanging clothes, and many wheeled hampers. There were a half dozen setups for pressing, each with a steam table, ironing board, steam finisher, and Suzie, a form for blocking and pressing dresses.

Sloane was intrigued. "I worked in a dry-cleaning shop before I joined the Navy. This guy has a nice setup."

"What's that smell? I don't like it."

"Cleaning solvent, perchloroethylene. Won't hurt you." He looked upward. Hanging from the ceiling were a great many long dresses and drapes. "Look at that. The hausfraus of Munich are either going to dances or doing spring cleaning—or both. This guy is prosperous."

"How do they get the stuff up there?"

"It's called a pleater. Gowns, drapes, stuff too long to fit on the conveyor are put up there to let the pleats hang out."

"I still don't know how they get the stuff up there."

"Easy. See that rope? It's attached to the wall." He went to the side and unhooked one of the ropes, slowly lowering the loaded pleater. "Works like a Venetian blind. Release the rope and the whole thing comes down." He raised the pleater again and hooked it.

"Okay, I already know more about dry cleaning than I want to." Rogers was tense, on guard, impatient. He strode toward the back and turned to check the line of sight from the street. Good. They couldn't be seen from here, either. He went to the rear, unlocked the sliding door, opened it. It moved easily with a rumbling, metallic sound. Not too loud. He stepped out onto the loading dock. An alley wide enough for a medium-sized delivery truck bisected the whole block. The walkway beside the building continued across the alley, leading to the street behind. He looked down. There was a four-foot drop to the street.

Sloane joined him, making the same discoveries. "Good place. It's an island, lots of ways out." They re-entered the building, closing but not locking the sliding door.

Sloane went to check out the shop's equipment. He was always fascinated by things mechanical and how they worked, and the machinery provided him momentary diversion. "This is the washer." He stood before something that did resemble a frontload machine, but it was much larger, at least five feet across. "Only solvent is used instead of water." He pointed toward the bottom of the washer. "This is the tank for the perchloroethylene. It goes through this pipe into the washer, then out the back here into this filter." He examined a tank behind the washer. "It takes all the dirt out of the solvent. If the solvent isn't clean the clothes aren't clean."

"How do they get rid of that foul odor?"

"Over here, in the dryer. The heat takes the odor out."

"That's what you think."

"Maybe the sniffer's not working." He went to another tanklike apparatus. "This pulls the fumes from the air, evaporates out the water, and leaves the dry solvent. Expensive stuff. Can't waste it."

"The sniffer needs a nose job, if you ask me."

Sloane pointed toward the corner. "That's the boiler for making steam. Gas fired, electric start it looks like. This guy's got great equipment."

Rogers moved a chair into position before the washer. "Okay. Enough fun and games. He'll be coming."

Sloane nodded and followed Rogers to the lobby, where they stood in the shadows watching the street, one behind each window. They were alert to every vehicle and passerby, any detail which might strike them as out of the ordinary. There were none. Everything was as it should be. So they waited. Khruchenko was to come by taxi.

In better light David Sloane would have been seen to be tall, an inch or two over six feet, with Irish coloring, wavy dark hair, and penetrating blue eyes. He had an even, almost boyish handsomeness, and when it was useful to him possessed a disarming smile. He could be charming. In happier, less tense days he had laughed a lot and told a good story. Women were attracted to him. Harry Rogers was a couple of inches shorter, a black man of the coloring that used to be called mulatto. His dark hair was straight, worn short, and his eyes were a hazel brown. He possessed little of Sloane's charm. Instead he had a cold, catlike quality, and most people were instinctively afraid of him, although they were unsure why. Even Sloane thought of his partner as "wild sometimes."

Race was the only significant difference between them and it didn't matter. They were of the same age and came from amazingly similar backgrounds. Both had been runaways and had no close family ties. They had separately joined the Navy at age eighteen, then been selected by CSA computers on the basis of their profiles.

They had been together ever since as partners, learning the same information, receiving identical training, developing similar attitudes. Both had survived three years in the field. Thus there was between them a symbiosis, which even veterans of intelligence work thought uncanny. They had implicit trust in each other. They knew what the other would do in any situation, and they could even read each other's mind. It was not uncommon for one to start a sentence and the other to finish it.

"I don't like this. It doesn't smell right."

Sloane glanced at him. "I told you. It's perchloro—"

"I'm not talking about—"

"I know you're not."

They were silent for a time. Rogers picked up on a taxi moving slowly along the street. It didn't stop and picked up speed. "That could be him."

"Very likely."

Almost unconsciously Rogers reached inside his windbreaker, pulling out his 9mm Walther PPK, checking the clip and attachment of the silencer. He put it back into the holster. "We could let this go."

Sloane understood. Khruchenko was now meaningless to them. They were going to take a walk, simply disappear, and they had worked out exactly how to do it. It would mean leaving the Agency, country, home. But what had any of them done for them lately? They would take new identities somewhere else, start over, try to forget all the killing and dying, all the double-crosses and betrayals, three years of danger and incredible tension. Three years! It might as well have been three centuries. They had changed and both knew it. Having once been rebellious runaways, they now wanted what they thought of as a "normal" life. They each wanted a job, wife, kids, a picket fence, safety, and relief from tension so badly they could taste it.

"We don't have to do this for Mother." It was a term of derision, used by field agents, to refer to Brandywine and its minions there. It connoted the addition of two more syllables vulgarly used to refer to copulation. Brandywine disapproved of the term.

In the near darkness Sloane nodded. "I know we don't." He shared his partner's apprehension about meeting Khruchenko. Once burned is twice something or other. But he disliked unfinished business.

Almost a year ago Khruchenko had wanted to talk to them in Prague. It was not that unusual for opposing agents to meet. They had agreed, but only after taking every possible precaution. They used a safe house, which does not necessarily have to be a dwelling. In this case it was an area near the elephant house at the Prague Zoo, popular, filled with women and kids. There were great sightlines to observe the whole area, which Sloane did, standing with his back to the bars surrounding the elephant cage, as he and Harry straddled Khruchenko. He repeatedly scanned the whole area. Nothing. Then he turned. He had no idea why. He sensed rather than saw the gun barrel in the darkened doorway of the elephant house. He pushed Rogers and Khruchenko to the ground and fell atop them, hearing the thud of bullets into the ground behind them. They had escaped, but barely. While Harry ran to the rear of the elephant house, finding no one, Sloane drew his Walther and shoved it into Khruchenko's ribs. There was fear in his eyes, desperation, pleading. "I had nothing to do with it. It wasn't me," he said in Russian. Sloane had killed several times for far less provocation, but somehow his finger was now restrained. "It was your people—Parsley, not me," Khruchenko said. Then he ran and Sloane had let him go.

"I believed him, Harry," Sloane said now, knowing his partner would pick up on his thoughts. "He would never have stood so close to us if he had arranged the hit. I have to find out who Parsley is."

"I know you do."

"But you wish I didn't."

Rogers shrugged.

"There have been too many close calls. Somebody or something called Parsley wants us dead."

"Because we know too much?"

Sloane nodded. "We're close to him, Harry. Khruchenko will give us the last piece of the puzzle."

"All right." There was authority in Rogers's voice now, his doubt replaced by conviction. "He'll talk, we'll listen. He'll tell you who Parsley is. Then I'll kill him. I'm tired of the game, Dave."

To them the intelligence activities of the US and the Soviet Union were an endless game, using nearly identical methods, played incessantly for no worthwhile purpose. Though they had once believed, they were now cynical. There was not a particle of difference between the two sides of the intelligence game. But they played on, on and on and on, notching a victory here, a defeat there, chewing up men's lives, wasting time and endless money—for what? Victory meant they lived and got to play again. They had been players for three years. They were masters of the game. They would play no more. They would disappear.

Rogers spoke again into the silence. "Suppose Khruchenko tells us who or what Parsley is. What are you going to do about it?"

"Nothing. I just want to know."

"Just another puzzle to be solved?"

"Yes. I'm tired of the game, too." Sloane glanced at the shadowy form of the only real friend he had made in his life. "It'll be all right. We've taken every precaution."

"I know."

And they had. The defection of Yuri Khruchenko had been going on all day. Sloane and Rogers had done it by the numbers that in intelligence parlance was known as "flag him, flush him, run him, ask him, send him." A man had stood that morning on a busy street corner in downtown Munich. He thus was "flagged." On instructions from Sloane a minor US agent had hired a commercial taxi driver to stop at the curb and ask him if he was "Mr. Mueller," a prearranged signal. When he said he was and entered the cab—"flushing"—he was taken to another location and dropped off. This process was repeated with several taxis to "run" him. Finally he was taken into custody by agents who strip-searched and interrogated him—the "ask him" process. The agents had no need to know who they were supposedly questioning or for what purpose, and so they did not. Regardless of the answers Mr. Mueller gave, he was released. "Send him."

Sloane and Rogers knew Mr. Mueller was a decoy. Khruchenko would never put himself at risk by turning himself in to strangers. Nor would Sloane and Rogers accept him. After all, they had barely escaped death in Prague and didn't trust the KGB official at all. At midday another man stood on a busy street corner. This was Khruchenko. The very fact he had allowed the decoy to return to him and had obeyed instructions to stand on that particular corner was proof that he wanted to defect. Or at least talk.

The entire process had been repeated. Khruchenko had been flagged, flushed, run, asked, and sent—this time with a black raincoat, which he was to have dry-cleaned on Wernerstrasse. He had yet to lay eyes on Sloane or Rogers and had no idea what awaited him at the dry cleaners. He only knew he was dealing with professionals. All this was standard practice, used by the KGB, British MI5 and the better intelligence agencies the world over.

Rogers saw him first, strolling with seeming carelessness down the street, a black raincoat over his arm. He was in his early fifties, gray-haired, trim, rather handsome really. He wore a Dunhill suit and Gucci shoes.

"I see he's wearing his Sunday best," Sloane said. "What a shame to get blood all over it."

He really wasn't interested in gossip, but "Washington Off Guard," gushingly written by socialite Evelyn Cushman under the pen name "Curtis Eustace," was required reading for Parsley. He forced himself to read the array of near-libelous drivel about congressmen, bureaucrats, and assorted politicos until he found the item he had planted himself: "What very married senator was seen emerging from a prominent D.C. watering hole with a knockout blonde on his arm last night?"

He had simply made it up. Chances are several senators were out with blondes last night—and very nervous today. If none were, who could prove it? Actually the piece of gossip was a coded message for a person in the Soviet Embassy whom he had never met and could not possibly identify. The embassy official, a top KGB operative, would read the item and know that Parsley, code name for the Soviet mole high in US intelligence—a person he did not know and could never identify—was taking care of the Khruchenko matter. Moscow was to stay out of it.

The bit of gossip was thus a one-time pad, unbreakable by CSA computers. Parsley had devised the method himself and was extremely proud of it. Genesis of the idea had been "Deep Throat," the celebrated informant used by Bob Woodward and Carl Bernstein in their Watergate exposés. What if the two reporters were simply sold a bill of goods? Apparently American reporters would believe anything, especially if it came from a high-ranking official with a fancy title on the door. It was a simple matter to plant misinformation with an official who told another official then another official who mentioned it to pet reporters, where the "news" was reported as coming from the peripatetic "reliable" or "informed" source.

It was a simple matter for Parsley to devise a series of one-time pads. The coded message lay not in the words—these could be changed by reporters—but in the event, in this case a married US senator going out with another woman. In simplest words it meant: "Parsley will act." He was motivated by an item he had read two days earlier in *Pravda:* "Sergei Koransky has joined the Soviet trade delegation in Munich, Federal Republic of Germany." The meaning was clear to Parsley. From a meeting of The Committee he had learned Khruchenko wanted to defect. Parsley could have alerted Moscow and had him killed, but he had other fish to fry, two of them in fact. He wanted Khruchenko as bait, and the *Pravda* item told him his whereabouts. He was on the hook. Yuri Khruchenko—"Sergei K."—was going to Munich.

The system of sending highly classified messages in code via seemingly innocuous news items and gossip worked to perfection. Parsley used Eustace-Cushman a lot, simply because she was gullible, never checked anything, and used material very quickly, often overnight. But on occasion he had planted messages with some very famous reporters on *The New York Times* and the *Wash-*

ington Post. If speed was essential, they could easily use the news broadcast from a local Washington radio station. On a few occasions they had even made the plant on national network television news. Parsley was quite proud of the time Dan Rather had unknowingly sent a message for him.

He read the item about the philandering senator again. "Parsley will act." Yes, he already had. Yuri Khruchenko, that traitorous bastard, was as good as dead, those two troublesome American agents with him. The three of them were a menace and should have been eliminated a long time ago. He had almost gotten them in Prague, but the hit had been bungled. Unbelievably, Khruchenko had survived, managing to convince everyone he had met the American agents to kill them and would have if Parsley had simply stayed out of it. Parsley had known better, but deep underground in Brandywine, knowing he must do absolutely nothing to jeopardize his cover, he could not confront Khruchenko. So he had waited in certain knowledge this day would come, and he would finally eliminate the one man with even a remote chance of identifying him.

There would be no bungling this time. Sloane and Rogers had set their own trap and lured Khruchenko into it. American agents, sent by himself, would eliminate all three in mere seconds.

"Drop the raincoat, Yuri." Rogers spoke in Russian. He stood in the office behind the partition, Walther in hand. Sloane was to the rear of the lobby, behind the wall next to the conveyor. He was also armed. Both were able to see Khruchenko as he entered the shop and stood at the counter.

The Russian obeyed, laying the raincoat slowly and carefully across the counter, as though it were a garment of great value. His hands bore no gun, and there was no flicker of expression on his Slavic face, at least none visible in the poor light.

"Now remove your suit jacket and pants." Rogers's Russian was soft, yet had authority to it.

In English Khruchenko said, "I have no weapon."

"I said strip." Rogers's voice, in English now, took on edge. "Jacket, pants, shirt. I get turned on by men's underwear." A minute later Khruchenko had complied. He wore white boxer shorts, no undershirt. Silk socks were held up by garters. His body was very hirsute and trim for a man his age. "You know the drill, Yuri. Shoes and socks." In a moment he was barefoot. "Drop your drawers, bend over." He did. Khruchenko carried no bug. "You can pull 'em back up now. I'm not *that* crazy about you." Then he commanded, "Walk around the counter, past the conveyor to the rear—*slowly*. I'd sooner kill you than look at you."

When Khruchenko obeyed, Rogers came from behind the partition, locked the front door, then quickly checked the discarded clothing for a weapon and bug. There were none. Khruchenko had come clean.

Rogers looked toward the rear, pushing aside some garments on the conveyor so he could see. Khruchenko, incongruous in bare feet and underdrawers, had reached the rear. He turned around, still blinking against the light, trying to find his captors, neither of whom he could yet see.

"I came to defect," he said in loud English.

"Just like Prague." Sloane stepped from behind the conveyor.

Khruchenko saw him, then turned to see Rogers to his right. Both had Walthers leveled at him, but these did not frighten him. Their eyes did, cold, remorseless. They were ready to kill. He had seen it often and knew his own eyes must have looked that way at times. "I had nothing to do with Prague."

"So you said."

"It was the truth. I was to be killed, too. You saved my life. I'm grateful."

"You lie, Yuri." Rogers's voice was as taut as the hand on his Walther. "No one wanted to kill you. You stayed at Dzerzhinsky Square. That ain't Siberia."

"I told them I'd planned to kill you. They believed me."

Rogers stepped toward him. "We believe you too, Yuri. You did plan to kill us. It was a setup."

Khruchenko saw the menace in him and knew fear. "Yes, but not by me. It was Parsley. Parsley did it. It was your own people."

"Who is Parsley?"

Almost in relief Khruchenko turned to the softer, less menacing voice of Sloane. "Parsley is our agent, a mole as you call him, high in American intelligence—your own agency."

"How high?"

"Very high." The Russian smiled, but it was tight, forced by fright. "You shouldn't kill me. I can tell you many things."

"Who is Parsley?"

"I told you, he's—"

"His name, Yuri." Rogers now shoved the end of the silencer hard against Khruchenko's ribs, making him flinch. "We are not interested in vegetables."

"I don't know his name—only Parsley. But I think I can figure out—"

"Sit down." Sloane motioned to the single, straight-backed chair. It was badly scratched, most of its varnish gone.

Khruchenko sat, then registered fear as he saw Sloane extract two small syringes from the pocket of his windbreaker, then return one. "Please. I will tell you all I know, but not here." There was pleading in his voice as he saw Sloane snap the cover from the needle. "It is dangerous. You have to know. It should be done with doctors—in a hospital."

Sloane knew. The drug was powerful. It would cause a man to tell all he knew. Nothing could be held back. But the dose had to be precise for a man's body weight. Not enough and he could lie. Too much and he fell asleep. Way too much and he became a vegetable.

Sloane looked at Rogers and grinned. "About a hundred and sixty-five pounds, wouldn't you say?"

Sound burst from the Russian. "Seventy kilos, not a gram more. I've weighed seventy kilos my whole—"

"Thank you, Yuri." Rogers's grin was broad. "Better give him a double dose."

"No, no, *please*—"

His voice ended with an audible sucking in of air as Sloane plunged the needle into his left arm.

It only took a second. Khruchenko's body relaxed, almost as quickly as a snap of the fingers, and he slumped heavily against the chair. His head, a great weight now, fell forward until his chin rested against his chest. For a moment Sloane thought he had given him too much and he had gone to sleep, but Rogers picked up his head by the hair and asked, "What is your name?"

"Yuri Ilyich Petrokovsky."

Rogers glanced at Sloane and smiled. Both understood. Petrokovsky was his real name at birth. Khruchenko was a phony one given him by the KGB. The Russian was telling the truth.

Rogers turned back to him. "Where do you work?"

"*Komitet Gosudarstvennoi Bezopasnosti.*"

It was the Russian name for the KGB.

"What are your duties?"

Khruchenko answered immediately, describing himself as in charge of the American section, overseeing all Soviet intelligence activities within the continental United States, Canada, and Mexico. He was a big fish, all right. But as the guttural voice droned on listlessly in Russian, Sloane grew impatient. He didn't want to know Khruchenko's life history. And there really was nothing he didn't already know.

"That is enough." His voice was sharp. "Who is Parsley?"

"Parsley is the code name for our agent in Washington. He is high in the Central Security Agency, very trusted. He is the only person we permit to work independently on his own initiative. He has never failed us."

That in itself was interesting. Sloane knew the KGB never granted independence to its agents. They were not trusted and had to do everything by the book, follow orders precisely, report verbatim everything they learned, then await further instructions. It was a cardinal difference between the KGB and the CSA and gave the US a distinct leg up in the intelligence wars. If Parsley had the status to initiate operations and work independently, he must be important indeed.

But that knowledge didn't identify him. "Who is Parsley?" Sloane asked again. It was a mistake. Khruchenko began again, listlessly repeating the same spiel. Sloane slapped him hard to stop him, then changed the question: "What is Parsley's name?"

Silence.

"He has a name, an American name. What is it?"

Again silence.

Rogers tightened his grip on the Russian's gray hair and pulled his head back farther. "If you are in charge of the American section, you must have a name for him. What do you call him?"

"Parsley."

Sloane and Rogers looked at each other in consternation. Here was Khruchenko, Parsley's superior in the KGB, supposedly in contact with him and controlling him, yet he knew him only by his code word.

Sloane pursued it. "Is Parsley the only name you know?"

"Yes."

"Is Parsley a man or woman?"

"Man."

"Is it one man or more than one?"

"One."

Rogers now. "You say he's high in the agency. How high?"

"The Committee."

Again Sloane and Rogers looked at each other, their minds registering the same thought. A Soviet mole on The Committee! It couldn't be. The damage he could do! National security could not possibly be more threatened. But there was no time to consider this. Sloane turned to Khruchenko. "If you control him, how come you don't know his name?"

"No one ever knew it."

Rogers jerked his head back hard. "You lie. He's your mole. Somebody had to put him in place."

"He came to us."

"Impossible!" Rogers leveled his Walther toward the Russian's head. "I'll kill you now if you don't tell the truth."

Sloane touched Rogers's arm, restraining him. "Explain, Khruchenko. How did he come to you?"

"We knew someone was helping us, someone very knowledgeable, but we didn't know who."

"How was he helping you?"

"We received information which enabled us to know what was going on. Your operations failed, ours succeeded. We deduced that someone in the CSA was helping us."

Sloane waited for him to continue. He didn't. Apparently that was a complete answer to Khruchenko. It wasn't to Sloane. "One thing at a time. How did you receive information?"

"As we always do. Mostly through your coded messages which we could break. Some in newspapers and technical journals. We realized there was someone who knew what we already knew and was giving us the additional information to enable us to figure out the rest. We didn't know who it was."

Yes, it would work. A member of The Committee would have up-to-date analyses of what information the Soviets possessed. It would be a simple matter to leak the additional information they needed.

"You said he spoiled our operations. Which ones?"

"Many. I can't remember them all—Vietnam, Angola, Iran, Central America, Pakistan. You were party to some."

Rogers's eyes widened as he looked at Sloane. It was an explanation—the botched jobs, the narrow escapes. They had been trapped in Pakistan, had to shoot their way out, barely got away. They knew someone had been tipped off, but never knew how or by whom. It was one of many. Parsley. That sonofabitch.

Sloane forced his mind not to react. He wanted information. "Your operations were helped. Which?"

"Many. Vietnam, Iran, Afghanistan, Nicaragua, Libya. Many. All the way back to Cuba."

Sloane saw Rogers's reaction, anger leading to violence, his hand tightening on the Walther. "Parsley helped you with all this. How?"

Silence.

He didn't know or was unable to say. "How did

Parsley help you?" He sighed. "Never mind. I already know."

Rogers now spoke to Sloane. "It would be so easy. A mole on The Committee would know our operations. He could alert the KGB."

"Or simply foul it up from our end—give wrong information to men in the field, send them up blind alleys."

"Or into traps."

"Like Prague—and Pakistan."

"Sonofabitch."

"He could use CSA equipment, methods, and people to help the KGB. Nobody'd know the difference—if he was clever and careful enough."

"If he's on The Committee you'd better believe he is."

"Yes." Sloane turned back to Khruchenko. "How did you know Parsley was helping you?"

"For a long time we didn't. We thought it was just your usual mistakes. Many still do. But I know better. I had more respect—for you, the agency. I just knew someone was behind it."

Sloane waited, impatient for more. There was none. He wanted the whole story, quickly, and Khruchenko's terse, literal answers were maddening. "He made contact with you?"

"Yes."

"How?"

"By phone. The usual way."

Yes, a phone call from a phone call from a phone call. "Where did you meet him?"

"Vienna."

"Where in Vienna?"

"A church confessional."

"Did you see him?"

"Very little through the screen."

"Then you don't know him."

"I would know his voice. I have not forgotten it."

Sloane shrugged. "That's something anyway. What did he want?"

"Money."

"Lots?"

"Not really."

"Where?"

"Zurich."

A Swiss bank account. Untraceable. "You paid him?"

"Yes. He wanted a hundred thousand Swiss francs for past work, ten thousand a month in the future."

Rogers now. "Cheap. Why so little?"

"He did not want to change his lifestyle very much. He said it would blow his cover."

Sloane nodded his head, several times, quickly. A very smart man. "You trusted him enough to pay him?"

"It was a risk. I was severely criticized. I felt I had no choice. He could be invaluable to us."

Rogers: "And he was?"

"Yes."

"Christ Almighty!" The words escaped Sloane as a half sigh, half epithet. "It explains a lot, Harry."

"Damn near everything." Rogers turned to the Russian. "Why did he do it? Is he a Commie?"

"No."

"Did he give a reason?"

"No. I asked. He said it was none of my business."

"Jesus Christ! Sonofabitch!"

Sloane's reaction was similar, but he forced it aside. "How often did you see him?"

"Just the once."

"Somebody must contact him."

"No one."

"No one but you has ever seen him?"

"That is correct. He will not permit it."

Sloane looked at Rogers, who spoke first. "No

one must see him or know him—or even that he exists, for that matter. It would blow his cover."

"Which is why he tried to kill Khruchenko—the only man who has ever seen him—in Prague."

"Us along with him, because we suspected a mole."

Sloane turned back to the defector. "How do you control him?"

"Very little. He is independent. He does what he can when he can."

Rogers understood. "He would have to be extremely careful, Dave. Security would have to be everything to him. He wouldn't take orders from Moscow."

Sloane nodded. "You must have some contact with him."

"Yes. Newspapers, television, radio. It is a code he devised."

"How does it work?"

"News items, gossip."

"I don't understand. Give an example."

"There are code names, Igor, Boris, Natasha, many of them. The name plus an event is the code. An agronomist named Igor reporting a failing wheat crop means our people are in place. A ballet dancer named Irina twists her ankle, a swimmer named Petro ties a record. It all has meaning. It is complicated yet simple."

"How does Parsley contact you?"

"The same way. Your decadent gossip columns are most useful."

Sloane was admiring. "Simply beautiful. All Parsley has to do is read *Pravda*."

Rogers finished the statement. "And all the Russians have to do is read American papers—the *Washington Post* and *The New York Times* most likely."

"If the code is simply a news event, they could use radio and television. Damn clever."

"If done well—and I'm sure it is—hell, no one

would ever guess the code even exists." Rogers saw Khruchenko raise a hand and rub his eye. "He's coming out of it. Let's finish him and get the hell outta here."

Sloane shook his head. "In a minute." He turned to Khruchenko. "Why are you defecting?"

"Because of Parsley."

Sloane furrowed his brow. It didn't make sense. "Explain. What has Parsley done?"

"It is what he could do. Parsley is a most dangerous man. If he can manipulate US intelligence, he can manipulate ours, too. He has not yet, but one day he will. I feel it. I know it. I have warned of it, but I am not believed."

Rogers smiled. "Then you haven't suddenly become a capitalist."

"No, never. You are corrupt."

And Rogers laughed. "Now I really do believe you, Yuri. You're a patriot, saving the world for Communism."

"Parsley is most dangerous. He must be stopped."

Sloane now. "Why?"

"He wants power. He controls your intelligence now. He helps us. We are grateful. But one day when we trust him enough he will manipulate us. We will be destroyed. It is too much power for one man."

"And power is what he wants?"

"Yes, he is mad for power."

Sloane looked at Rogers. Both understood. Power was the prime motive in the intelligence game. There was little money and not an iota of glory. But power was heady stuff. A man on The Committee could—

"He's almost out of it, Dave. I'm gonna finish him."

Sloane hesitated. "Let me think a minute." He walked away from Rogers, leaving him standing, gun in hand, over the Russian. "Should we report this, Harry?"

"To whom? Parsley?"

"You're right." Sloane had moved perhaps a dozen feet away. He stood behind a steam table, idly running his hand over the pressing surface. "Whoever we talk to, it will just get back to Parsley, alert him, drive him deeper under cover."

"And so will this bastard." Rogers lowered the barrel of his Walther toward Khruchenko. "There's no point to him. I'm going to take him."

"Wait. He says he can recognize Parsley's voice."

"Maybe, maybe not. What're we gonna do, hold on to him until we get everybody in Brandywine on tape?"

"Not everyone. He said The Committee, remember?"

"Bullcrap! We don't know who's on The Committee. Nobody does. Nobody's even sure the damn Committee exists." He heard Sloane sigh in acquiescence. "Dave, we're getting out, remember? We can lie on the beach, stick our feet in the sand and wonder who Parsley is for the rest of our lives. Let's just get out of here. Parsley must want Khruchenko dead. If we try to hold on to him, he'll have a death warrant for us, too."

Sloane sighed. Harry was right. His was the only way. He nodded approval. He watched the Walther, silencer attached, swivel toward Khruchenko's head, then looked away, down at the steam table. He could kill, had many times, but he didn't like to watch someone else doing it. Inwardly he waited for the quick pop and splat, which meant Khruchenko was dead.

He never heard it. Instead there was the sudden loud rumbling of a sliding metal door, then the quick *spit, spit, spit* of automatic weapons. For Sloane it was a tabloid, frozen in time, two men bursting in the back door, two Uzis with silencers attached belching fire, Khruchenko blown off the chair by the impact of the heavy 9mm bullets, Rogers thrown backward, blood spurting from his chest.

Sloane's mind never willed it. His hand, long-practiced, self-governing, instinctive, drew and fired, the Walther spitting death. He saw one man fall, even as the second Uzi swiveled toward him, muzzle vomiting flame. He heard the splatter of bullets into the metal press, against the wall behind him, as his finger repeatedly pressed the trigger of the Walther.

He dropped to the floor behind the press, aware the Uzi had stopped. Must have hit him. Then he heard steps and rolled around the press, looking up. He didn't see the man, only the gun pointing down at him. Again he rolled, under the conveyor filled with clothes. They offered no protection. He heard, sensed the bullets, twenty a second, smashing through the garments, then felt the hammer blows of bullets into his shoulder, thigh, and side.

Still he rolled, all the way to the other side of the conveyor, where the door to the alley was. He got to his feet, hoping to run, but he had only one good leg. He lurched three steps, reaching the wall, and turned toward the door. The Uzi was there, not six feet away, held by a man. He stood, legs apart, weapon leveled for the kill, blond, green eyes cold, wearing a trench coat. Sloane's hand moved sharply to fire. It was only then that he realized he had lost his weapon when he was hit.

"You're gonna die now, you Commie bastard."

To Sloane this man was unprofessional. A person shot first, talked later. But that thought was lost in a new, incredulous one. It was an American voice. "No, wait!" Sloane leaned against the wall, trying to raise his arms in surrender, but only his one good arm, the right, would move. He lifted it as high as he could. "Wait, I'm an American."

"And I'm Little Bo Peep."

Sloane knew it was no use. The man's eyes told him that. He was a killer like himself. He had no qualms. He just wanted to torment a helpless man a moment before he killed him. Harry did that sometimes. "Do it, friend. Get it over with."

"Have no fear. I will."

Sloane's hand was unbidden. Perhaps it was looking for something to hold on to. It found a cord, hooked tight to the wall. Sloane's mind knew. He resisted the impulse to glance upward. There could be no warning.

A quick jerk, an even quicker release of the cord, and the pleater fell on the gunman, knocking him down, covering him with heavy drapes and ball gowns. The Uzi went off with the impact, but harmlessly into the floor. The bullets whined in ricochet.

Using his good leg and dragging his right, Sloane made his way past the gunman, now thrashing wildly to throw off the mound of drapes, the bulky pleater. He made his way to a point near the chair where Khruchenko had sat, bent, picked up Rogers's Walther, turned, and leveled it toward the man just now emerging from the drapes. Part of him wanted to disarm him, ask him who he was and what he thought he was doing. But he already knew. Parsley. And there was the Uzi. Sloane watched it being extricated from under a bagged set of drapes. He fired then. Three times. The drapes would have to be cleaned again.

He turned and saw the two gunmen who had entered first. He hadn't missed. Both were dead. This third man must have been outside opening the door. He turned again, saw Khruchenko. And Harry Rogers. Sloane gave no visible reaction. But he spoke aloud: "It was a setup, Harry. I'll find out who did it. I'll find Parsley."

Only now did he consider himself. He did so

with detachment, clinically, deliberately dissociating his mind from the wounded body as though outside it. There were three wounds. Left shoulder. Arm useless. Maybe a smashed bone. Right thigh. Had to drag the leg, but it would support some weight. Probably a flesh wound, no broken bones. Gut, right side. That could be serious, real serious. He was puzzled. Three wounds and he still lived. One was enough. A hollow point bullet made a huge hole in a man. He glanced down at Rogers's body. Yes. He never had a chance, the others either. So why was he still standing? And then he knew. The third man, the one who opened the door, must have had armor-piercing bullets in case he had to shoot through the door or a car or something. Sloane nodded. Sometimes you're just lucky.

The pain struck him then, lots of it, terrible, getting worse. He wouldn't think about it. Pain never killed anybody. And he had been wounded before. Pain was no stranger.

He looked down. Blood on his pants, shoes, dripping on the floor, pooling. That was serious. If he lost too much blood he'd pass out. Had to get to the safe house quick.

Sloane lurched three steps toward the side door, then stopped, imagining how he looked: blood all over him, Harry's Walther still in his hand. He holstered that inside his windbreaker, then went to the conveyor, selected a black raincoat, ripped open the plastic bag and draped the garment around his shoulders.

In a moment he was outside in the walkway. He would go to the rent-a-car he and Harry had stashed two blocks away. But which way did he go to reach it? Not at all like him to confuse directions. Probably the loss of blood. Becoming disoriented already. Think. To the south, yes. They had approached the shop from its rear, walking around the block to reach the front.

He made his way down the walkway, across the

alley, lurching down the narrow passageway, using the side of the building for handholds to pull himself along until he reached the next street. He forced himself to remember the name, Steubenstrasse. Good. His mind still functioned. He looked across the street. No walkway on the other side. Should be one. Maybe farther up the street. Which way? Had to decide. He elected the right.

He let go of the wall and forced himself to stand erect, squaring his shoulders. He grimaced in pain, but did not cry out, then stepped out onto the sidewalk and turned right, trying to walk as normally as possible, minimizing his limp. Lots of people limped. If anyone asked, he'd say it was a skiing accident. But it took great effort. The bad leg had to support his weight longer. Sweat dripped into his eyes off his brows. Must look awful. He used his right hand to pull out his handkerchief, then wipe away the sweat. He saw. Not sweat, blood. He wiped some more, then used his fingers as a comb, smoothing out his hair. Had to look like he belonged.

He crossed the street, passed shops. Most were closed, but a few still did business: wine shops, groceries, confectioners. In front of a bar a group of revelers emerged and almost knocked him down. They spoke to him in German. He knew German. Considered it his best language next to English, but he didn't understand them. Probably an apology. He smiled, nodded, continued on. Had to stay alert, be more careful.

He kept looking to his left, hunting the walkway. There was none. Must have turned in the wrong direction. Have to walk around the block. Damn! He looked ahead. The intersection was an infinity away. Then he would have to make it to the next street and halfway up that. He could do it. Had to.

He forced his attention on the street ahead, counting the cars that moved through the intersection. But he lost count and the headlights became fuzzy. His mind was going. Couldn't let it. Had to concentrate. He looked at passersby, trying to give them names: Werner, Hilda, Rosa, Erich, Wilhelmina, Friedrich. Couldn't think of any more German names. Multiplicaton tables. That would be good. Six times seven is forty-two. Eight times six is forty-eight. Nine times seven is sixty-three. Too easy. Twelve times eleven is one hundred thirty-two. Twelve times fourteen is ...

He was at the corner now. Not too much farther. He turned left. The moton made him dizzy and he had to stop. No, can't get dizzy. He plunged on. Twelve times fourteen is ... Twelve times fourteen is ... is one hundred and fifty-four. Twelve times seventeen is ... No use. Couldn't think. Had to. What is the name of this street? It had a name. Harry and he had memorized the names of every street in the area. They had tested each other. Why couldn't he remember? He knew. He was going fast, way too fast.

He stumbled into a woman, making her drop her bag of groceries. She spoke in angry German. "I'm sorry, I—" He lurched on. His leg was dragging badly now and he couldn't seem to stop it. Must look awful, stumbling around like a drunk. He lurched against a lamppost and held on with his good arm. Rest, he needed rest. No. There wasn't time. He had to get to the safe house.

It was then he knew he'd never make it. Everything was blurring, fading in and out, and his head felt very heavy. He had to rest the weight against the lamppost. He was so sleepy. All he wanted to do was close his eyes, rest. Just a minute and he'd be fine.

He caught himself sliding down the pole. No, not here. He'd be dead if found here. But he had to lie down. Where? Doorway. No. Police would find him.

Taxi, you dummy. Momentarily more alert, he scanned the street. He saw none. No good anyway. Taxi driver would just turn him over to the cops. Where? A car, any car.

He released the pole and leaned against the side of a parked car, trying the door handles. Locked. He lurched to the next car. Locked. Next car. No, loading zone. He threw himself across the space, barely reaching the hood of a parked vehicle. He groped along the side. Front handle. Locked. *Oh God! Please!* Back handle.

Unlocked. He crawled inside.

TWO

When Freddie Falscape entered the shop she had her mind set on purchasing a bottle of Liebfraumilch. It was the best bottle of Rhine wine she knew, indeed the only brand she knew by name, and figured it would be a good house gift for Erika Hartmann. Now she wasn't so sure. Wasn't it a little like carrying coals to Newcastle? Germans might consider Liebfraumilch pop wine and slop for all she knew.

Freddie tried to remember. At Mount Holyoke College, Erika Schmidt, as she was then, had drunk what? Beer. That was all anybody could afford. Couldn't take beer. Newcastle didn't need any more coal. She looked at the array of bottles on the shelves. Then she knew. Something American. That's what she'd take.

She turned to the proprietor, a short, balding man in his fifties, and rendered her most dazzling smile. During her year's sabbatical in Europe she'd discovered a smile was the best substitute for not knowing languages. "Do you have American whiskey?"

"American whiskey? *Jawohl*. Much Americans come here."

Freddie ruefully admitted his accent might be thick, but his English was still far better than her

German. When she returned to the States in the fall, she was going to do nothing but study languages. That was a promise. He motioned and she followed him deeper into the shop, where he stopped pridefully before a shelf of bottles. She saw the American labels, but that didn't help a bit. She knew next to nothing about booze. Old Granddad. She'd heard of that. Straight bourbon, whatever that was. Erika and Rudy—she was thinking his name whenever possible to help remember it—probably hated the stuff, but they might like to own a bottle. "I'll take it." Again she punctuated her words with a smile.

While he bagged it and she paid him in deutsche marks, she remembered her other reason for stopping here. "This is a gift for a friend. She lives on Königstrasse. Could you tell me where that is?"

He hesitated, blinking repeatedly, as though comprehension of her words was sinking into his brain in a process of osmosis. "Ver?"

"Königstrasse, number 1347."

He brightened at once. "*Ja, ja,* Königstrasse." He came around the counter, took her arm and led her to the front window. He spoke rapidly in German, giving ample directions, she was sure, only she didn't understand a word. But his flamboyant gestures more than made up for it. Up to the corner, turn right. He held up a thumb and his first two fingers. Königstrasse was three streets up. He made a cutting motion in front of himself with an extended hand. Königstrasse went in both directions. She was on her own in finding 1347.

Another smile. "*Danke schön, mein Herr.*"

He replied in German. All she understood was "*Auf Wiedersehen, Fräulein.*" A traitorous thought sneaked into her mind. *Fräulein.* He was right about that—regrettably. All of a sudden she dreaded a visit to the very married Erika. She didn't want to meet her flawless husband and doubtlessly peerless offspring. It was not an exercise calculated to improve her disposition.

As she left the shop and walked toward her German Ford, usually exiled thoughts entered and rummaged around her mind as though seeking a permanent domicile. Marriage and family had always been on her list of priorities, but for a long time they weren't that high on it. Career, achievement, independence, travel topped them. But these were in the process of being crossed off. She had her Ph.D. at twenty-four. She was now assistant professor of political science at Calvert College, a regarded women's school in southern Maryland. She had published a couple of papers on American government. "Foreign Policy and a Free Press" had been best received. Tenure seemed likely in a few more years. She had acquired a mortgage on her own house. This sabbatical year in Europe certainly qualified as travel. The bottom of the list was rising to the top. Did that make it cream?

Hardly. Since high school there had been no shortage of boys, men-boys and men. There'd been lots of dates, some romances, even a couple of affairs. Lustrous brown hair, luminous brown eyes, lots of orthodontia and her own house had seen to that. She had heard enough I-love-you-I-can't-live-without-yous from men she never laid eyes on again to last a lifetime. But she couldn't complain. There had been a couple of genuine opportunities. Nice men who would probably make good husbands and fathers. But why rush into it? There was plenty of time.

Now at twenty-nine, thirty lurking in August ready to pounce out and molest her, time seemed cramped. Those damn studies showing how women in their thirties have a harder time becoming pregnant. Women should have babies first, career second. Now they tell her. And where suddenly were all those great catches she had thrown back into the water? Sizzling in other frying pans, no doubt. *Stop it, Freddie. There's nothing more disgusting than a manhunting broad.*

She inserted the key in the lock, opened the door and slid behind the wheel, depositing the bottle of bourbon on the seat beside her. In so doing she dropped her car keys, then opened the door a little to turn on the dome light. There. She retrieved the keys and selected the one for the ignition. She was just reaching to insert it when a hard object was thrust shockingly against her head behind her right ear.

"*Shut the door!*"

She froze with fright, her hand suspended halfway to the ignition, body rigid, eyes wide, breathing stopped.

"I said *shut the door!* Do you understand English?"

She had no voice. She could only nod.

"Then, shut it. *Now!*"

A hard shove of the gun barrel made her head fall forward. Terror seized her and she began to tremble. Another, harder nudge from the gun. Timorously she extended a shaking left hand, grasped the door handle and pulled. The interior light went out. The darkness seemed deeper than it really was.

"I'm not going to ... hurt you. I just want you to ... to drive me to my car. Go ... to the corner ... turn left, then ... left again. Can you ... do that?"

The voice sounded strained, the breathing labored. There was less menace in the voice now. He was appealing to her. She swallowed hard, then nodded. Voice came. "Just don't hurt me."

"I said I ... wouldn't. Just drive. Think of yourself ... as a taxi."

"Yes." She glanced in the rear-view mirror, but could see only the hand with the gun on the back of the seat. He must be crouched behind her seat or lying down. "How did you get into my car?"

"Back door . . . open. You should be . . . more careful. Drive!"

She bent forward, away from the gun against her head, inserted the key, started the engine.

"I know you're . . . scared, but if you do . . . exactly as I say . . . it'll all be over . . . in a minute. Then you can . . . go on your way."

She heard reassurance in the voice and believed it, if only because she wanted to. There was something else. "You're an American, aren't you? So am I."

"Small world. Drive!"

Pulse racing, still not thinking clearly, she put the car in gear and started to let out the clutch.

"Hold it . . . car coming. Let it pass."

Now she turned her head and waited before pulling into the street. The car seemed strange, the act of driving foreign to her. "Which way did you say?"

"Left. Left again . . . at the next corner."

There was something about the voice. She had to hear it again. "Where you from in the States?" It was a silly question under the circumstances, but all she could think of.

"Cut the talk and drive."

She prided herself on accents. Flat *a* in *and*. Midwestern. Something else. He was having great difficulty saying anything. "Are you ill? You sound awful."

"Just drive."

She was at the corner now, waiting for the light. Green came and she made the left turn, staying toward the center of the street. "You're in pain, aren't you?"

"Doesn't . . . matter."

"Do you need a hospital? I'll take you."

"A hospital is . . . last thing . . . I need."

Sloane had very nearly passed out the moment

he entered the car, but he fought it, struggling to maintain a wavering consciousness. Just had to. He was anything but safe. Then he revived a little. Apparently just resting and not moving helped. He lost track of how long he was there, five, maybe ten minutes, but he was prepared when she came. Had to get to his car, then to the post office to pick up the travel pack. It was the last escape hatch. Harry and he left nothing to chance. He felt the car turning left. "About the middle ... of the block—on the right. Brown Audi. Should be ... fireplug ... in front."

She moved slowly, staying in second gear. "I see it."

"Pull in ... front ... by the fireplug. Close to the ... curb."

"I—I can't pull into the space. I'll have to back in."

"Do it."

She pulled in front, stopped, shifted, and backed in. Her mind, seizing trivialities, noted she did it surprisingly well.

"Keep ... motor running. Don't leave ... car and don't ... look around. When I get out ... you leave."

"All right." Her voice sounded calmer than she felt.

"If you ... want to live—forget you ... ever saw me."

She felt her hands tighten on the steering wheel. "If I leave, how can you kill me?"

"I can't. Others will. Stay away from ... police. Forget ... all this."

"But—"

"No buts. Believe me, I'm doing you ... a favor."

"Great favor!"

Sloane had a problem. He had only one good hand. He needed it to get out of the car, which meant he couldn't keep his gun on the girl.

Couldn't be helped. He holstered the weapon, then pulling on the back of the seat and pushing with his good left leg, he managed to sit upright.

In the rear-view mirror Freddie saw the gun disappear. Her impulse was to leap out of the car, run, scream. But she didn't. A pronounced groan from him stopped her. Then she saw his face in the mirror, but it was back-lighted, indistinct.

Sloane fumbled for the door handle, found it, pulled, shoved it open. The interior light came on.

She squealed. Both her hands came to her mouth to suppress a scream. His face was a bloody mess, contorted in pain. She turned, looked over the seat, and gasped. Blood all over him. It welled up and streamed from his shoulder. The seat was smeared with it. "You're hurt."

"I'm ... fine."

"In the pink—bloody pink."

She watched him slide toward the door. His left arm was useless. He shoved the door open, gripped the side of the door with his right hand, pulled himself toward the opening. Then he lifted his right leg and thrust it out the door. She saw the bloody hole in the thigh. The leg was useless, too. He tried to pull himself out of the car, but the leg wouldn't support his weight. He fell back inside.

"You're badly wounded. You can't even get out of the car."

"Yes, I can." He drew his gun. "Get out. Come ... help me."

She looked at the gun, unsteady in his hand. What was that thing on the end? A silencer, she guessed. No one would hear the shots. She obeyed him, slowly getting out of the car, walking around the front. She really did not think of escape. This man was in too bad a shape.

Freddie stood in the open doorway, strangely unafraid of the weapon in his hand. She watched him thrust his left leg out of the car. It seemed okay.

"Take my wrist ... pull me out."

She shook her head. "This is silly. You're half dead now. You'll finish it if you don't get to a hospital and quick. I'll take you."

"No. No hospital." He extended the gun hand toward her. "Pull."

Still shaking her head, she obeyed, grasping his wrist, planting her feet. Leaning backward from the weight of him, she slowly pulled him out of the car. At once he turned and leaned over the trunk of her car. He twisted again and took one lurching step, dragging his leg, to lean over the hood of the car at the curb. She heard his labored breathing. Must be wounded somewhere else, ribs most likely.

"You can't drive. You're all shot up."

"I can." Sloane took another lurching step, then another, around the side. He was at the driver's side now, leaning against the windshield.

"You have one arm and one leg. How do you expect to drive?" She looked at his shoulder. Blood was streaming from it now. "Every time you move, you just lose more blood."

She was fading in his vision and he closed his eyes. Everything was swirling.

"Get back in the car. I'll take you to the hospital."

"No hospital. No ... doctors."

There was a rattling sound to his voice. "You're dying. You need medical attention."

"No." His voice was more air than sound now. "I'll be killed."

She shook her head. No point in arguing. "All right. I'll take you wherever you want to go."

"Post office."

"Post office! It's closed."

"Lobby's open."

Again she shook her head at him, adding a sigh

of frustration this time. "Okay, stupid, you're the boss." She went to him. "Put that dumb gun away and I'll help you into the car."

Freddie had trouble finding the main post office. She had to stop, get out, and ask directions—from a cop. Part of her mind wanted to bring him back to the car, turn this wounded man over to him. But she didn't, couldn't and she was far from sure why. There was something about him, half dead, probably dying—only his wheezy struggle for breath told her he was not already gone—which brought out the mother hen in her. She always had been a sucker for wounded animals. As a child she'd brought assorted bunnies and birds to her father to fix up—and he was a surgeon, not a vet.

She was no longer afraid of him. That gun was bravado. Probably didn't have the strength to pull the trigger. And he was desperate. That most of all. How far had he come to reach her car, dragging a useless leg, his arm dangling? God, the pain! He wanted to live. So badly. He had to have a good reason.

Somebody was after him. Probably the ones who shot him. No hospital, he said, no cops, tell no one. *I'm doing you a favor.* If he could think to say that in his condition, who was she to argue with him?

She dazzled the cop with a smile, returned to the car and drove to the post office, stopping in front. She let the motor run. "Are you awake?"

"Yes." Her voice snapped him to awareness. He had lain in the back seat only semiconscious. Apparently lying down had revived him again. "You stopped ... got out. What'd you—"

She couldn't resist. "I talked to a cop."

"Goddamn, I told—"

"I only asked directions. I figured he'd know where the post office was."

"A cop is the last—"

"What cop? You don't see one, do you? Just you and me in front of the good old Munich post office. Unless you plan to bleed to death, you'd better tell me what we're here for."

"Help me ... out of the car."

"Lord, not that again."

"I gotta get ... inside."

"Up those steps? You're bananas. Those steps are your graveyard. Tell me what you want and I'll get it."

He groaned. "Just go ... leave. I'll make it. ..."

"Fat chance. Look, I'm not going to leave you and have your death on my conscience. You're probably going to die anyway, but at least I'll have tried. Now, what do you want at the post office? You got a letter to mail?"

"Leave, I tell you."

"God, you're stubborn!" In her exasperation she turned around and leaned over the back of the seat. "Look, fella, I'm—" His good hand snapped around her wrist. It was like a vise, hurting her. He still had strength. "You're hurting me."

The grip tightened. "Who are you?"

She shook her head in despair. "You want introductions? Okay, my name is Fern Falscape. M-my friends call me Freddie. Who are you?"

More pressure on her wrist. "What do you ... do?"

"I teach." He was bending the wrist now. "That hurts enough. Please. I—I teach at Calvert College, poly sci. It's a small women's—"

"I know ... what it is. What you ... doing in Munich?"

"I'm here—Jesus, you're hurting me. Stop it!"

"Tell the truth."

"Dammit, I am. I teach at Calvert. You can check. I'm on sabbatical. Been in London all winter. I came here to visit a college friend."

"What friend?"

"Erika, Erika Hartmann. Used to be Schmidt. Her husband is Rudy Hartmann."

"Rudy ... Hartmann." He said the name slowly, as though scanning it for meaning. "What's he do?"

"How would I know what he does? Oh, yes, I do. He's in cameras—I think. He sells them." She saw him blink, as though confused, and felt his grip weaken on her arm. "Look, I'm nobody. I don't know nobody—anybody. I can't hurt you." His hand fell away. His burst of energy was used up and he was exhausted. She quickly rubbed the soreness out of her wrist. "My friend, I'm the only game in town just now. If you won't let me help you, you're going to die. You're on borrowed time as it is."

He was unable to think or act. He could only groan in helplessness. "Box 5497. There's an ... envelope."

She mentally repeated the number to memorize it. "Have you got a key?"

"Why are you ... helping me?"

"Damned if I know. Beats an evening with Erika and Rudy, I guess."

"What?"

"Never mind. Have you got the key?"

"Combi ... nation." He tried to think, then shook his head to clear it. "Eight right, five left ... there's a third ... I can't—"

"Okay. Eight right, five left. I'll figure the rest."

She did, by turning the dial to the right until the box opened. She retrieved a large manila envelope. It was postmarked Munich and addressed to Stewart Grady, Box 5497, Munich. Stewart Grady. So that was his name. She shrugged.

Back in the car Freddie said, "Here's your precious envelope, Stewart."

"I'm not ... Stewart. That's Harry. He's dead."

"God!" The word of exasperation was almost inaudible. "You're going to bleed to death while you argue with everything I say. Tell me what to do with this envelope."

"Open it."

"Figures." She did, ripping off one corner, sliding her finger through the seal. "What next?"

He couldn't think, but memory served him. "There should be ... two passports ... two visas ... two airline tickets ... two—"

"Is that what you wanted this for? Believe me, Stewart, Harry or whatever your name is, the only trip you're taking is to the mortuary."

He shook his head to clear it. "There's a ... hotel key. Take me ... there."

She fished inside the envelope, her fingers finding the metal key at the bottom, pulling it out. She read the ornate tab. Hotel Columbia, Room 112. "Um, the Columbia. You live well. Couldn't afford it myself."

She drove in silence, listening to his disordered breathing as a sign he still lived. In a few minutes she said, "Are you still with me, Stewart?"

"I'm not ... Stewart."

"I'm sorry, but I like to personalize the bloody people I drive around. Are you sure you want the Hotel Columbia? It's one of the busiest places in town."

"That's why. Nobody'll ... pay attention. Just another ... tourist."

"Have you looked in a mirror lately? When you make your grand *bloody* entrance through the lobby, I guarantee everybody will notice."

"In back ... service entrance."

"Figures. The hotel is coming up on the right." She made the turn, then, moving slowly, found the driveway to the rear.

"There should be ... steps ... up to a ... loading dock."

"Yes, I see it." She stopped so the right rear door would open at the steps, then turned off the motor and lights.

"Help me . . . out. Then you can go."

"Thanks a lot." She climbed out and looked around. It was dark and she didn't see anyone. How long could that last? She walked around the car and opened the rear door. "What if someone sees us?"

"Tell 'em . . . I'm drunk."

"*Bloody* drunk." She reached in a hand, took his good arm, and pulled him to a sitting position. "Can you scoot this way?"

"Yes. I'm fine."

"Perfect specimen—of a sieve." She waited a moment, then reached down to lift his bad leg out. "God, your trousers are soaked in blood." She saw him bring the good leg out of the car, then she took his hand and pulled him outside.

"Put . . . coat around me."

She reached inside and pulled out the stolen raincoat, feeling rather than seeing that it was also soaked with blood. "That'll never cut it. Take mine." She slipped out of her raincoat and draped it around his shoulders. "Little small, but we haven't much to work with."

He was standing more or less erect now, a few inches taller than she was in her heels. "I've forgotten . . . your name. But . . . thank you. I caution you . . . not to—"

"Freddie, and I'm not leaving yet. You'll never make it up those few steps. Here, lean on my shoulder."

He hesitated, then reluctantly obeyed. As pain scoured through him with each step, he was grateful.

On the loading platform she said, "Don't we have to check in or something?"

"Not we—me. And we don't . . . have to." He paused, panting for breath. "It was done . . . week ago. Manager . . . was told the room"—he paused to painfully suck in air—"was for . . . storing equipment—computers. No one clean . . . bother."

"It's all paid for?"

"Yes."

Still holding him she looked around. "Only one trouble. How do we get in? Everything looks locked."

He groaned. "Didn't get . . . key made. Mistake. Have to . . . pick lock."

She was impressed. "So you're a burglar. Is that how you were shot?"

"No." He tried to think, remember. "Pick is . . . my pants . . . left pocket. You'll . . . have to get it."

She was on his right side, his good arm around her shoulders, and couldn't reach his pocket. "Here, lean against the building." In a moment her hand was in his pocket. "This is great fun, very sexy, but what am I looking for?"

"It feels . . . like a knife."

"I got it."

"Hand it here."

She did, then saw him try to move toward the door. It was hopeless. "Tell you what. You sit on the step, take a rest. Tell me how to use this gadget and I'll open the door." He hesitated, looking at her, then seemed to resign himself to his helplessness. He nodded and she helped him sit, taking the pick from him.

"It's like a . . . knife—only there are shivs . . . folded inside. Several."

She tried it, folding out several thin metal strips. "I got it. What'll I do now?"

"The first is covered . . . with powdered graphite." He swallowed. God, it hurt to breathe. "Stick . . . in lock."

"Okay, let me try." In a moment she said, "It's in. What now?"

"Work it . . . a little. Gently. Not too . . . hard."

"Okay, it's worked."

"Slide it out . . . carefully. There should be . . .

black marks on blade. Just match up marks . . . with one of the . . . shivs."

"You gotta be kidding. It's dark. Who can see?" She looked around. "I know." A moment later she sat in the car using the dome light. With some fascination she saw the marks. An impression of a key in the graphite. How clever of somebody. She tried several of the shivs, lining it up with the marks. Maybe. No, this one. She came back to him. "I think I got it."

"Try it. Not too hard. Don't . . . force it."

She wiggled the shiv in and out, twisting gently. "I feel something." Then she felt the lock give. "Hot damn! I did it."

She opened the door, propped it open, stepped inside. Long tiled hallway with passages off to the side. No one around. Then there was, a short, swarthy man in a white jacket. Looked Spanish, maybe Portuguese. Wore a white jacket and carried a tray with a bottle and glasses on it. He didn't see her—or at least care that she was there. He pushed a button. An elevator opened. He was room service.

Freddie retreated outside. "Stewart?" She whispered the name. No sound. She bent over him in the darkness. He was sprawled on his back and she thought him dead until she heard him wheeze. "Are you with me, Stewart?"

"I'm not . . . Stewart."

"Then give me a name to call you."

He hesitated. Couldn't remember the name he was using. Must be far gone to forget something like that. "Dave."

"Okay, Dave. I got the rear door open. The service elevator is close, but I'm afraid of people."

"Take back stairs. First door . . . on right."

In a moment, supporting his weight, she opened the door to the stairwell and gasped. He'd never make it. "C'mon, let's give it the old college try."

Stopping frequently they made it to the first

landing, turned, faced the second flight. "Does it hurt a lot?"

"If anybody ... comes, just say—"

"I know. You've been swilling Bloody Marys—*real* Bloody Marys."

At last they were at the door to the hallway. "Stay here." She opened the door and stepped out into the carpeted hallway. No one was visible. "I'll find the room."

"First on ... right. We planned it that way."

"Did you, now?" She went to the door, unlocked it and stepped inside. Bath to the left, closet on right. Smallish room, double bed, two chairs, desk, one window, drapes closed. View of the alley no doubt. Had to be one of the worst rooms in the hotel.

She returned for him, opening the door to the stairwell, where he leaned against the wall. For the first time she really saw his face in good light. He looked a ghastly gray. Probably not a drop of blood left in him. His eyes were glassy, dazed. He was out on his feet. "C'mon, just a couple of steps."

In a few minutes she had him on the bed. She looked down at him, so bloody, so terribly wounded. Now that she had him here, what did she do? How did she save his life?

She fought against her panic. Clean him up at least. See how bad off he is. She turned to the bathroom for towels.

His voice startled her. She thought he was out. "The car. Get in ... go. Even if ... I live, I'm ... a dead man. You will be too. Go ... while you can."

THREE

Freddie felt profoundly helpless. The damp towel in her hand was a pitiful tool to keep life in him. She had wiped his face, discovering a crease in his scalp over his left ear. Already clotting. Not a serious wound.

But the one in his shoulder was a virulent black thing, blood oozing from it constantly. And his thigh. Another black hole bearing his life away in a rivulet of blood. He needed a hospital, emergency surgery to stop the bleeding. There was no hope otherwise.

No hospital, no cops, tell no one. I'll be killed. Who was he? A crook, shot in a robbery or something? Hardly. He wouldn't come all the way to Munich for that. Too many opportunities at home. *It doesn't matter who or what he is, you sap. He wants to live. Are you going to help him or not?*

Again she bent over Sloane, unzipping his windbreaker. The damn gun. She unbuckled the strap and pulled it off him, then unbuttoned his shirt and pulled it away from his shoulder. She gasped and almost cried out. The wound was horrible, bleeding more now because she had pulled the shirt away. The jagged edge of his broken clavicle stuck through the skin. The bullet probably passed clean through him, meaning there was a wound on the other side. May have shattered the shoulder bone. God, what would she do with that?

Then she saw blood on his right side and pulled out the remaining shirttail. Another spill of blood and she gasped. A bullet had passed through his ribs. May have cracked a couple. And the bullet was still inside. Probably had massive internal bleeding. It was hopeless. The thigh. She touched his wet trouser leg, then passed her fingers beneath it. Another double wound. But only in flesh. Missed the bone.

Panic welled in her. It was no use. He was as good as dead. A hospital probably couldn't save him. And hadn't he told her to leave him? *Even if I live I'm a dead man.* She picked up the towel and dabbed at the flow of blood from his shoulder. She jerked it away, looking at it in horror, then ran to the bathroom, dropping it in the basin, running water on it. *Out damn spot.*

She leaned over the sink, both arms extended, head down. Her eyes were closed and she breathed deeply, trying to calm herself. *You can at least try.* Yes. She was not without medical knowledge. Her father was a thoracic surgeon and a damn good one. Her mother was a graduate nurse. She had grown up listening to tales of operations and treatments. She had worked part-time in her father's office, been a candy striper. Her parents had wanted her to be a doctor and been disappointed when she rejected medicine. It wasn't too late. *Dr. Freddie Falscape, healer of shot-up strangers.*

Calmer now, she went back to the bed and stood over it. What would her father do? Suppose this happened when he was out camping or hunting and he didn't have a hospital or even his black bag. What would he do? Stop the bleeding. Yes. And she knew how. Pressure bandages. Dad would use anything he had, sheets, blankets, towels. She turned back to the bathroom. At least she had towels. Then she stopped. She was better off than Dad. There had to be a drug store open at this hour.

She headed for the door and again stopped. She must look awful, a fact confirmed by the dresser mirror. From her purse she extracted brush and lipstick, using both. Then she saw a large blood stain on the right side of her suit. Damn! Her best travel outfit, kelly-green wool. It was ruined. She looked like a Christmas tree. God! She removed the suit jacket. Her white blouse with a jabot was okay. But the skirt had a stain at the hip. *Really, Mr. de la Renta? Blood stains are in? Are you sure?* If she carried her shoulder purse on the other side and let the strap out . . . yes, have to do.

She headed for the drug store in the hotel lobby. It was still open. But she was dismayed—mostly cosmetics, perfume, souvenirs, tourist junk. She needed real medical supplies. There was a shelf with Band-aids, gauze, adhesive tape. So little. She reached, then stopped. If she bought all this and asked for more, eyebrows would be raised, questions asked. Better go elsewhere. Then she remembered her car. Had to move it. She headed for the rear exit.

Freddie cruised streets hunting an all-night drug store, finding none. Finally she saw a cop. Harry or whoever he was wouldn't approve, but she couldn't waste time. She got out, went to him, smiled, said she needed aspirin. Three blocks down, two over. *Danke schön*. She was blessed with abundance, two competing pharmacies on the same block. She divided her purchases. In the second she didn't have enough deutsche marks and had to cash a twenty-dollar traveler's check.

Back at the hotel she parked in front and passed through the lobby, acting as though she belonged, climbed the main stairs and found her way to the room. She went to work immediately.

On the drive from the drug store she had plotted precisely what she must do. Now, her mind alert, she took it step by step. First she stripped down to her bra and panty hose. Had to keep her outfit clean. God knows when she'd get back to her hotel for a change. Then, using her newly acquired scissors, she cut away his clothing until he was naked. Nice body, slender, trim. Twenties most likely and in good health. He'd need every bit of it.

She had bought a small pail which she now filled with warm water. Using a cloth and disinfectant soap she bent over his shoulder. At her touch he groaned. God, the pain he must have. How could he walk or move? Then he groaned more and pushed at her with his good arm. "Please, I'm trying to help." Again he pushed. "I know it hurts, but—" Had to do something. He was unconscious but still fighting her and only making his bleeding worse. If she only had some morphine.

Freddie did what she had to, taping his right wrist to the head of the bed, his left leg to the foot. He would struggle, but not interfere. When she finished she smiled, her sense of humor surfacing. "This really is very sexy. Hope you're into S and M."

She worked as rapidly as she could while concentrating on being thorough. The shoulder first. She cleaned the area, front and back, with soap and water, then poured a half bottle of peroxide into the wound. It figured to foam the dirt and whatever else was in the wound out without burning the tissue as alcohol or iodine would. Then she applied a mass of gauze over both holes and bound the shoulder as tight as she could. When she forced the broken clavicle in place he struggled at his bonds and screamed until she had to gag him. She was nauseous, near to vomiting from knowledge of the pain she was causing him, but she forced the bone back in place then taped it heavily, winding the adhesive as tightly as she could around both shoulders, his chest and back. His upper body was covered with tape, already turning red from his blood. It had to stop or he would die. There was nothing more anyone could do outside of an operating room.

Now the wound in his right side. It was by far the most serious, she knew. God knows what it had torn up inside. Missed his heart obviously, but it had to have hit something, liver, kidney. Either was a death warrant. He was probably bleeding to death inside and there wasn't a blessed thing she could do about it. As she applied gauze and bound his ribs and torso as tightly as possible, she took what comfort there was in the fact he still lived. Maybe the internal wounds would clot by themselves. Hope he took lots of vitamin K. Then the right thigh. Another pressure bandage. This was easier. She didn't have to struggle with the weight of his body.

Finally she tended to his head. With her scissors she snipped away a swatch of clotted hair. "Nice hair," she said. "Latest hair style—the bullet bob—but it'll grow back—if any of you lives to grow that is." She cleaned the wound with peroxide until she saw fresh blood, then squeezed the cut together and bandaged it tight.

Only then did she become aware of a sharp ache in her back from bending over him. She straightened up, stretching backward, both hands at her hips. Her breath expired in a long, audible "Wow" sound. Lord, she was tired. What time was it? Quarter to three. She had to have worked on him four or five hours. Now she looked at him, listening for his breathing. Ought to be easier with his ribs taped. She smiled. Not a bad job. He was solid adhesive from his waist to his neck, another large wrapping on his right leg.

"The rest is up to you, friend. I've done all I know how."

No, she hadn't. That arm had to be kept immobile or the clavicle would never heal. With a towel she made a sling, tied it around his neck and inserted the arm. Then, hating to move him again but certain she had to, she wrapped the arm tight against his chest with an Ace bandage. Good. He couldn't move the arm and shoulder if he tried.

She had a sense of completion now. Everything she could do had been done. It wasn't enough. He needed a surgeon. He needed whole blood. With all he'd lost he probably needed a bucketful. And he needed an IV. She'd tried to buy a kit at the drug store, but couldn't without a doctor's order. She sighed. Have to try to get as much liquid in him as possible. But not right now. He needed sleep. Sleep, hell. The man was unconscious.

Freddie hesitated over whether to untether his hand and foot. Couldn't have him thrashing around, yet he ought to be as comfortable as possible. She made up her mind, reached for the scissors and snipped him free, letting his good arm fall at his side. The tidiness in her wanted to remove the tape from his wrist and ankle, but she didn't. It would pull out hair and hurt. It might be the least of all the pain he felt, but she could spare him that. She smiled. "Just wait till I change the bandage. You'll be an ex-hairy-chested man."

She covered him with a blanket, bending low once more to make certain he still breathed. She took his pulse for fifteen seconds. Forty. Times four. God, his heart was racing. She shook her head in despair. "Old ticker's not finding much red stuff to move around. Nothing I can do about it." Finally she turned away from him, suddenly bone weary. God! She caught a glimpse of herself in the mirror. She was smeared with blood, almost covered. You'd think she had been wounded.

In the bathroom she washed her hands, arms, and face, and dabbed at a spot on her hair. Her bra and pantyhose were hopeless and she removed them, washing her torso and legs. Good thing she removed her suit. Back in the bedroom she slipped into her blouse, glancing at him. "Too bad you're out of it. You missed an eyeful." The stain on the skirt commanded her attention, and she returned to the bathroom, rinsing the spot thoroughly. Improved. She donned the skirt still wet.

Once again in the bedroom she plopped into the only comfortable chair, moaning from the pleasure of being off her feet. Lord, she was tired. Better sleep while she could. She closed her burning eyes, but only for a moment as realization shocked her awake. She stared and her eyes did not deceive. There was blood all over the place. Bolting to her feet, she quickly organized a clean-up. The bedspread, blankets, and sheet were probably ruined. She'd have to get rid of them later, his cut-up clothes, too. Fortunately she had thrown them in a vinyl chair, which wouldn't stain. She'd get rid of them in the morning.

It was the trail of red across the gold carpet that concerned her the most. Quickly she filled her pail with cold water and on hands and knees began to wet the spots and rub vigorously with a coarse towel. They didn't come out, but improved. If she got the right cleanser, maybe they would. She was near the doorway when she realized there must be a trail of blood down the hallway and stairs. It would lead right to them.

Fortunately the hall carpet was red and didn't show the blood, but the back stairs were a mess. She hesitated. What if she were seen cleaning them? Ask another question. What choice did she have? With fresh water and her last towel she tackled the stairs, moving backward down them till she reached the first landing.

There was a big stain where he had stopped to rest. She stopped, too. Why was she doing all this? He was a total stranger. He could be Jack the Ripper, Charles Manson, and Son of Sam rolled into one for all she knew. But she only sighed and continued down the stairs, rag in hand. She knew the answer. *Show me a wounded creature and I turn into a charwoman.*

When she reached the door to the loading zone she stopped. Probably enough blood out there to qualify for Red Cross disaster relief, but it was dark and she couldn't see to clean it up. All she could do was hope somebody'd figure a wounded man tried to get in the back door but failed. She carefully wiped the entrance way again, then retraced her steps to the room, dabbing at a couple of spots she missed. Inside she worked on the carpet some more. *Enough. Even the best charwomen get a rest.*

When she stood up she saw his clothes on the chair. Better get them into the empty pharmacy bag to carry out in the morning, then clean up that chair. He said no one was supposed to enter the room, but who could be sure of that? She saved his shoes, socks and belt. The rest was hopeless. Carefully she emptied the contents of his pockets and set the items on the bureau, stuffing the stained apparel in the pharmacy bag. When the chair was wiped clean, she dumped her pink water down the toilet. Then she ran water in the tub and dropped in all the soiled towels, her undergarments, and his socks to soak.

Physically exhausted, but still alert, she stood in the hallway trying to see what a chambermaid would see. Just a man sleeping in bed under a blanket. *So he has a small bandage on his head. Lots of people do. Well, some. A few maybe?* She looked around. Nothing else out of order. God, yes there was. His damn gun on the nightstand. She went over, picked it up, saw blood on the holster. In the bathroom she washed the leather carefully, the grip and barrel of the gun. Heavy. Cylinder on the end. Silencer. He wanted to kill people quietly. She didn't like guns, never had. In the bedroom she started to put it in a dresser drawer. No, might be found there. She looked around. Yes. Between the mattress and springs. As she inserted it beneath his feet she said, "You won't be needing this for a while."

Moving farther up the bed, she pulled back the blanket. The stains on his bandages were a deeper red. Still bleeding. "If you know any prayers, my friend, this might be the time for them."

Friend. Had to have a name. Wasn't Stewart Grady. He said that was Harry's name and Harry was dead. Who is Harry who is dead? She shook her head. Very confusing. She went to the bureau to examine the items from his pockets. A clip of bullets attracted her. This she put under the mattress with the gun. A small cheap transistor radio. Smashed. She examined it carefully. Hole clean through it. What pocket had it been in? Windbreaker. Yes, the bullet had passed through the radio before entering his side. Lucky. Just might save his life.

A small plastic syringe full of some liquid. What was that for? A wad of deutsche marks in a money clip. She didn't count them. German coins, keys to a Hertz Rent-a-car, bloody handkerchief. Throw that away. Cheap ballpoint pen, red Bic lighter, half-empty pack of Winstons. He smoked. Bad habit. Kill him. Silly. That wasn't what was going to kill him. Bodies weren't intended to be sieves.

Wallet. She opened it. US dollars. She didn't count but saw some hundreds, fifties, on down to tens. Loaded. At least he'd be able to pay back the money she'd spent at the drug store. Maryland driver's license. Lionel Twilley. So that was his name. *Lionel!* He didn't look like a Lionel. And that wasn't his name. He'd said it was something else. Yes, Dave. But there it was, Lionel Twilley, 617 Portnoy Street, Silver Spring, Maryland 20907, age 25, height six-two, 170 pounds, dark hair, blue eyes. That was his photo, too. Lionel Twilley. If he was a Lionel she was a Gladys. She fished into another compartment. Cards—Hertz, Amex, MasterCharge. All in the name of Lionel Twilley. Social Security card, also Lionel Twilley. What was this? A press card. Lionel Twilley was an official photographer for a travel magazine. Sure, and she was Mary Poppins. Instead of a camera he carried a picklock and gun that killed people quietly.

She shook her head. Sure was strange. Then she had a thought. If he were an American in Munich he ought to have a passport. There wasn't one. The envelope stuffed in her purse. She retrieved it and dumped the contents on the dresser. Two of everything, passports, international visas, international driver's licenses, airline tickets. Lots of credit and identification cards. She began with the passports. The first was his—Dave's. She was determined to call him that. The name now wasn't Lionel Twilley but William Hatch, and he was from South Bend, Indiana, where he was a botanist. *My eye!* She opened the second passport, saw a dark-skinned man, maybe black. Aha! Stewart Grady, Wilkes Barre, Pennsylvania, mail carrier. That must be Harry. She was making progress.

Everything else was in the same two names, William Hatch and Stewart Grady—and duplicated, two of everything, visas, licenses, credit cards, even two press cards. *Botany and delivering the mail are just sidelines for these two famous photographers, I suppose. Something sure is fishy or these two are suffering a horrible identity crisis.* She fingered through the stuff again. *No Dave and that's what he said his name was. Must be it. In his shape I doubt if he could think to lie.*

Finally she examined the airline tickets. No names, but all paid for. Lots of cities: Copenhagen, Stockholm, London, Madrid, finally Cape Town, South Africa. Supposed to leave this morning, 7:40 A.M. She turned to the bed. "Somehow, Lionel, William, Dave, or whatever your name is, I think you're going to miss your flight."

Suddenly too weary to stand, her head throbbing, she went to the chair and dropped. "You'll forgive me if I crash for a couple hours." She made a mental note to wake up at first light. Had to get rid of his clothes. And the car. Must be blood all over it. Had to clean that up before anyone saw it. Yes, first light. Sometimes she could will herself awake when she wanted to. Had to hope it worked this time.

Sprawled in the chair, her feet propped on the chair from the desk, Freddie was most uncomfortable, but that didn't keep her from sleeping past first light. It was close to eight o'clock when a groan from Sloane awakened her.

Disorientation lasted only a second, then she was at the bed. He was trying to roll to his side, first left, then right. Both had to hurt. She touched his chest and made him lie still. "Best stay on your back"—she remembered the name she had decided on—"Dave." He was quiet now, breath shallow but fairly regular. She pulled back the blankets and shook her head. His bandages were deep red. She slid her hand under the sling and touched the bandage on his shoulder. Not too wet. Maybe the bleeding was letting up. Again she shook her head. Not much she could do about it if it wasn't. Change the bandages? No, that would just start the bleeding again. She took his pulse for a half minute, computed. One-nineteen, down from one-sixty. Wasn't that a good sign? His blood supply was being replenished. Heart wasn't working so hard. Maybe his bleeding was stopping.

"Dave baby, you're on your own now. The reinforcements have run out of ammunition." She covered him up, then tucked in the bottom sheet more tightly. For a second she looked down at him. Not bad-looking. Wonder what color eyes he has? She'd seen them but couldn't remember. Oh, yes, the driver's license had said blue. But what shade? She hated light blue eyes. She was tempted to raise an eyelid and peek, but was afraid of waking him. She felt his forehead. Little cool and damp. She shrugged. No idea what that meant. "Got to go out for a while, sweetie. If the phone rings for me, just take the message."

She ran a brush through her hair, applied lipstick, grabbed her purse, then hesitated. Something wasn't right. She checked the room. Okay, just a man asleep in bed. What? Then she knew. His clothes. Had to get rid of them.

By daylight the back stairs and hallway to the rear looked clean, freshly mopped in fact. She checked the loading platform in back. No blood, just damp concrete. She smiled. Thank God for these tidy Germans. Find a mess of blood, just clean it up.

Freddie went out through the lobby to the parking lot. The car was as she feared, the back seat covered with blood. Fortunately they were vinyl seat covers. It would clean up. She looked around furtively. Not many people up and around. Maybe no one had seen it.

In accordance with a plan already worked out, she drove to the Isar River, crossed the bridge and passed through the park, hunting an isolated place near the water's edge. There was none. She drove out of the park into the streets, trying to stick close to the river. Finally, when buildings looked seedy, she turned down one alley, then into another behind some buildings. The river was on her right, down a sharp embankment of six feet or so. She parked, got out, opened the right rear door, then swore. She had forgotten her little bucket and something to wipe with. Farther up the alley she found a cracked plastic bucket which would do, then remembered the bag with his clothes. She hated even to touch them, but squelched her squeamishness. Repeated trips to the river were hard work. Her bare legs were scratched and her wool skirt ruined, but the back seat came reasonably clean. Finally finished, she tossed the bucket and remnants of his clothing into the river and watched them float downstream.

Freddie felt a sense of urgency. She couldn't leave him alone too long, but there were certain things she had to do. She returned to her hotel, stripped, showered and shampooed, then dressed in clean clothes, pants, sweater, and jacket, her normal attire. A bra felt heavenly. All that jiggle wasn't for her.

Finally she faced up to a decision. Should she pack, check out, and move in with him? He was going to need a lot of care, and she'd be spending most of her time there. *Have a grand time in Munich, heart of Bavaria.* Paying for a hotel room she didn't use bothered her thrifty soul. His room was small, but she could manage. True, the sleeping accommodations weren't the greatest, but she could sneak in a cot—or crawl in bed with him for that matter. Wouldn't be the first time; besides, he was in no shape for heavy breathing. Yes, moving over there was practical. The Hotel Columbia was a lot better than this second-rate flea trap.

She sighed. On the other hand, moving in was a commitment she wasn't sure she wanted to make. *Even if I live I'm a dead man. You will be, too. Go while you can.* Out of his mind, already unconscious, he'd said that. Couldn't say she wasn't warned. And what did she know about him—except that he was American, used several names, carried a gun so he could kill people silently—which hadn't kept him from being shot full of holes. Oh, yes, he knew how to pick locks—and so now did she. He could be anybody or anything, including a mass murderer and child rapist. She could be harboring a fugitive. *Freddie Falscape, you are hereby charged with— Stop it!* He warned her, told her to leave, say nothing. *I'm doing you a favor.* Yes. Had to be a victim, not a perpetrator. And she felt no menace in him—just helplessness.

She began to throw things into her suitcase and shoulder grip. *You're an activist, aren't you? Do something even if it's wrong. I guess I must be. All I know is that man needs me. If there is a piper to be paid, I'll try to come up with the change.*

She packed quickly and checked out, flashing generous smiles but leaving only a modest tip. Her next stop was dictated by the fact she was famished. Eating like a horse and keeping her figure was probably her one real blessing in life. She longed for a real meal, on the order of a two-inch porterhouse smothered in mushrooms, but she restricted herself to a quick trip to the market and a modest bag of sandwich meat, cheese, bread, condiments, milk and fruit. Then she headed for the drug store she had visited last night, but found another one first. She bought more peroxide, gauze, and adhesive tape, then items she had forgotten the night before: thermometer, bent straws, tweezers, scalpel, blood pressure kit, and the strongest painkillers sold over the counter. At the cash register she remembered sleeping pills. Just antihistamines, but might help a little.

In the parking lot she started to get her suitcase out of the trunk, then thought better of it. He said the room had been paid for but was supposedly unoccupied. If she carried luggage, she'd attract the doorman, bellhops, people at the desk. Better come back after dark. Besides, her arms would be full with her groceries and medical supplies. She did sling the flight bag over her shoulder, however, passed through the lobby unnoticed and up the stairs. She walked past the room, stopping before the wrong door until a couple got on the elevator and the hall was empty. Then she returned to the right room, having trouble only in freeing a hand to unlock the door.

The sight inside almost made her scream. He was rolling about the bed, thrashing, emitting loud groans, hitting at his sling and shoulder. "No, *don't!*" She dropped her parcels and ran to him—just in time to keep him from rolling completely out of bed. Even then it took all her strength.

"*Harry! Look out, Harry!*"

"God, please! Stop!"

He pushed at her with his good arm and she fell backward several steps, almost falling.

"*Harry!*" He pushed himself to a sitting position, trying to get up.

Freddie lunged at him, pushed him down, threw her weight over his body, holding down his right arm with both hands. Even then he struggled, trying to free the arm, kick at her with his good leg, bellowing with rage. She held on, pressing down hard against him. How could he have so much strength?

"Please, please, *don't*. Just rest. Be quiet. Everything is all right." She tried to make her voice as soothing as possible. Then, after one last fierce struggle, he seemed to collapse. Slowly, untrustingly, she released him and stood up. He lay quietly on his back. He seemed to be in a deep coma. She looked at his bandages and saw the reddening stains. "I fear you've done it this time, my friend. Never should have left you alone. Should've kept you tied up and gagged."

Wasn't too late. Quickly she got more tape and bound his arm and leg to the bed. Hated to, but what choice did she have? The gag? She hesitated, squeamish at the thought of it. But his bellowing had probably already wakened the dead. No choice. She installed a light gag in his mouth. Then she checked his bandages. No point in changing them. She repaired minor damage to the sling. At least he hadn't broken the clavicle loose. Pulse. Racing. She didn't count.

She stood over him. He looked so still, deathly still. God! "Please don't die. I don't know who you are or what you've done, but please don't die." Her wit, virtually irrepressible, surfaced. "I can't have done all this work for nothing. It isn't fair."

FOUR

Gordon Adams remained calm all day Saturday. He received a series of messages indicating the defection of Yuri Khruchenko was on schedule. His decoy had been flagged, flushed, run, asked, then sent back to Khruchenko, who had repeated the process. Apparently Sloane and Rogers had done this much by the book. But where were they going to take Khruchenko? No one seemed to know. Adams wasn't even sure it was happening in Munich. It could be anywhere, for Christ's sake.

His mental swearing was a symptom of his concern about the entire operation. By nightfall, when he had received no final word on the taking of Khruchenko, concern gave way to worry then to exasperation. What were Sloane and Rogers doing? When all of Sunday passed with still no word, Adams was reduced to a cold inner fury which made him appear icy calm to his subordinates. His mind was under rigid control, thus no more mental swearing. Something was wrong in Munich, seriously wrong. He spent the night at Brandywine, phoning his wife to say a problem had come up at the Naval shipyard in Newport News and he would be gone a couple of days. She didn't seem to care.

The ultimate exasperation came about three A.M. on Monday when Adams learned what had happened in Munich, not from his own men, but from the Reuters wire. He had gone to bed on a cot in his office, leaving word to be awakened if any news came from Munich, however insignificant it might seem. When he read the teletype, he recognized the demise of the Munich operation. Five men were found shot to death in a dry-cleaning shop on Wernerstrasse. Killings believed to have occurred some time Saturday night. Police identified the dead tentatively as three Israelis, an American, and an East German. Shootout believed to be the work of an Israeli anti-Nazi terrorist group.

Adams quickly read the rest of the article. No names, but he knew it was Sloane and Rogers. They would use a dry-cleaning shop to take Khruchenko. Closed for the weekend, it would be perfect for them. But five dead! How? Who? He didn't believe the phony identifications for a second. The Israelis had no involvement in this. That was just a cover. Sloane and Rogers might have posed as Israelis. Were they dead? And the East German. Could be Khruchenko. God, he hoped not. He dispatched a Code One message to Munich ordering operatives to find out everything possible about the dry-cleaning murders at once. He would rather have used a higher priority code, but a Code One agent was the highest he had in Munich. In the message he included a one-word command to Sloane and Rogers, who were Code Three, to report at once. He suspected the message was futile, but if by chance one or both were still alive they would get it. If not, no one else would know the message was there.

By eight A.M. Brandywine time, Adams had pieced together most of what must have happened and it was all bad news. Khruchenko was dead, so was Rogers. Sloane was missing. The two had taken Khruchenko in the back of the dry-cleaning shop. An empty syringe had been found. Apparently they were debriefing him right on the spot—the bastards. They were going their separate way, learning all they could, then withholding their knowledge from the agency. Damn 'em! If they'd done it by the book none of this would have happened.

Apparently there had been a setup. Three men had burst in the back door firing Uzis. Rogers and Khruchenko never had a chance. Who the three men were was unknown. German police were still saying Israelis, but Tel Aviv was denying any involvement. A sixth man, surely Sloane, was missing. But he was badly wounded. Police followed a heavy trail of blood down the street and around the corner, where it ended. The entire neighborhood was searched, but nothing was found. Police believe he may have driven off in a car. All German authorities were alerted to watch for a wounded man in a vehicle. But the search was concentrated in Munich. From the amount of blood lost in the trail, police deduced he couldn't have gone far. He was seriously wounded, and now probably dead or dying.

By ten A.M. Adams had the results of ballistics tests. Khruchenko and Rogers had been killed by multiple rounds from two different Uzis, both of which were found at the scene. Two of the "Israelis" had been killed by Sloane's gun, which was found, the third by Rogers's Walther, which was missing. Somehow Sloane had switched weapons with his partner. Wasn't hard to figure. Sloane had lost his weapon when hit, then somehow gotten to Rogers's to kill the third man.

None of these deductions comforted Adams. This operation was routine and should have succeeded. He had set it up himself. Sloane and Rogers might be tired, used up, so cynical they were working for themselves and not the Agency, but they were also damn good, maybe the best there ever was. They had survived in the field by being exceedingly careful, totally wary. They simply never would have fallen into a trap set by Khruchenko. After the near miss in Prague, they trusted him not at all. They would have taken him only in a situation that they deemed foolproof. But it wasn't. They were set up, doublecrossed by someone they trusted, someone who was working against them.

Adams leaned back in his swivel chair and elevated his feet to his desk. He rubbed his eyes. They felt gritty. Two hours sleep wasn't enough. He forced himself to think. He had been totally careful. Only seven people in the Agency knew Khruchenko wanted to defect. Two were Sloane and Rogers. Khruchenko had contacted them— just how, they wouldn't reveal. They were the only American agents he trusted, and he would surrender to no one else. Adams hated to use them even this one last time. They had become a force unto themselves, a vast mistake for which he was held personally responsible. But Khruchenko left him no choice.

It was possible the two operatives had messed up and fallen into a trap set by Khruchenko. Adams found that most difficult to believe. Sloane and Rogers would have bugged out at the first inkling of danger. And those two had radar for a setup. It was always possible the KGB had laid the trap, dangling Khruchenko as bait. Rogers and Sloane had been amazingly successful against them, and the Russians had no love for them. But, no. Khruchenko knew too much ever to be risked as bait just to catch two American field operatives. If the KGB knew Khruchenko was even thinking of defecting, they would have killed him before he ever left Moscow.

That left an unthinkable possibility. The mole. Sloane and Rogers had long suspected a mole high in the agency and made no bones about it. Their operations in Pakistan, Prague, and a half dozen other places had soured. A couple of times they barely escaped with their lives. They trusted no one, not even himself. And their distrust had triggered his, at least to the extent of recognizing the possible existence of a mole. Khruchenko would know, thus his importance. Since Sloane and Rogers would never put their hides on the line by telling anyone of the Khruchenko defection, since he had not told anyone himself, that left the four other members of The Committee. They were sworn to secrecy about any matters before the group and should have told no one. But one of them had. Was there any other explanation for those five bodies in a Munich dry-cleaning shop?

Without willing it or being aware of it, Adams sat upright in his chair, then leaned over the desk, both fists under his chin. He was trying to think like Sloane and Rogers and he should be able to. After all, he had trained them. Sloane and Rogers had set up the whole operation. It had run all day Saturday and gone fine. They had used commercial cab drivers to run first the decoy then Khruchenko. A couple of other operatives were involved, particularly in the "ask 'em" phase. But they wouldn't have "need to know" who they were questioning and for what purpose, and so wouldn't know. Sloane and Rogers would see to that.

They selected the dry-cleaning shop for the meeting. That was most unlike them and surely a mistake. They normally used the most public places, hotels, tourist traps where there were lots of people, and they could go unnoticed. But they had selected a dry-cleaning shop closed for the weekend. They wanted to be alone with Khruchenko. They wanted to chemically debrief him, find out what he knew before bringing him in.

No. They could have done that in a hotel room, most anyplace. Adams now swore under his breath. They wanted to be alone with him in an empty shop because they planned to debrief then kill him. They couldn't do that in a public place for fear of being seen with him. But they could leave his body in a dry-cleaning shop while they had a whole weekend to escape. And not just from that murder, but from the whole Agency. The two planned to bug out. The bastards!

Adams got up and walked around his desk, forcing his pique at his star operatives out of his mind. Unless Sloane and Rogers had picked up Khruchenko in the last cab and taken him to the dry-cleaning shop, which was extremely careless and unlikely, then *someone* had to have told the hit men where to go. *Someone* knew about the dry-cleaning shop. Find that someone and he had a large piece of the puzzle. Had the mole made a mistake?

Adams picked up the phone and reached Cash, his assistant for Middle European operations. "I want a complete report on the Munich operation from everyone involved. I want to know *everything*. No detail should be considered insignificant."

He made a second call to Boggs, his administrative assistant. "Any news from Munich? Have they found the wounded man?" No word. "Let me know the second there is."

Adams resumed his pacing. Khruchenko dead, Rogers dead, Sloane half dead, dying or already dead. Had to hope not. Sloane's living was the only sail left in the wind. He and Rogers had chemically debriefed Khruchenko before the shooting—or at least tried to. How far had they gotten? What had they learned? Only Sloane knew the answers. He had to be found, brought in, and made to talk.

But carefully, very, very carefully. Sloane was badly wounded, maybe fighting for his life. He'd be like his code name—Wolf—a wounded wolf defending his den. His partner, Bear, was dead. He wouldn't take kindly to that. He'd want vengeance. There had been a trap and he above all would know it. Probably figure it came from Brandywine—which it well might have. He would trust no one from the Agency. Probably kill anyone who came near him. Adams shook his head. Bad situation. Maybe he was too badly wounded to be able to kill. It was a straw in the wind. Had to grab it. There was another chance. If he sent someone whom Sloane knew and trusted. Yes. But who?

Adams entered his walk-in safe and retrieved a locked box—Sloane's file. Ordinarily this sort of information was in a computer to be read off a screen. But someone—nobody ever learned who—had tapped the computer. Adams never trusted the gadget again. Sloane's file was bulky, intimidating in size, but Adams started at the beginning with his security check. To earn a classification of Top Secret Category Three, Cryptographic Code Word Three, the highest in the land, Sloane's life had been put under a microscope. Everything he had ever done, everyone he had ever known was there.

Adams looked for names of friends, relatives, service buddies, anyone he'd known, liked, trusted even a little. Several times he shook his head. They had done too good a job. Sloane was selected because, aside from being a highly intelligent problem solver, he was a loner. Ran away from home at sixteen. No ties to family, few friends even as a kid. There had to be someone. Adams read for over an hour before he found something. At Pensacola, during cryptology school, Sloane had roomed with one Duane Forbes. Both had known each other by different names, but no matter. Sloane and Forbes had been buddies, gone out drinking together, even bought a car together. Not bad. Maybe, just maybe. He picked up the phone and asked Boggs to bring the file on an inactive agent named Duane Forbes.

It was much slimmer. Duane Forbes had been selected for the same training as Sloane and Rogers, but he had flunked out. Just couldn't assimilate all the information. Bad in electronics, impossible in languages, except German. Never made Code Word Three—but he had been cleared for it. Just never received the classification. His training ended after cryptology school and he was sent into the field as a Code Word One. Mistake. Lousy in the field, which is why his partner was killed. A really messed-up operation in the Philippines. Because Forbes was cleared for Code Word Three, some thought was given to bringing him into Brandywine. But he had a reputation as a foul-up. He had been allowed to retire.

Adams studied the remainder of Forbes's file. Lived in the Cleveland area. In the insurance business. He had performed a couple of assignments satisfactorily, just surveillance and make a report. Married. Adams looked at her photo. Blond, young, pretty. A daughter one year old. Another on the way. He nodded. Forbes might do.

Adams delved back into Sloane's file, searching for any involvement between the two after Pensacola. A half hour later he found it. Sloane and Forbes had had a drink together in Manila. He checked the date. Two and a half years ago. It was just after Forbes lost his partner. Sloane had known him and sympathized. Forbes said he was getting out, retiring, going back to Cleveland. Sloane told him he was smart to do it, a lucky man. That's what he'd like to do. Sloane's cynicism was already starting.

Another few minutes of checking showed no further involvement between the two. But it was enough. They had been pals once, gone to cryptology school together. Forbes figured that was all there was, and he was a top agent. He had no idea what Sloane had gone on to learn—and do. He had no idea how much higher classification Sloane was, and Sloane had never told him.

Good, all good. If a Code Word Two agent was sent to find Sloane, he'd never trust him. Kill him if he could. But a Code Word One, so far out of it as to be ridiculous, particularly since he had been retired for two and a half years—now that was possible. Sloane wouldn't view him as a threat. Since he knew him, had once been a pal, he might figure Forbes was really there to help him.

Adams closed and locked both files. Forbes. Just had to work. He picked up the phone.

Parsley also read the Reuters wire and the news disturbed him greatly. Five dead, one wounded and missing had instant meaning for him. He had sent Schwartz, a Code Word Two agent, one of the most capable men from his own zone, to Munich. He was told a high-ranking man from KGB was meeting two American Code Three operatives who had turned double agents. Posing as a Code Word One newly assigned to Munich, he would participate in the drill with the decoy until he learned where the meeting was to take place. Then, using his authority as a Code Word Two, he was to borrow men from Army Intelligence at Rhinebeck AFB, surprise the three at their meeting and dispatch them. Parsley himself had arranged for Schwartz to receive a packet containing complete Israeli identifications for three men. A trio carrying Uzis ought to wipe out a dozen men.

Parsley swore audibly. The three were dead, including Schwartz. That was a virtue. He would never be able to speak of his orders. The East German had to be Khruchenko. Dead. Thank God for that. One of the Americans, either Sloane or

Rogers, dead. But one still lived, at least enough to get away. He swore again. How had it happened? All that firepower and he still had escaped.

Dead or alive he had to be found. He knew far too much already and after meeting Khruchenko ... Khruchenko couldn't ID him, still ... God knows what he could figure out. There was no safety until he was dead. Someone had to be sent to find him—preferably his body, but if alive finish him. He knew who to send—Schwartz's partner. He would want vengeance. Parsley got out his code book and began to draft a message.

Freddie was down in the dumps and feeling a bit sorry for herself, both highly uncharacteristic of her. And she knew why. She had spent twenty-four hours at this man's bedside. His only activity had been another spate of tossing and turning. Tethered to the bed he hadn't moved much, but for good measure she had swiped a sheet, along with fresh towels, from the linen closet and tied his whole body to the bed so that he couldn't move. After that, nothing, just an unconscious man who somehow still breathed. His blood pressure was low, but his pulse was dropping, now close to one hundred.

She felt helpless. There was nothing she knew to do. She tried a few times to get water down him. It wasn't very successful. He coughed most of it out. She was bored out of her mind, claustrophobic from being cooped up in the room. The view from the window was as she feared, the alley, a patch of sky above, gray, raining. She needed activity, movement, people, involvement, and there was nothing to do. The TV, even the American reruns, were in German, and it made her feel like a boob-tube freak. She turned it off.

After dark Sunday, she went for a walk, but was afraid to leave him too long. She brought in her suitcase through the back, having left the door ajar with a wedge of paper. Unpacking, hanging up a few things, gave her momentary diversion. Then what? She had brought the bottle of bourbon in from the car. Maybe it would jolly her up. It didn't. Tasted ghastly, even diluted with water. *Face it, Freddie. You're never going to be the town drunk.*

Ultimately she lay down beside him, carefully, making sure he was not disturbed, listening to his shallow breathing, worrying. He didn't have much chance. Even if his bleeding stopped—and most likely his guts were already filled with blood—infection would get him. Peroxide wouldn't help much and with all the blood he'd lost, he couldn't have enough white corpuscles left to have any more than an occasional get-together. She felt his forehead. Still cool, but how much longer? The infection was probably just getting started, little bugs copulating, having babies who had babies who had babies. He needed antibiotics, lots of them. Fat chance she had of getting those without a doctor.

Why had she listened to him, not gone for help? If it were so important to her to save his life—and God knows why—she should call an ambulance. So he was in trouble with the law. Better bars than dead. No doctors, he had said, no hospital, no police, tell no one, leave while you can. *I'm doing you a favor.* Why did she believe him? Because he was desperate, already unconscious on his feet. It was no con. Those words were part of his fight for life.

Okay, she couldn't betray him by turning him in when he was helpless. But what was she going to feel when he conked out there in bed and she hadn't taken him to the hospital? Yeah, lousy. "Ol' buddy, you just better not die on me. I don't like guilt trips." She made a decision then. She'd go along with him for now. No hospital, no doctors. But as soon as he woke up, if he woke up, she'd convince him to go himself, get patched up, get that bullet out of his gut, get some antibiotics. Yes, she'd do that.

To her surprise she fell asleep, but awoke early—first light, as luck would have it. She untied his sheet, pulled back his blanket and checked him. No change as near as she could tell, except his blood pressure was a shade higher and his pulse down to ninety-two. Wasn't that progress? Did it mean his bleeding had stopped? No sign of fever—yet. *Be good little bugs. Go elsewhere for your hanky-panky.* She fastened him back in bed, then showered. For something to do she spent a long time pampering herself, shaving her legs and underarms, brushing her hair, fussing over makeup, and changing her attire twice. She ended up in a pale blue shirtwaist cotton dress, hose, and heels. Another five minutes were consumed in deciding on jewelry. She selected a blue and pink silk scarf at her throat. Changing her purse consumed another bit of time. She found the picklock. *At least I learned something useful. Freddie Falscape, girl footpad.*

She had run out of things to do and stood looking at her handiwork in the mirror. Not a bad-looking broad. She had always felt good about her looks. Nothing flashy, nothing spectacular. Nobody stopped and gaped at her, but she wore well. She liked her hair, brunette, worn to the shoulders, flipping out naturally at the ends. All she had to do was tease the top a little. And she liked her eyes, big and brown. Long ago she'd gotten over wishing they were blue. Men noticed her eyes, and if the truth were known she helped them out by practicing eye contact, if she were interested in someone, that is. But her mouth was her best feature, she knew: lips well turned out but not too full, wide, the corners turned up a trifle, and symmetrical.

She shook her head. All dressed up and no

place to go. Oh, there was, all right. She'd read *Fodor's*. Munich was the gayest city in Germany, all that beer, wiener schnitzel and naughty, naughty nightlife. She turned to the bed. "I guess you're the main tourist attraction in downtown Munich." She smiled, remembering a stunt she pulled once in an English castle. There was a sign: WATCH STEP. She'd just stood there, looking at it. Everyone wondered what she was doing. She said she was watching the step but nothing was happening. "That's you, Dave baby. I watch but nothing happens."

She stood over him a moment. "Know what? I'm famished. Suppose you could amuse yourself while I run down and grab a quick bite?"

She did, only the bite was a goodly portion of the breakfast menu. The hot food, being with people, feeling ordinary and accepted lifted her spirits. She longed to go outside, even though it was raining, but knew she had to get back to him.

Emerging from the coffee shop she saw the newsstand. Yes, there must be something to read. That would pass the time. The paperbacks and most of the magazines were in German, although she did pick up last week's *Time*. There were newspapers, *The New York Times* and the *London Times*, both of some vintage. Oh well, old news is better than no news. Then a headline leaped at her: FIVE KILLED IN SHOOT-OUT. It was the Monday edition of the English language paper published in Munich. She paid for everything and hurried back to the room.

The story depressed her terribly.. Five men dead in a dry-cleaning shop on Wernerstrasse, a sixth man, believed to be the assassin, subject of a massive search by police. He was known to be badly wounded. She read the details even though she already knew them. It had to be him, the trail of blood ending at a curb on Wilhelmstrasse. May have entered a car. Police found blood a block away at a brown Audi rented from Hertz. They were checking to see if it came from the same man. *It did, oh it did.* Police believe his escape was aided by an accomplice and were appealing to citizens to report any wounded men or bloodstained vehicles.

She stared at the unmoving figure in the bed. No wonder he didn't want doctors, hospital, police. Five dead. *My God!* What had she done? Loathing, fear, disgust, revulsion welled up inside her. A mass murderer. She had suspected it but— What a sap she was! Her impulse was to run, go to the police. They would believe her. She wasn't an accomplice. She was just a dumb, misguided fool who had tried to help a fellow American.

American. The paper was still in her hand and she looked again. "Dead are three Israelis, an East German, and an American. Police withheld identities, but a police informant said the American was a light-skinned Negro." She went to the dresser and scooped up the passport. Stewart Grady. But that wasn't his real name. Harry, yes. *Harry's dead.* Had to be him.

She stared at Sloane lying in the bed, as though the nearly lifeless figure could provide an answer. She turned away. Had to think. She began to pace a little. *Harry's dead.* They had to be working together. The trip to the post office. Had to go there for the envelope. It was so important he had been determined to get it himself if she'd let him. All that stuff inside, two of everything. Phony names, phony identities. Yes, they had to be working together. Harry and Dave. No last names. Working together, partners. If they were, then— She stopped in mid-stride, turned toward the bed. He wouldn't have killed Harry. The newspaper was wrong. It came almost as a relief to her. Then she remembered. There was a way to check. She reached under the bed and pulled out his gun. Holding it gingerly at arm's length, the muzzle pointed at the floor, she fumbled with it until she managed to extract the clip of bullets. Three gone. And there were five dead. He couldn't have killed them all.

Wonderful! So he only killed three, not five. Just think how much of a better person that makes him. Practically ready for sainthood! She shook her head. Maybe he didn't kill anyone. He wouldn't have killed Harry, his partner. Somebody else had to do that. Maybe he was only protecting Harry, defending himself. Yes. *Yes!* He didn't shoot himself. Somebody else had to, and hardly Harry.

Calmer now, she shoved the clip back into the weapon and placed it back under the mattress. Standing over him, she said, "All right. I don't know who you are or what you've done, but I'm going along with you a while longer. Tell no one, you said. I gather the risk is not just to you, but to me if I do. Is that the favor you're doing me? Wonderful! Thanks for crawling into my car. You also said that even if you live you're dead. Great prognosis! Okay, can't be helped. But I'll tell you one thing, buster. When you wake up—if you wake up—you just better have some splendid explanations."

That was her decision. She had no idea whether it was the right one—probably not. But without a crystal ball, she had no idea what was right. She could only stumble along as a cockeyed optimist. She could remember Mitzi Gaynor singing the line in *South Pacific*. She tried but couldn't remember the tune. But she remained depressed, uncertain, frustrated, full of doubt. All she could do was wait.

Duane Forbes opened the door marked 2-D and stepped inside. It had been three, close to four, years since he'd been here, but everything was familiar. Little had changed. The cryptography classroom. Lord, the grueling hours he'd spent here. Tough stuff to learn.

He walked around the room, examining some of the equipment. Different stuff. The codes he'd learned were probably old hat by now. He turned and spotted his old desk, walked over and sat. He remembered and quickly found his initials carved in the surface. D.F. Nobody could connect it to him. He was known as Bob Arthur then. His code name was Kingfisher.

It had all happened so fast. A voice on the phone. Pack a bag. Be at Cleveland-Hopkins Airport at eight P.M. Ticket waiting at United. He was Robert D. Arthur, No. 8964, one-thirty A.M.

He told Addie he was going to Washington. Had to meet an insurance executive early Tuesday. Might be a big promotion. At the airport he saw his flight was to Norfolk, Virginia, then to Pensacola, Florida, via Piedmont. At Pensacola he went to Corry Field, then to the gate of the CSA compound. He punched his number, 8964, into a cypher lock and entered. Then he signed in with a Marine guard as Robert D. Arthur. It was precisely one-thirty A.M. The Marine took his suitcase and made him empty his pockets. Go to Classroom 2-D. Okay, he'd done the drill. He was in 2-D. For what? There was nobody here. He shrugged. Hurry up and wait. That was the Navy.

He and Addie had been doing it when the phone call had come. He smiled. Most people probably didn't do it at four in the afternoon, but then most people weren't him and Addie. She was ready anytime. And with Jana down for her nap, time was a-wasting. He let out a snortlike sound. Addie never wasted any time. Morning, noon, evening, night was fine with her. She couldn't get enough. Wearing him out—only she always seemed to find some way to turn him on. Addie'd do *anything*. It seemed the most important thing in life, sometimes the only thing. He'd asked her once. She'd said, "When another woman looks at you, she's going to see a very tired man."

He had no complaints. Oh, yes, he did. Addie didn't have all the brains in the world. Her interests didn't go beyond television, movies, rock music, and clothes, which she kept him strapped buying. He hadn't wanted to marry her—anybody for that matter. But he had the hots for her and she wouldn't give in. Kept saying he wouldn't be sorry. He guessed he wasn't. She was good to Jana and busted her ass for him. He had no complaints about his sex life—unless it was too much. Sometimes he wondered if she wasn't a nympho. Naw, she just liked it.

Good to get away though. He missed all this sometimes. Exciting. Dangerous. Kept you on your toes, sharp. You felt like all your faculties were honed to a fine edge. It was a battle of wits. You'd better outwit the other guy if you wanted to live. He had. He was a survivor. Poor Jamie. One lapse and he was gone.

Forbes got up from the desk and walked to the blackboard in front. Somebody'd cleaned it. They always did. Security was everything. That's probably why they'd flown him here. This was a secure space. Somebody wanted to talk about something that couldn't be known to others. All right, he was ready—for anything they wanted. Must be important to fly him to Pensacola in such a hurry, then clear him through security. Had to be something more than the piddling little surveillance jobs and security checks he'd done in Cleveland.

Adams watched him on the video monitor while he waited for the final security clearance to come through. Yes, this was Robert Arthur, codename Kingfisher. Fingerprints, voice, signature checked. Good. Pensacola security didn't know him as Duane Forbes, only as Arthur. He stood up, then paused a moment, mentally reviewing what he wanted to say. Two hours sleep wasn't enough for him anymore. Hated flying to Pensacola, but Forbes wasn't cleared to enter Brandywine. There were Space Twos closer to Cleveland than Pensacola, but he figured the familiar setting would put Forbes at ease and off his guard—if he had any. He entered Classroom 2-D.

Adams did it by the book. He made no greeting, simply motioned Forbes to a desk in the front row and sat next to him. He was performing as a briefer who normally gave orders to field agents. A briefer was a nameless, faceless person who passed on rote, utterly meaningless words to an agent. There were no questions. Neither ever saw the other again. A briefer acted like a talking piece of furniture. Adams had thought about using a briefer for Forbes but abandoned the idea. Too many instructions were needed, if only because Forbes was so far out of everything. No briefer could be permitted to know that much. Also, he couldn't risk having the mole, if there were one, learning from a briefer anything about Forbes.

"Do you remember David Dickson?"

Forbes's brow furrowed. "Dickson, you say?" Then he grinned. "Sure, Dave Dickson. He was my roomie when I was here."

"Yes, you bought a car together."

"Sure did. A 'fifty-five Chevy. Been wrecked. Motor bad."

Adams's expression showed no change, but he was appalled. This man was totally unprofessional. He had forgotten everything—if he ever knew it. Maybe that was for the best. Sloane might trust someone so obviously unprofessional as this one. "You met him later in Manila?"

"Yeah, sure did. How'd you know that?"

Lord! "Have you had contact since?"

"No. I wondered whatever happened to him. Is he in some kind of trouble?"

That was a good lead in. "Yes. Dickson has remained on active duty, various assignments. He is known to be wounded. He may need help. You are to go to him and provide that help."

Forbes was surprised. "Me? Why me? I'm retired."

"So you are. You are also a friend of his."

"That was years ago."

"He will remember you."

Forbes glanced at the man beside him. Didn't know him. And his deadpan impersonality made him nervous. Wouldn't even look at him. "Where is he?"

"Munich."

"Munich? Germany?" He shook his head. "Why me? You must have somebody there already."

"We don't. You will go. That is not a request."

The sharp words brought Forbes up short. "All right. What do I do?"

Adams knew this was the hard part. Forbes had to be told what he needed to know to do the job, but not one syllable more. "First, you find him. Read this and memorize it." He handed him the latest Reuters dispatch from Munich. It reported the details of the shooting and the hunt for the wounded man. He waited until Forbes finished. "Take all the time you need. Memorize all the addresses, every detail." Finally Forbes handed it back to him. "Have you got it all?"

"Yes. Dickson is the wounded man?"

"Yes."

"Who shot him? What was he doing?"

"You have no need to know. You are to go to Munich and find Dickson."

"Based on what I just read? If the police can't find him, how can I?"

Adams suppressed his exasperation. "Dickson is using the identify of either Lionel Twilley from

Silver Spring, Maryland, or William Hatch from South Bend, Indiana."

"Which the German police don't know."

"Correct. That may help you, although, of course, he may use another identity entirely. He's either stolen a private car or forced someone to drive him to a safe house known only to himself. Since he is badly wounded, he would be unable to travel far. He is in Munich, holed up, in need of medical attention."

"Holed up where?"

"He will not be hard to find. Prior to the shooting, he would have established a safe house. Most likely it would be a major hotel, frequented by tourists, especially Americans, so that he would not attract attention. He would have paid for the room in advance, said it was for storage, and would not require any type of service. It will be a room on the first or second floor, easily accessible from the street, probably by a service entrance. Got all that?"

"Yes."

"There aren't very many such hotels. Start at the airport. He most likely went there."

Forbes nodded. "What do I do when I find him?"

"He will need medical attention, but be unable to go to a doctor or hospital. Aid will come to him as soon as you phone this number." He handed him a slip of paper with seven digits on it. "Memorize it. Do not forget it." He waited. "Got it?"

In a moment Forbes said, "Yes."

Adams took back the piece of paper. "Repeat it."

Forbes did and Adams was impressed. "Good. When you phone use a pay box. You will reach a local message service. Simply say you have a message for Post Office Box 233. Have you got the number?"

"Yes, P.O. Box 233."

"No need to identify yourself. Your message will be forwarded to Box 233 where it will be picked up within the hour."

"What's my message?"

"In the travel pack I'm going to give you is a street map of Munich. If you should lose it you can buy a similar one anywhere. Hotels are numbered on the map. You will form a number with the first two digits being the number of the hotel, the remaining digits the room number where you find Dickson. If, for example, you find him in Room 147 of Hotel Number 10, your message for Box 233 will be 'Have placed an order for 10147 pairs.' Have you got it?"

"Yes—only what if I don't find him at a hotel?"

"We are almost certain you will, but if not your message will simply ask for delivery to be made at whatever address he's at."

"Is that all I'm to do?"

"Yes. After you make the phone call you may return home. It should be a short, easy assignment. As soon as you locate Dickson, you are finished. Just be certain it is Dickson. You do remember what he looks like?"

"Yes, I think so."

Adams heard the hesitation in his voice. "You have a problem?"

"I don't know." He paused, firming his mouth into a hard line. "Dave and I were buddies, sort of, but it has been a while. If he's stayed in field work, gotten into trouble and been wounded, I'm not sure he'll want to see me."

"It is precisely because he is wounded and needs help that he will be glad to see you."

"I suppose, still I—"

"You may want to approach him with caution. Then recall your past association, assure him you are there to help him."

"He'll believe me?"

Without hesitation Adams replied, "Yes, of course." Then he handed him a manila envelope. "Here is your travel pack. It contains a passport and other identification in the name of Robert Arthur. Also the street map of which I spoke. There is a plane ticket from Pensacola to Munich, also an open-ended ticket from Munich to Cleveland. You need only make a reservation when you are finished."

Duane Forbes watched the man rise. The interview was over. "But—but what if something goes wrong?"

"Nothing will go wrong."

"What if I need to contact someone?"

Adams stared at him. "You won't. This is a very simple mission."

Deep under Dzerzhinsky Square, Dimitri Galenkov pondered the loss of Yuri Khruchenko. Like himself, he was an old warrior in the intelligence wars, one of the survivors from the days prior to détente, that stupid policy. Andropov, Brezhnev, the whole Politburo had panicked after the CSA success of North Korea. They needed time, they said, time to reorganize the KGB. Détente! Impossible! The CSA had merely taken advantage of their weakness. Détente! Thank God it had ended.

He forced his mind back to his problem. There never had been any question of the loyalty of Yuri Khruchenko. His own knowledge of the man, his long-time friend and confidant, left no doubt. Yuri was his brother-in-law. His sister had not wanted the arranged marriage, but the KGB had considered it wise and she had made a good life with Yuri. But Yuri worried too much about Parsley. His usefulness was undoubted, he insisted, his aid, unsolicited, often subtle, had meant success many times, but he should not be trusted. He is not one of us, Yuri had said. He is a capitalist who wants power. One day he will betray us. Yes,

Yuri had said it many times in their private conversations. He had himself tried often to reassure his friend. True, Parsley may try to betray us, but you will know and so will I when that happens. We are not fools. Parsley is not that clever. He always knew his friend remained unconvinced, however. Perhaps Yuri should have been told of the control secretly placed on Parsley.

Galenkov shook his head. Sad. Yuri's mind must have broken. He must have become more obsessed with the danger from Parsley than he realized. But defect to stop him? Unthinkable, yet it happened. Dead now. Gone.

Galenkov's attitude changed abruptly. It was as though he had held a brief, private wake for an old friend and comrade. Finished now, he tended to business. The decoy had been recovered, debriefed. He did not know whom he had decoyed for or what his intentions were. He had simply followed orders. No sense in disciplining the man, but he should be observed closely.

The troublesome question was how long Khruchenko had been in the dry-cleaning shop. The empty syringe meant he had been debriefed on the spot. Extraordinary and risky. But those two Americans were very good. They had been marked for death for over two years, but they each had the lives of a cat. How much had Yuri told them? He was in a position to compromise every agent in North America and a dozen operations. Had he time to do so? Galenkov shook his head in frustration, then characteristically decided what he must do. There was no point in panicking as before. Changing agents and operations would take years. He would alert everyone to danger, put all operations on hold, then wait to see what developed. A few days, a week or two would reveal how much the Americans knew.

A bigger danger. Three words kept returning to his mind: "Parsley will act." Yes, Parsley had acted—but not well enough. One of the Americans had found yet another life in his cat's body. Wounded, missing, at least half a life. Perhaps he had not yet reported what he learned from Yuri Khruchenko. He must never do so. He must be found. If not dead yet, he must be eliminated. There would be no reliance on Parsley this time. He would act himself.

FIVE

Sloane's dreams were terrible, chaotic, full of flashes of fire, searing, agonizing pain from which he could not escape, no matter how hard he tried. He was held immobile, as though in a vise, so tight he could hardly breathe, while the flashes, hot, scalding, bore into him, again and again, constantly, excruciatingly. He wanted to scream his agony, but somehow he could not.

Then it stopped and his consciousness rose. He opened his eyes. Strange, unknown. A woman, smiling, saying something. Who was she? She removed something from his mouth. So dry. Couldn't swallow. Water. Oh, please, water. Her hand on his forehead. So cool. Then behind his head, lifting. Water trickled into his mouth. God, thank you, thank you. She said something, but he couldn't hear. She was floating away, beyond his vision. Flashes now. Oh, the pain.

It happened again. He saw her clearer now. So beautiful. Water. Oh, yes, cool, like her hand. He tried to touch her but somehow couldn't. Then she floated away again. His dream was different now. He was in a desert, hot, sand burning his body as he crawled over it, and the sun beating down on him. Had to keep moving. Thirsty.

Ahead was water, cool, blue. He could see it. Had to reach it.

He was brought to full consciousness by the sensation at his stomach, cold, sharp. What was it? It moved upward toward his chest. He opened his eyes, saw her. The sharp movement stopped. Brown hair, brown eyes, very beautiful. He didn't know her.

"I do believe you're awake this time."

He stared at her, blinked. Who was she?

"Do you want some water?"

"Please." His voice was strange to him, a cracked whisper. Then she was holding a glass and bent straw to him. He sucked, hard, deep. It was good. But he couldn't keep his eyes open.

"That's it. You must be the Gobi Desert."

He heard her, but it made no sense to him. He registered only that her voice was pleasant, somehow soothing. He liked hearing it. He finished and let go of the straw. His lips were wet. He moved them. It felt good.

"You're in an awful lot of trouble, friend. You're a sieve—four wounds. Your left arm and shoulder are useless, your right leg not much better. There's a bullet in your side. You have a fever of 101 and climbing. I think that qualifies as one foot in the grave. You need a hospital if you are to survive."

"No hospital."

"Look, I'm no doctor, not even a nurse. I can't do surgery, which you badly need. I can't buy morphine, antibiotics, IV, whole blood, anything that might keep you alive." She saw him shaking his head, or trying to. It had to hurt. "My, but you're stubborn. Are you awake enough to understand you're going to die if you don't get medical attention?"

"I can't. I'll be—"

"I know. You told me. But does it matter which way you die? The police want you for five murders. You're all over the newspapers. Isn't it better to live behind bars than die here in this bed?"

He opened his eyes. Who was she? There was something about her he should remember, only ... His eyes closed again. Couldn't keep them open.

"Dave or Lionel or William or whoever you really are, you can be suicidal all you want, but I'm not. You're in big trouble and so am I. The police are looking for you everywhere. If they burst in that door and find me with you, I'm in trouble, too. It's called harboring a fugitive. I'm an accomplice."

He forced his eyes open. "Who are you?"

"I've a better question. Who are *you*? I don't make a habit—at least not a regular one—of protecting mass murderers."

It made no sense to him. "I don't know ... who you are."

She shook her head. "I guess you don't remember. You were shot in a dry-cleaning shop on Wernerstrasse. You crawled or walked, I don't know which, a couple of blocks and got into the back seat of my car. At gunpoint you forced me to drive you first to your car, then the post office, finally here. Don't you remember any of it?"

He did, a little, flashes of fire. "I—I remember ... shooting." Then more, a tabloid, Harry flying backward. "Is Harry dead?"

"Yes, Harry's dead."

He stared at her, blinking repeatedly as though trying to cling to wavering consciousness. "Where am I?"

"Where you told me to bring you, Room 112, Hotel Columbia."

It came back to him, the loading platform, picking the lock, but nothing beyond that. "Please ... your name. I have ... to know."

She sighed. "I told you once, but I guess you

had other things on your mind. My name is Fern Falscape. My friends call me Freddie. I think you'd better call me Fern—even better, Professor Falscape. I'm far from certain you're a friend." She saw his eyelids slowly close, flutter. "May I point out that I don't know your name—at least not for certain. You are maybe Lionel Twilley, maybe William Hatch, maybe somebody named Dave. Which is it?" She waited. He didn't answer. "It seems to me I've a right to know. After all, I've done a whole lot more for you lately than you have for me." Still no answer. She turned away, figuring he was unconscious again.

"Dave—David Sloane."

His answer surprised her. "At least that's something. Tell me, Mr. Sloane, exactly what do you do—besides kill people in dry-cleaning shops?"

"Field op."

She furrowed her brow. "Field op? I don't understand. What's an op?"

"Operative."

"Field operative?" She shook her head. "You're a farmer?"

"No." He was tired, sinking away. "Intelligence."

She repeated the word in her mind. *Intelligence.* "Oh, I get it. You're a spy?" She heard him moan. "Are you on some kind of—what do they call it?—oh, yes, mission in Munich?"

"Can't talk . . . tired."

"Wait. Have some more water."

He felt the straw at his lips, sucked hard, too fast. Had to cough.

"Dave, I have to know what to do. I can't save your life. And if I stay here, I'll—"

"Go . . . tell no one."

"You said that before. Why should I tell no one?"

"You'll . . . be killed."

"Why me? I've done nothing."

"Because of . . . what I know."

He had passed out and Freddie knew she would learn no more from him now. But what she had heard filled her with relief. He wasn't a crook, a mass murderer, but an American agent, a spy on some kind of mission, serving his country. And he had been wounded while doing it. If he had killed it was in the line of duty. It was *right* for her to help him. *Thank God!*

She picked up the scissors and resumed cutting away the bandages. They had to be changed. Probably causing the infection. His wounds were horrid to see, black, festering, surrounded by angry reddish-bluish flesh. Everything seemed so much worse than before, and she didn't know what to do. But, struggling against her squeamishness and fright, she began to clean the wounds, each in turn, scraping away dried blood and pus, even to the edge of the holes. When fresh blood appeared in his shoulder, she jumped back, almost screamed. Maybe it was good. Who knew? She repeatedly poured peroxide into the wounds. Did it help? Had to wash away some of the dead stuff, didn't it?

When she finished applying the last of the bandages and the sling for his arm, it was long past dark and she was exhausted. Her back rebelled and her head was reeling.

A shower refreshed her, the last of her meat and cheese in a sandwich even more. She sat now in her pajamas, munching and thinking. An American agent. She could not doubt it. All those phony identification papers, his gun, his wounds. And the people who had tried to kill him in the dry-cleaning shop would still be after him. No wonder he wanted no hospital, no doctors, no police. Tell no one. And she was in danger, too. *Because of what I know.* Yes. Even if she really didn't know anything, she would be killed simply because she had been with him and *might* know something. *Wonderful, Freddie. Simply jolly. Have a good time in Munich.*

Yet, she felt good, better than in days. There was virtue in what she was doing. She wasn't being silly, helping a wounded man who might be . . . Yes, he needed her. *Need, commitment.* That's what was missing from her life.

Freddie stood over him and learned something about herself. She wasn't just an academician, a precocious Ph.D. who was a whiz at the books and had a flawless memory for taking tests. Sometimes her heart could rule her brain. This man, this field op—had to remember the term—was . . . what? She didn't know. And it didn't matter. *Oh, Lord!* Next Week East Lynne. *It is the tragic story of a woman who—oh, shit!*

She ungagged and untethered him, wanting to make him as comfortable as possible. He awoke in the night, moaning, and it awakened her. She gave him water. In the morning she went out, bought chicken soup at a deli, awoke him and spooned some down him. In the afternoon she changed the menu to beef broth. A little color came to him, but his fever hovered around 101. *Dr. Kildare, I'd like you to meet Nurse Nightingale. Some people call her Flo, but those who know her best call her Flop.*

At precisely 10:45 A.M. Gordon Adams left his office at Brandywine and made his way to Elevator C, activating it by using his red card and pressing a numerical code on a cypher lock. Alone, he descended to the four-hundred-foot level, the lowest at Brandywine.

The security checks he now encountered were even more rigorous than when he first entered the underground complex. It began when he approached a Marine at a table, logged in, then emptied his pockets. He deposited his wallet, change, keys, nail clipper, cigarettes and lighter, handkerchief, watch, pen, pencil, and even his wedding band. He carried nothing but the clothes on his back, not even a piece of paper. Then he was subjected to a variety of surveillance devices: photo identifier, voice scanner, X-ray, metal detector, weight evaluator, fingerprint analyzer.

Only then could Adams approach the final room. He came to a heavy metal door, not unlike those which seal watertight compartments on submarines. To open it he had to compress a long series of numerical buttons which both opened the door and identified him as being authorized to enter. These codes had to be rendered with great precision. One error and he set off alarms. He was at risk of being shot on the spot, no questions asked.

Adams was precise and entered. The door closed behind him, sealing hermetically. He took a few steps down a passageway and repeated the process with a second door, using a different code to open it. A flawless memory for numbers was a prerequisite in the intelligence game.

At last he entered Space Three, one of five in the country, a room measuring twelve by fifteen feet. Deep underground, its walls were four feet of reinforced concrete with a lead shield around that. It was indestructible, even at Ground Zero. The Space Three was utterly self-contained. There were no communications in or out. It was equipped with its own electrical supply, plumbing and air conditioning, and it was provisioned with food, water, sleeping accommodations and other necessities to support a half dozen people for a year. The Space Three guaranteed the nation's nucleus of leadership would survive a nuclear holocaust.

Adams took a seat at a small table. He was the last to arrive. The other four men, very much like himself, had come alone in accordance with a prearranged schedule. The Marine on duty outside had been replaced after each one. Thus, there was no person alive who could identify all five men or even know they had gathered in one place. They were The Committee. They were meeting there not because they feared nuclear attack, rather because it offered total security. The words uttered in the Space Three would be known only to the five men. There were no recording devices. No minutes were kept. Participants neither made nor referred to notes. A perfect memory was essential even to be considered for membership on The Committee.

The five had been meeting in this manner for years and were well-known to each other, but in the unlikely event any one of them was ever "chemically debriefed" and made to tell all he knew, he would be unable to identify a fellow Committee member other than by his code name. Adams was Green. In his early days with the CSA, particularly when in the field, he had used a variety of names. When he was brought into Brandywine, he was Frank Young for a long time. When he was elevated to The Committee he became Mr. Green. No first name, just Mr. Green—always. It was the same with the others at the table: Mr. Black, Mr. White, Mr. Brown, Mr. Gray.

The five men possessed virtually total anonymity. By Act of Congress, unwittingly passed in 1959 as a minor amendment to an even more insignificant bill, no employee of the Central Security Agency, with the exception of the Director and Deputy Director—and they were uninformed figureheads—could be publicly identified. It even became illegal to state how many people worked for the CSA, although their number was believed to exceed one hundred thousand. The five men were not even listed in the highly classified personnel records of the agency. They were all on detached service from civilian or military departments, which paid their salary and never knew who they were. Indeed, the entire

CSA budget, billions annually, was unknown to the President and his Office of Management and Budget, which submitted it, and to Congress which appropriated it. The CSA billions were simply tacked on to the budgets of other federal departments as secret projects, heads of those agencies having no idea what the money went for. Whenever Gordon Adams heard politicians talk of cutting the budget, or Presidents such as Carter and Reagan demand the line-item veto—or do-gooders decry the fact that a ten-cent nut or screw cost ten dollars, a ship, plane, or missile millions more in "cost overruns"—he had to suppress a laugh. The CSA had to get its money somewhere. And it would never permit itself or national security to be threatened or nickel-and-dimed to death. If a president didn't know it when entering office, he soon discovered he had absolutely no power over the CSA.

The anonymity of The Committee extended to CSA employees, even the high-ranking ones, not one of which could be sure exactly who was on The Committee or even that such a group existed, no matter how much they might believe that it did. Even those on The Committee did not know each other. Although all five lived somewhere in the environs of the District of Columbia, they rarely encountered each other outside of Brandywine. They certainly never met at social gatherings where they might be introduced and learn another's cover name, a feat accomplished in the small world of official Washington by filing and sticking to a rigorous schedule of activities. They lived exceedingly dull lives outside of Brandywine, joining no organizations, eschewing all publicity. To have their photo in a newspaper or any claim to fame, however slight, was to be thrown off The Committee, out of the Agency, and probably receive a death warrant. More nameless, faceless people were hard to imagine. They had no title on the door, no visible authority, no fame, little wealth. Few noticed or paid attention to them, including most of those who worked closest with them.

Yet, as they sat around the table in the austere Space Three and began their meeting, they were without doubt the five most powerful men in the most powerful nation on earth. Each headed and was responsible for an intelligence zone. Green was Europe, White North America, Gray South America, Black Africa, Brown Asia. By tacit agreement between the CSA and KGB, Australia, New Zealand and Antarctica were off limits. This arrangement was sometimes inconvenient. The Soviet Union fell in two zones—as did the war between Iran and Iraq.

Each man was of equal rank, although White presided, keeping the meeting orderly and efficient, simply because he was senior. It would come to each of them in turn.

No one appointed them, if only because no one, including themselves, knew who they were to make such an appointment. They had in effect appointed themselves, rising to their lofty status by reason of ability, hard work, personal sacrifice, circumspection, and luck. Over the years, a total of more than a century for the five of them, they had accumulated—and jealously guarded—so much information about what had happened and was happening in worldwide military, diplomatic, political, economic, ideological, and intelligence affairs that no decision concerning vital national security matters could be made without their knowledge and participation. Authority in the CSA, like the KGB and all the better intelligence agencies, came not from inheritance, money, title, friends, popularity, or any of the usual means by which persons rise to power, but from *knowledge*, specific, detailed, all-encompassing.

The Committee meetings were highly efficient,

devoid of small talk, witticisms, or personal observations. Under unwritten rules, The Committee did not concern itself with the day-to-day routine of any zone. That was left to individual members. Indeed, to question the routine actions of a member, such as in assigning personnel, was an insult. If a man said, "I'm handling it," that usually could not be questioned.

The Committee restricted itself, or tried to, to important problems, plans, and projects that affected the security of the nation and most especially of the Agency itself. They had long since systemized procedures for masking their own activities; for concealing information from the White House, Pentagon, Congress, and the entire government, as well as press and public; and for controlling the information available to all those groups and thus manipulating their knowledge, beliefs, and actions. They were the parent organization of the CIA, which they used as a front for their own activities, and maintained direct operational control over the Defense Intelligence Agency, National Security Council, the separate intelligence branches of the military services, indeed the entire intelligence community of the United States.

The meeting began with a roll call of members, each of whom reported information and activities of interest to the whole group. This was in accordance with the unwritten rule for full disclosure. Each offered the others total trust. Even though their existence as a group remained secret, there were no secrets among them. Jealously guarding information, the means by which a person forced entry onto The Committee, was now forbidden. To be discovered to have withheld information from the others involved at best a lengthy and hopefully plausible explanation or, at worst, death. What one knew all knew, at least in priority matters commanding The Committee's attention.

The members were interchangeable. Any one could run another's zone, and it had happened once or twice in an emergency.

When Adams's turn came, he spoke of a few matters throughout his European zone, then brought up the Khruchenko matter. He had already made up his mind to withhold certain information and even lie if necessary. Whatever consequences might occur, he felt it had to be done. "You are aware Khruchenko is dead. He would have been useful—apparently too useful, which is why he was killed."

Black: "Do you think they took him to stop the defection?"

"Possibly. I'm not certain."

Gray: "What else can it be? Khruchenko was head of the North American section. He could identify agents, operations, much more. Of course they killed him. They had to."

"I agree it is the first and most logical assumption, Mr. Gray. But it is still an assumption. I am trying to determine what happened with certainty. We do not yet have the precise identities of the three 'Israelis.'"

White: "Who were our people?"

"Wolf and Bear. Bear is dead, Wolf missing, presumed badly wounded."

White: "Has he made contact?"

"Not yet. Presumably he can't. We're trying to locate him."

Brown: "Wolf and Bear, huh? Those two again—the last of your little experiment."

There was a tinge of sarcasm in Brown's voice, which annoyed Adams. Brown was a trifle sarcastic with everybody, and Adams knew he wasn't being singled out for special treatment, but that didn't make him like it any better. The "little experiment" he referred to was a plan he had proposed over four years ago when he had first joined The Committee. It had been approved, but the experiment remained "his," especially when it turned out badly. The idea was to train ten pairs of agents, one pair with backup for each zone. They would be Code Word Three agents, possess the red card, but be given special training and information so they could operate worldwide, in any zone. They were to work independently and on the highest priority operations. They would have access to any and all information necessary to their assignment.

Adams still thought it a good idea, but it turned out to be a mistake. The special agents were too independent. They knew too much and learned too much. Worse, they withheld information for their own use until they knew more about certain matters than The Committee. They even came to be a threat to Committee functions. All were gone now—a couple of them executed as too dangerous to live—except for Rogers and Sloane. They were the first pair trained and still the very best. Now just Sloane remained.

When Adams made no reply to Brown, he persisted. "Why did you use those two on something as sensitive as the Khruchenko thing? Those two should have been retired a long time ago—or better yet killed."

Adams bristled. This was perilously close to interfering in the affairs of his zone. He would not dignify it with an explanation, but he did say, "Khruchenko would surrender only to Wolf and Bear, no one else. It was part of the deal."

Gray: "Why?"

"He trusted them."

Brown: "Which is more than I do. So they messed up. Bear is dead. Good. Maybe we'll be lucky and Wolf will join him."

"That will not be at all lucky, Mr. Brown. Wolf is the one person who can tell us what really happened at the dry-cleaning shop. We intend to find him."

White: "You have people on it?"

"Yes. Munich is looking for him. Shouldn't be hard to find."

As the roll passed to Gray, Adams was relieved. He had withheld two pertinent facts: that some chemical debriefing of Khruchenko had occurred and that he had sent Forbes to search out Sloane. In the unlikely event he was ever called upon to explain, he would be able to.

Parsley did not miss the omission of the debriefing. Quigley, partner to the dead Schwartz, had already reported the empty syringe. Why didn't Green mention that Sloane might have learned valuable information from Khruchenko? Strange. It was highly unlikely Green didn't know. Why say nothing about it? Parsley kept his face a mask while he studied Green closely. Nothing visible, but he was now a man to watch. It was impossible that Green was on to him, yet. . . . A person could not be too careful.

SIX

Duane Forbes approached the desk of the Hotel Columbia. He wore jeans and a windbreaker and carried a box with the name of a prominent Munich computer outlet emblazoned on it. In his best German he said he had a delivery for Herr Hatch.

The clerk, middle-aged, officious, bored, and worried about his bunions, said, "The service entrance is in back."

Forbes smiled. "I'm not sure I have the right hotel. Would you check your register for Herr Hatch?"

With some petulance the clerk checked. "No Herr Hatch." It brought him some small pleasure to report that fact.

"Herr Hatch is an American. He took a room to store some equipment."

"We have no Herr Hatch."

Forbes sighed. "I may have the name wrong. Would you check a Herr Twilley or a Herr Dickson?"

The clerk glared at him, then dutifully and ever so formally checked the register. "No Herr Twilley or Herr Dickson. You have the wrong hotel—as you said."

Forbes sighed, picked up his package from the

counter and left. The clerk stared after him. Stupid foreigners. Coming here, speaking bad German, taking jobs from our own people. Couldn't even get the right hotel for deliveries. The only room rented for storage here was 112, Herr Grady.

Forbes sat over a stein of Hackerbrau, hoping to drown his discouragement. It had seemed so easy when he started, but having hit every hotel in the environs of the airport and all the major ones downtown, even some not so major, he accepted the fact that no one named Hatch, Twilley, or Dickson had rented a room for storage. Dave must be using another name and that could be anything. He was down a blind alley.

After drinking another half liter of beer, this one washing down a plate of sauerbraten, he had decided on a whole new approach. He would retrace Dave's steps and see what he could come up with. He drove to Wernerstrasse, parked near the dry-cleaning shop, and started from there. Newspapers had run a map of the trail of blood, hoping to find someone who had seen or talked to the wounded man. This turned up a woman who said he had bumped into her. She thought he was drunk. When last she saw him he was hanging on to a lamppost. That was no help. The trail of blood already indicated that.

Not knowing what he was looking for, but bereft of any other idea, Forbes arrived at the lamppost. Dave had left blood stains on a couple of parked cars, then staggered across that loading zone where the trail ended. Police believed he had gotten into the car just beyond the loading zone, and either had driven away or had been driven away. They had no idea whose car or what make of car. All attempts to find the abandoned vehicle and all appeals to anyone who might have driven him away came out negative. A line from this morning's newspaper came to Forbes: "Since no car that the suspect might have used has turned up, police now believe he has an accomplice who is sheltering him."

Forbes knew better. There was no accomplice. American intelligence agents work in pairs and the American killed in the shootout was probably Dave's partner. Besides, there was a rented car stashed in the next block. There was blood on and around it. Dickson had gone to the car but was too wounded to drive it. Had to be.

If Dave Dickson did not have an accomplice, then there were two choices. Either he was grabbed by the same people who made the hit and wounded him, in which case he was being held by them and probably dead; or, he had forced someone to drive him . . . someplace. Forbes weighed the choices. If this was some kind of intelligence operation involving the Israelis or Russians, the first choice was too tough for him. He didn't even have a weapon. Besides, his orders were just to find a friend and help him. The second choice was easier.

He stood at the lamppost and looked up and down the street. The cops had combed this area for Dickson and anyone who might have helped him. Zero. Therefore the person must not have been a local. A person from out of the area had stopped here, parked his car. For what purpose? Visit someone, maybe buy something. There weren't many places open at this hour.

The wine shop was the third place he tried. The short, bald man behind the counter was wary. "Why do you ask me these questions? Are you the police? I have already told them everything."

Forbes rendered his most engaging smile. "I'm a reporter for *Der Stern*. I'm here to—"

"*Ja, ja,* journalist." His manner changed abruptly. Effusively, he remembered all his customers. There had been only one stranger Saturday night, an American woman, young, very pretty. She had bought a bottle of American whiskey. He went to the shelf and produced a bottle of Old Granddad to indicate the brand. She had paid in deutsche marks, then asked directions to Königstrasse. He had given them to her.

"How do you know she was American?"

He made a waving gesture with his hand to indicate the question was beyond doubt. "Who else buys American whiskey? She spoke English, no German. She was American, believe me."

"Why did she want directions to Königstrasse?" When the proprietor rendered an elaborate shrug, Forbes asked, "Did she say where she wanted to go on Königstrasse?"

"I don't remember if she did. I told the police all this. Unfortunately it is a large street. Many people live there."

"She gave no name?"

"No, why would she?"

Forbes nodded in resignation. "Could you describe her?"

"Young, pretty, very nice smile. I remember that."

"What was she wearing?"

"Who notices clothes on a woman? A raincoat, I think, light in color."

"Color hair?"

"Brown, I think. Yes, and brown eyes. I remember them." He threw out his hands in a gesture of futility. "There is nothing more to remember. She was an ordinary person, very nice, very friendly."

Forbes thanked him and turned to leave.

"Do you think she had something to do with the murders on Wernerstrasse?"

"I don't know."

Searching for he didn't know what, Forbes drove to where the rented Audi had been. Nothing. Then he drove up and down Königstrasse a couple of times. A forbidding facade of apartment buildings. Thousands of occupants. Let the police work that. They had the manpower.

Finally he just drove, slowly, aimlessly, around the city, trying to think. If it was the American girl whose car Dickson had entered, she had not come forward. With all the news the murders were making, she'd have to be blind and deaf not to know about them—either that or he was holding her and she couldn't get away. Maybe she didn't want to. Maybe she was an accomplice. No, couldn't be. He remembered his own brief experience. No agent in the field ever risked his cover with a stranger. And if she worked for the Agency, Mother would have known about her. Why send him to find Dickson?

Puzzle. Hard to figure. Then he had a thought. She was American, so was Dickson. Maybe he convinced her to help him. Yes, possible. Try it. Okay, she helped him. What help would he need? Reach his safe house. Then what? He was wounded, bleeding bad. He'd need— Yes.

In less than a half hour he was parked in the block with the two all-night pharmacies. The first druggist remembered a pretty girl with brown hair. Possibly American. But she hadn't worn a raincoat. The girl he remembered wore a white blouse and a skirt, green he thought. What did she buy? Adhesive tape, gauze. Quite a lot now that he thought of it. Scissors. Some peroxide, his largest bottle.

Forbes reacted. It had to be her. "Did she say anything?" A shrug, a doubtful shake of the head. "Did she happen to give a name or where she was staying?" More slow shakes of the head. "How did she pay you?"

"In deutsche marks. I don't recall how large the notes were."

Forbes was equally frustrated at the second drug store—same girl, similar purchases—until he asked about payment. Traveler's check. American Express. She tried to cash one for one hundred dollars. Too large. He had accepted a twenty-dollar one.

Forbes forced himself to suppress his excitement. "Do you have the check?"

"No, no, no. I took it to the bank first thing Monday. It's long gone, I'm sure."

Forbes had a visual image of trying to trace the check, surely one of thousands cashed that day in Munich. "You don't happen to remember the name on the check, do you?"

"But of course. I keep a record of all checks, even traveler's checks. They can be stolen, you know."

"Would you look it up for me?"

The druggist looked annoyed. "I suppose I can, but I have another customer. You will have to wait."

It was agonizing for Forbes. There seemed to be a succession of customers. Wouldn't you know it? Then the druggist fooled around, or so it seemed to Forbes, with his bottles of pills, typewriter, records, and cash register. Forbes felt forgotten and spoke to the druggist.

"I've decided I really shouldn't give out that information."

Forbes swore inwardly. So close. His mind raced. Had to have a reason to know. Journalist ploy wouldn't do. He winged it. "I know it's a lot to ask, but you see I think this woman may be my wife. We quarreled—we live at the military base—and she left me. I'm trying to find her. Our baby daughter is very sick." He tried to make his distress as genuine as possible.

"I see. What is your wife's name?"

"Addie—Addie Arthur. But she may have used another name—just to keep me from finding her. That's why I must know the name on that check."

The druggist hesitated, then shook his head. "I

really don't think I should become involved. I'm sorry."

"Please. Our baby is so sick. She cries for her mother—constantly."

The druggist sighed. "All right." It seemed a century, but he finally returned from his office, handing him a slip of paper with a name written on it. Fern L. Falscape. Excelsior Hotel.

Sloane heard the rustle of footsteps on the carpet outside the door, then the crackling of paper. Instinctively his hand found Harry's Walther, retrieved from under the mattress yesterday and inserted inside his sling. Now came a gentle tapping, her fingernail against the door, one, three, two. He relaxed. It was her signal, arranged yesterday. He waited, key, lock, latch, door closing, then she was there, her arms full of paper bags.

"Good morning. It's a lovely day. The rain has stopped, the sun is shining and all is right in the world of the Munchkins—or whatever they're called. They have broken out their liederhosen. Can't say men in short leather pants are a big turn on." She dropped her parcels on the desk and came to him, feeling his forehead. He still had a temperature, although not a high one. "How're you feeling?"

"Better." It was true. He was terribly weak and pain came from so many places he couldn't locate them, but his mind was clear for the first time. His previous awakenings had a fuzzy quality, an unreality, and he had not been entirely certain where he was or what was happening. He extended his hand. "Help me up."

She screwed up her face in an expression of grave doubt. "I don't know. I'm afraid you'll rip something open."

"I didn't yesterday."

It was true. To her dismay he had insisted on

getting up to go to the bathroom. He had leaned heavily on her, but had made it to the john and back with no apparent harm. Maybe moving was good for him. She took his hand and pulled him to a sitting position on the edge of the bed. At once she saw his distress and smiled. Yesterday he had discovered for the first time that he had no clothes on. She had teased him, saying she had seen naked men before, indeed *better* naked men. Angrily he had insisted a towel be wrapped around him. To her it was ridiculous. Of all his problems modesty was the least of them. "I went shopping. What do you want first, food or clothes?"

"Clothes."

"Figures." She laughed and went to the desk to open parcels. A windbreaker was in the first. She held it up. "It's dark blue like your other one, only it snaps instead of zips. That all right?"

"Fine."

She opened a bag. "Pants, shirts, socks." She held up two of each. "Oh Lord, I forgot underdrawers. Which do you prefer—boxers or jockeys? I can't remember what you wore."

"Doesn't matter."

She brought him a pair of blue chino pants. "I'm glad to see you're not an exhibitionist." He had no witty reply and that surprised her. A dozen men she had known would never have let that crack go by, but he had. She catalogued information. He wasn't good with women. He was handsome, but he didn't use it. Strange. He seemed almost stunted emotionally. She watched as he inserted his good left leg into the pants, but he couldn't manage the right.

"Let me help you." She squatted before him, lifting and thrusting his bad leg into the pants, then shimmied them up to his hips. He slid off the bed to stand, but had to hold on to her shoulder to steady himself. She pulled the pants around his waist and fastened them. "Perfect fit."

She zipped up the fly. "There. A magical disappearing act. Your modesty is restored." She looked at him and laughed. "You really are shy, aren't you?"

"Just not used to being dressed by girls."

"That's a no-no. We're women these days." She returned to the desk. "You have a choice of shirts, brownish plaid and blue. I thought it might go with your eyes."

"Neither now. It won't be very comfortable with my shoulder."

"I see. We just cover up the usable parts." And she laughed. "I'm sorry. I'm just a hopeless tease."

This woman with a man's name was unfathomable to him. She couldn't be an agent, KGB or any other kind. He was all but helpless and she had his gun, at least until yesterday. If she was KGB—or Parsley had sent her—she would have killed him. She had not. Instead she helped him. Yesterday he had grilled her on everything she had done, everyone she had talked to while he was unconscious. He could find no fault. She had brought him here, kept him from bleeding to death, then hidden him. It made no sense. Any woman he could imagine would have run from him at the car.

"Why are you here—helping me?"

She turned from him and paced across the room. When she looked at him, her face was screwed up into a grimace that expressed doubt. "I've been thinking about that—a lot. I think you and I have to talk."

"I know."

"You've been my sort of wounded-bird number. My father's a doctor, a surgeon. When I was a kid I used to bring him animals to fix up, baby birds, rabbits, squirrels, things like that. Couldn't see anything suffer and die."

"I thank you for that."

"But I never ran a menagerie. Dad would fix up the animals, then I'd let them go." She pursed her lips. "I guess you get the idea." She saw him nod. "I can't stay here much longer. I have to go back to London, get ready to go home. I just flew down here for a few days to see Munich and visit a friend. I haven't done either yet. Don't misunderstand. I wanted to help you. I'm glad I did. I feel good about it. But I can't stay here till you're well. That's going to take a long time and"—she shrugged—"and if you don't go to a hospital, get that bullet out of you, get sewn up properly and some antibiotics, it may be never. But I guess you know all that."

He looked away from her, trying to think. He couldn't somehow. *Harry's dead.* Harry and he had been together so long, it was as if part of himself had died. They had planned everything together, then done it. He was alone now and on extremely unfamiliar turf. In his whole life the only person he had ever depended upon and trusted was Harry, and Harry was gone. This girl was all he had. He couldn't even make it across the room without her. *Her!* All he knew about women was how to fuck them. Even then it was authorized whores, hired by Mother to service agents in safe houses. They had security clearances and reported back to the Agency every word he uttered. To meet a woman any more than casually was to be compromised. James Bond was a joke. To pick up a woman, have the slightest involvement, screw her, was unthinkable. He wouldn't know who she was, who she knew, who she really worked for. A woman named Freddie. Could he depend on her, trust her? What choice did he have? Better question: how did he even begin to start trusting someone besides Harry? *Harry's dead.*

He turned to her, met her gaze. She was very beautiful to him, soft brown hair, enveloping brown eyes, maddening lips, tall, slender, lithe, long-limbed, fragile arms. He was aware of the rise of her breasts beneath her sweater. It was green, a little lighter shade than her skirt. "Do you wear green often?"

She was surprised. It was the first notice he had ever made of her. "Sometimes."

"It's a good color on you. You really are beautiful."

"Thank you. I do the best I can with limited material." Now she smiled. "I thought you hadn't noticed."

"I have."

She saw him smile, boyish, a grin really. He had good, even teeth. "That's nice. I didn't think you owned one of those—a smile I mean."

"I'm sorry. I haven't exactly been myself."

"I'm sure of that."

"You have to be a very nice person to help me as you have. I'm most grateful, and I can't make it further without you—" He saw her start to speak and moved his good hand to stop her. "I know how much you've done already, and I hate to ask more, but . . ." He let the sentence trail off. "Look, if I stay here I'm going to be found eventually and killed. I have to go somewhere else. Will you help me?"

"Where will you go? This is the safest place. Didn't you pick it out because it was safe?"

"Yes, but we only took the room for a week. It will be up soon and the hotel will want it." He saw her open her mouth and knew what she was going to say. "Harry paid for the room and he's dead. If I try to pay or you try to pay, then one of us will become known."

She nodded. "I see. Where do you want to go?"

Sloane had no plan. He was unable to think beyond the realization he was a dead man. Parsley would never let him live, nor would the KGB. The Munich police might be the least of it, but they also hunted him. Escape was impossible. Escape to what? That's what he didn't know. Part of him wanted to go for Parsley, at least try to avenge Harry. But another part of him wanted to let it all go, just walk away and disappear. That's what Harry and he were going to do. And they would have, if only he hadn't tried to solve the damn puzzle of Parsley. Go for Parsley or disappear? He didn't know which and he couldn't do either with one arm, one leg, and a fever. He had to get well if he was to have any chance to do anything.

"Do you have any idea what you want to do?"

Suddenly he did. "Yes, camping. What I'd like you to do is buy me a vehicle, a VW van or something that's outfitted for camping. I'll give you the money. I figure I can stay on back roads and hole up in campgrounds till I get well. Will you do that much for me?"

She looked at him quizzically out of the side of her eyes. "No way. You can't drive one-handed and one-footed, let alone climb in and out, cook and all the rest."

"I'd thought of that."

She nodded knowingly. "And you thought I'd go with you."

He grinned at her. "Ever go camping? It's lots of fun. We could meander up the Rhine, through Alsace-Lorraine, anywhere you want to go. We'd be back in London in plenty of time for you to go home."

She studied him a moment, then turned away, pacing to the desk, leaning her backside against it. Camping through Germany and France in the springtime. She'd enjoy it, and it would give him a chance to get well—if he was going to get well. She sighed. He had just put her between a rock and a hard place, asking for a longer commitment from her at the very time she was determined to do a fade-out on this little soap opera and figure out a change of plot. *Will our heroine fall in love with Dave, her wounded spy? Or will she come to her senses and save herself while she can? Tune in—right now!*

She glanced at him. Fall in love? Impossible, yet the ingredients were there: a wounded, very vulnerable man who depended on her. His need, her commitment to somehow keeping him alive, lots of proximity. Yes, it could happen. *Tell me, Miss Falscape, when did you first . . . Oh shit!* "Dave, I'd like to ask a few questions if you don't mind."

"Shoot."

"An apt word. What happened in that dry-cleaning shop?"

"What do you think happened?"

"Are you a psychiatrist—answer a question with a question? All right. You said you were an intelligence agent—a field op. I want to believe that. It makes all this easier."

"I am."

"Okay. That makes Harry one, too. You were partners."

"Yes."

"You went to the shop on some kind of mission, met an East German. The Israelis came in and the shooting started. How many did you kill?"

"Does it matter?"

Her anger flared. "You're damn right it matters. Killing isn't exactly approved of by Emily Post or Amy Vanderbilt. I'm not going to harbor, then go camping with, a murderer."

"It was self-defense, them or me. How do you think I got all shot up?"

She would not be put off. "I asked how many you killed."

"Three. Harry and Khruchenko had no chance. I was able to fire back."

She gaped at him. It was what she figured—feared. Why was she so surprised now?

"Yes, Freddie, I killed those men. What do you want from me?"

Still she stared at him. "Try remorse. Be a little sorry."

"I'm not."

She shook her head in disbelief. "Can't say you're not honest."

"Freddie, the papers have it all wrong. The man Harry and I met in that shop wasn't an East German. His name was Khruchenko and he was a Russian, a high-ranking official of the KGB. He wanted to defect. The three men who came in the door weren't Israelis. They had phony identities"—he motioned to the dresser—"just like those over there."

"Then who were they?"

"You figure it out." It was the drill, standard operating procedure for Need to Know. Don't tell a person *everything*. Let them reach their own conclusions based on what they already know and believe.

She blinked. "Russians? They came to kill this man—the defector—to keep him from defecting? You and Harry were there and—"

"You're a very smart girl, Freddie."

She shook her head several times, as though trying to clear it. "Oh boy oh boy oh boy. What's happening to me? Why does it make me feel better to know you killed three Russians instead of three Israelis?"

"Don't think about it."

"Is that what you do?"

"It's the only way to play the game."

"What game?"

"The intelligence game."

She squinted her eyes at him. "Are you really a spy?"

"We hate that word."

"Sorry. Field op. Who do you work for? CIA?"

"I can't tell you that."

She shook her head. "Wonderful. Just wonderful."

"All right. I'm not CIA. I work for another US agency which most peole don't know about. It is the parent organization of the CIA. It uses the CIA pretty much as a front, which gets all the blame—and credit, I guess. My agency controls all the intelligence activity of the US worldwide."

"Sounds important." Part of her mind spotted the litter of bags on the desk. She began to fold them up, dropping them into the wastebasket. "If you want me to help you, don't you think you ought to trust me with at least a little information?"

She had a point. "Okay, I'm with the CSA, Central Security Agency."

She mentally repeated the name. "I've heard of it. Something to do with communications and codes."

"And a whole lot more. Very good."

"It advises the President on national security matters."

"Supposedly."

She looked at him sharply, eyes squinting a little. "You work for them?"

"Yes, I'm a special agent."

"I'll bet you're special. Can you prove it? You got a badge or something?"

He smiled. "No badges, sorry. That's the FBI. As a special agent I have the highest security clearance in the land, Top Secret Three, Cryptographic Code Word Three. It entitles me to the red card. With it I can go anywhere, do anything, but I never carry it with me. Aside from falling into unfriendly hands, it would be like hanging a sign around my neck urging people to kill me."

"I'm supposed to believe all this on your say so?"

"You have my travel pack, these bullets holes in me. I can't give you more proof than that." He watched her stare at him a moment, then turn, carry his newly purchased clothes to the dresser, and insert them in a drawer.

She turned back to him. "Okay, let's say I believe you. You're the world's greatest hotshot field op. You got all those category three whatever-they-weres and that handy-dandy red card, which you can't carry with you."

"I wish you weren't so sarcastic."

"And I wish you'd stop playing me for a sap. I don't like it."

"A sap is the last thing I think you are. Freddie, what's bothering you?"

She took two strides to the chair and sat on the arm, her legs crossed. "I'll tell you. If you're such an important man in this intelligence game, as you call it—five men dead, some game!—then why don't you pick up that phone, call your people, tell them you're wounded, and let them come and get you?"

Very smart girl, very tough question. To hide his hesitation he stood up and lurched to the dresser. With one hand he opened the whiskey bottle, poured a little into a glass, drank.

"I hardly think that's good for you."

"I hear it kills germs." Should he tell her about Parsley? No. She had no Need to Know. The knowledge would not help her at all and could kill her. But he had to tell her something. The drill. Stick as close to the truth as possible. "Freddie, I said I'm a special agent. That means that very few people, even within the Agency, know I even exist. Harry and I were sent here from Washington on a highly classified assignment. Very few people knew about Khruchenko—or me. I can't make the phone call you suggest without blowing my cover—and all our undercover operations in Moscow. I have to get back to Washington on my own. That's why I need your help."

"Why do you have your back to me? Are you lying?"

"No, I'm supporting my weight on the dresser." He turned so as to lean his back against it. "It's the truth, Freddie. I have to get back to Washington to report what I learned from Khruchenko before he was killed." And that was the truth—at least a form of it. Was this utterance forcing him toward the hopeless task of finding Parsley?

"Is that why the KGB is looking for you? Because of something this Khruchenko person told you?"

"Yes. And, Freddie, don't ask what it is. Believe me, you're better off not knowing."

"Am I? Do you remember telling me to go, tell no one about you? You were doing me a favor?"

"No, but it was certainly true."

"Later you said—oh, what's it matter what you said? Point is, I gather I'm in danger because I know you, because you *might* have told me something Khruchenko told you. Is that about it?"

"Precisely. They'll take you, shoot you full of chemicals that will bleed your brain of all it knows, then they'll kill you."

She heard the tone of his voice and it frightened her. "Wonderful! Thanks for crawling in the back of my car."

"I couldn't help it, Freddie. I was—"

"I know—desperate. Are you still desperate? Is that why you want me to go camping with you?"

Damn her! He swallowed the last of the bourbon from the glass. "Freddie, I was talking about your being in danger here, with me, in this room. If we can get out of Munich, and I can have a few days to get well so I can drive, then you can—"

"No way, Dave. Look at me." She waited. Finally his gaze joined hers. "I know you're lying."

"Yes. I'm desperate. I need you. I haven't got a prayer of escaping without you. Even with your help, there isn't much of a chance—but maybe enough, with luck, to gain some time. I can't do anything till I get well."

Her eyes held his a moment longer, then slowly she pursed her lips, biting at the inner surfaces. " 'O what a tangled web we weave, when first we practice to deceive.' "

"What?"

"Just a bit of poetry. I don't suppose poetry has much value in that intelligence game you play. I was trying to say I'm trapped. I can't leave you to be killed—and I'm scared to death to stay with you."

"Freddie, I—"

"Don't say anything. Just tell me what you want me to do."

"We'll need money. I want you to go to a bank. I'll give you a seven-digit account number. They'll hand you the money."

"How much?"

"Fifty grand ought to do it."

She raised a thick, well-tended eyebrow. "At least we'll live well—while we live. Whose money is it?"

"Do you really want to know?"

"Yes, my psychiatrist friend, I want to know. Is it our money?"

He smiled. "The KGB. Harry and I got their account number from one of their people."

"I suppose you killed him then."

"No." Now he told his first full and deliberate lie. "It was Khruchenko—and I didn't kill him."

She believed him. She had to.

SEVEN

Gordon Adams had left Brandywine early. The place was aggravating his claustrophobia and he badly needed fresh air. He left his car at a garage for a tune-up, then went for a long walk, which brought him to the Tidal Basin and finally West Potomac Park. He sat now on a park bench, enjoying the river, boats, people, cavorting squirrels, trees, grass, fresh air, and normalcy.

It was probably therapeutic for him, even though his mind remained preoccupied with his problems. Officially, all the five dead from the dry-cleaning shop remained unidentified, their bodies unclaimed. The US was never going to claim any of them, nor would the Soviets recognize the existence of Yuri Khruchenko. All was standard procedure.

What wasn't standard was the fact that *four* of the dead were Americans. Rogers he knew, of course, but he had not anticipated that the three "Israelis" would turn out to be Americans also. Two were Green Berets attached to Army intelligence at Rhinebeck Air Force Base, Sgts. Edward M. Wood and Scott R. Paslich—a fact which was concealed, covered up, and denied. This had taken some doing because German authorities had checked with Rhinebeck. Sorry, not our personnel.

Then there had been the problem of notifying next of kin. Harry Rogers was no problem. He was already "missing in action" and simply remained that way. The next of kin of Wood and Paslich were told they were killed in a Jeep accident. *We regret to inform you that* ...

The third "Israeli" with Wood and Paslich, the one Sloane killed with Rogers's weapon, was the person who intrigued Adams. His identification was confirmed. Name: Lt. Dean L. Schwartz; Status: CSA field op; Rank: Code Word Two; Code name: Terrier; Assignment: Tokyo.

Adams had known of him from his training at Pensacola. Good man. Would have made a Code Three if that program still existed. In fact Adams would have liked to have had him, but he had been assigned to Tokyo. Good record. Expert on Sino-Soviet relations.

The question was, what was he doing in Munich? Adams had no control over him and had not sent him. Yet he had shown up in Munich three days before the Khruchenko defection—complete with proper code words and recognition signals. He had participated in Saturday's drill of Khruchenko's decoy, then of Khruchenko himself.

Adams knew what had happened. Schwartz had been the last man in the drill, the "send 'em" phase. He had been the one person to know Sloane and Rogers were using the dry-cleaning shop on Wernerstrasse. He had then recruited—his Code Word Two status would make it easy—two men from Rhinebeck and gone to the shop, killed Rogers and Khruchenko, wounded Sloane. But not enough. Sloane had somehow managed to kill the two GIs with his own Walther, then gotten hold of Rogers's weapon to do in Schwartz. Must have been some gun battle.

How did Schwartz get to Munich? That was the question. Someone sent him for this special assignment. Kill Khruchenko, Sloane, and Rogers.

It wouldn't have been difficult, just a coded message, Code Word Two, which Schwartz could read. But who sent the message?

The mole. Had to be. Since Schwartz was in Tokyo, the logical assumption was Brown, who headed the Asia zone. But not necessarily. Anyone on The Committee could send the message. And, if he prepared and sent it himself, the origins of the message were untraceable.

Adams shook his head. He was no closer to learning the identity of the mole than he had been before. There was one loose end, however. Schwartz's partner, Quigley. He had left Tokyo and no one seemed to know where he had gone. Adams knew: Munich. He was after Sloane. Forbes just had to find him first.

Duane Forbes was having fun. The hunt for Dave Dickson had turned into a search for Fern Falscape, brown-haired, brown-eyed, pretty, American. Somehow she was a more appealing quarry. More than that, he liked playing detective. Finding Fern Falscape taxed his mental faculties and, he believed, his cunning. He really didn't want to go back to field work. He was content with Addie and his life. But wasn't it nice to prove to himself he could still do it if he had to?

He really had no proof that Fern Falscape was with Dave Dickson, but he was convinced she was. Dickson was holed up, badly wounded. He needed someone to help him. Fern Falscape had bought a ton of bandages at a pair of all-night drug stores. It had to be.

He went to the Excelsior Hotel. Checked out. No forwarding address. Figured. It was a dead end. Then he spent most of a day phoning every likely hotel in the environs of Munich, including the airport. No Fern L. Falscape registered. That figured, too, but he had to touch that base. He thought about following up on her traveler's check, but realized that under the best of circumstances all he'd learn from American Express was her stateside address. They wouldn't know where she was in Munich any more than he did.

He used what he had—a pair of all-night drug stores. It was relatively simple to learn the addresses of all such places in Munich. These he marked on his street map. It figured she would go to the closest ones. He drew a large circle around the stores she had used, then listed all the hotels which fell within it. There were a lot of them, but he reduced the number to those which were large, posh, touristy, and frequented by Americans. This list was further reduced by visits to the hotels. A badly wounded Dave Dickson wouldn't walk through the lobby. He'd enter a service entrance unseen. His room would be near it, probably one floor up. Several hotels on his list had no such configuration. He was down to a half dozen possibles.

The rest was easy. He did what Dave Dickson had done—taken a room for storage. In approaching reservation clerks he was most definite about what he wanted. He would be popping in and out a lot. Had to have something close to the service elevator or stairs. Then, when they had open rooms, he was indecisive. Didn't seem right somehow. Any other rooms available. What about the room next door?

He had some luck. The room he wanted wasn't available. Already taken; as a matter of fact it was being used for storage already.

Room 112, Hotel Columbia.

In a way it was hard for Jerry Quigley to believe. Wolf and Bear were a couple of years senior to him in the field. By the time he entered, they were already legends, two men so good they had survived a dozen missions behind the Iron Curtain. Dzerzhinsky Square supposedly had a price on their heads—at least a medal for the man who killed them.

Wolf and Bear were the model, their methods cited in classrooms at Pensacola. They succeeded because they had complete trust in each other. What one knew the other knew. They thought alike, acted together. It was said one could read the other's mind. It was the goal of all pairs in the field.

They were the perfect spooks. No one knew who they were—at least for certain. He believed he had spotted them once, two communications technicians working on the *Evansville*, an electronic surveillance ship in the Mediterranean. But he couldn't be sure. They were there only a short time and seemed so ordinary, just a couple of CTs doing what they had to and hating it. He had often wondered.

It was hard to believe Wolf and Bear had turned, yet he had to admit he could see how it was possible. Mother would drive a man to it, all those pencil pushers, computer analysts, and head shrinkers at Fort Belvoir and Brandywine concocting schemes to win the Cold War single-handedly. Most were disasters. All they were calculated to do was get a lot of good men killed, and if by chance one did succeed, it was a momentary victory, which the KGB quickly offset. The KGB and the CSA were two huge, impersonal, monolithic objects, one unstoppable, the other unmovable, grinding away at each other, chewing up money, minds, and people. He still believed in the Red Menace—better Dead than Red—although not as much as his partner Dean Schwartz had. But he had doubts, at least enough to understand how Wolf and Bear, so long in the field, so often sacrificed by the stupid, uncaring bastards at Brandywine, could have gone over.

But that didn't matter. Wolf and Bear had

killed Schwartz. His partner had put up a helluva fight in the back of that dry-cleaning shop. Got Bear and the KGB guy they were meeting. And he had almost gotten Wolf. Almost wasn't good enough. He would finish it. Death did not separate partners.

Wolf would be tough, make no mistakes about that. Vastly experienced, cunning like his code name, he would be hard to find, harder to kill. Quigley, himself Fox, would stalk him. Wolf would make a mistake. Then he would take him.

Freddie walked past the bank, trying to get up her nerve. "It's easy, nothing to it," he had said. "Just go to any international bank, give the teller the account number and tell her how much you want. She'll hand you the money."

Easy for him to say. He was up there having a snooze in bed while she was down here stealing money from the Soviet government. That's what it was, stealing, and no matter how many times he grinned and said "They do it to us all the time" would make it anything but stealing. She tried to hold on to her sense of moral outrage, but the plain fact was the whole idea of using Russian money to escape the KGB was utterly intriguing to her. It couldn't be possible. She had to find out.

She had queried him on anything she could think of that might go wrong. Suppose the account number's not right? It is. They could have changed it. They haven't. What if someone recognizes me? They won't. Suppose the KGB is looking for people tapping their account? They aren't. What if they don't have fifty thousand in the account? They will. What if I'm arrested on the spot and taken to jail as a common thief? He had laughed.

She reached the bank entrance, hesitated, then walked inside without looking up or around. She didn't want to know the name of the bank. It made her feel less like a crook. She was just running an errand, going where he told her to, doing what he said. *By such fragile rationale do we slide into moral degeneracy.*

"It would be best if you acted like you did this sort of thing every day, but if you don't, it still won't matter. You'll get the money." Those had been his last words. *The next words you hear from him will come through a metal grating at the jail.*

The bank seemed cavernous, austere, supremely dignified. It was an *institution*, an *international* financial institution no less. She felt like Jane and Michael causing a run on the Fidelity, Fiduciary Bank in *Mary Poppins*.

The woman behind the information desk was thirtyish, chic, with blond hair arranged in a French bun. She smiled. Such a nice smile. *Do you know you are about to become involved in an international theft?* "I'd like to make a withdrawal from a master account." She had rehearsed the words so much they were like the multiplication tables to her.

Another unwitting smile. "Yes, of course. Just a moment please."

Freddie watched her pick up the phone, dial. It would come now—uniformed men, maybe a stony-eyed bank official with a suspicious bulge under his jacket. She would be led away, interrogated.

"Mr. Hauptmann will see you. His office is . . ."

Freddie watched the manicured nail point off to her left, a walnut door, gold lettering on it. "Thank you." She felt like a lamb at the slaughterhouse. *Little lambie, just walk over there; see the nice man.* She pushed her sunglasses more firmly against her nose and pulled down the floppy brim of her hat. He had laughed when she insisted on wearing them, but what did he know?

"Good morning."

Mr. Hauptmann stood in the doorway to his office. He was in his forties, bald with a Caesar's wreath of dark hair. Behind his glasses he conveyed dignity, *integrity*. She stepped inside the paneled office, and he closed the door.

"Please have a seat."

She sat opposite his desk in a chair, genuine leather. Nothing plastic about this bank.

"You wish to make a withdrawal?"

She nodded.

"May I have the account number, please?"

He slid a piece of paper and pen toward her. She swallowed hard, and picked it up. Just a blank sheet from a notepad. The pen, just a standard yellow one like they use in school, felt strange in her hand. She hesitated. The numbers were burned in her brain. But were they? Maybe she had one wrong. Her hand moved: 747-858.1. She read them over. The .1 seemed like a sentinel guarding the portals to the Soviet treasury. All who tried to pass were liquidated.

She passed him the piece of paper and he read. "Very good. How much do you wish to withdraw?"

Freddie swallowed again. "Fifty thousand dollars." Her voice sounded strange to her.

"Is that US dollars?"

"Yes."

"I'll be with you in a moment."

He rose from his desk and exited through a door behind it. Freddie shivered. Now it would come. Behind her dark glasses she closed her eyes. Never had she been so nervous in her life. All she wanted to do was break and run. Not too late. Maybe she could escape before they came for her. Yes. She stood up. Just walk out. Tell the blonde with the French bun she had made a mistake. No, tell her she was going to be sick— which was true. She heard the handle on the door. Too late. She sat back down.

He was alone. "How would you like that, miss?"

Freddie stared at him in disbelief. He seemed so sensible. Surely he had more sense than to just *give* her the money.

"Would you like that all in US dollars?"

Anyway—roubles, kroners, yen, drachmas. Just let me out of here. She remembered. "Ten thousand in deutsche marks, twenty thousand in US dollars, the rest in Swiss francs."

"Very good. I'll be with you in a moment." Another long, agonizing wait, then he was counting out neat piles of money on his desk. "This is a great deal of money to carry, miss. Would you like some of this in traveler's checks?"

David had told her the bank would try to sell her traveler's checks. Made a little more on the transaction that way. "No, the cash will be fine, thank you."

"As you wish."

She watched him insert the money into a bank pouch, then hand it to her. She squeezed it into her purse. Then she knew. They would wait till she tried to leave the bank before seizing her. Wouldn't get blood all over the nice carpet in his office that way.

"Pleasure to serve you, miss."

She stared at him. Yes, his smile was diabolical. He knew what was going to happen. "Thank you." *For what? Spending the rest of my life in a German prison? Or will it be a Russian prison?*

Her heels marked her every step down the marble aisle. She clutched her purse till her arm hurt, certain any moment she would hear screams, shouts, clanging alarms. *Stop, thief! Arrest that woman—the dumb one!* The street offered no refuge and the walk back to the hotel was an eternity. The lobby was a trap. Only when she was in the hotel room, leaning heavily against the wall, could she breathe.

"Something go wrong?"

"Yes, everything. I'm a good girl from a good Christian home. Thou shalt not steal. I believe it, I believe it, I believe it. Oh boy, do I ever believe it."

"What went wrong?"

"Everything, I told you. I'm just not cut out for this sort of thing. You can do this cloak-and-dagger spy crap all you want. I'm finished. No more."

"You didn't get the money?"

He had shaved since she last saw him and now sat on the edge of the bed munching an apple. How could he be so calm? Easy. He hadn't just stolen money from the Soviet Union. "Yes, I got the damn money."

He grinned. "Then what's the matter?"

"I was scared to death, that's what's the matter. I was frightened out of my wits. I thought any moment I'd be grabbed. I'm still not sure they aren't after me."

Now he laughed. "Who?"

"The Russians. You did say it was their money, didn't you?"

"It is. All they'll know is that somebody in Munich hit up their computerized account. Some bureaucrat in Dzerzhinsky Square will eventually order an audit, demand an accounting. It will lead nowhere."

She stared at him. "You do this sort of thing—*for a living*?"

"All the time."

She shook her head. "I don't get it. I just walked into a bank, gave a number, and they handed me money. Nobody asked my name. I didn't sign anything. How can that be?"

"Think about it, Freddie. What's more valuable than money?"

"I don't know." She was suddenly depressed,

tired, and more than a little annoyed at him for putting her through this. It showed in her voice.

"Secrecy. Accounting for every penny would mean vouchers, signatures, the rest. It would also mean names and identities that could be traced. Covers would be blown, good men discovered and lost. It is simply easier to have an account anyone can draw from. All you have to know is a number. It wastes money, but saves lives."

Her next task was easier, more fun, but not much less surprising to her. He sent her to the American Express office to buy a vehicle, not inside but on the street nearby.

"This time of year there should be a dozen cars and vans for sale. It's the start of the summer season and everybody wants transportation. Buy anything that runs, the more nondescript the better. We'll get a tent, a couple of sleeping bags, and take off."

"You make everything sound so easy—when you don't have to do it."

"It is easy."

"No, it isn't. How do I register it?"

"You don't. Just pay the money and drive off."

"What if someone reports it as stolen?"

"They won't, but, okay, have the seller write you out a bill of sale."

"In longhand?" She was incredulous.

"God, he can print it if he wants."

"Sounds illegal."

He was exasperated with her and trying not to be. "It probably is, but who cares? It happens all the time. Where do you think all these kids driving around Europe get their vehicles? Probably violates motor vehicle registration laws, but the cops can't do much about it—and they don't want to. Hurts the tourist trade."

"I still think you make it sound too easy."

"It is. Oh, yeah, try to get one with Dutch plates."

"Why Dutch?"

"They issue a permanent plate. Won't have to worry about cops stopping us for an expired license."

It truly was easy. There were lots of choices, but she wasn't going to buy just anything. Her sense of thrift wouldn't permit it. For over an hour she kicked tires, looked under hoods, insisted on a test drive. Finally she acquired a six-year-old VW camper. It had a butane stove and cooler, water tank, electrical outlet, table, two chairs, and—her real reason for buying it—double bunks He would be able to lie down while she drove— and she would be able to sleep alone. It also had Dutch plates.

Smiling sweetly, but relating a tale of impoverishment, she even bargained down the Australian couple five hundred dollars. She paid in cash, resisted the urge to ask for a bill of sale, and drove off. She had trouble at first. She wasn't used to sitting so high up, and the van seemed so big and boxy, but she managed to approach the hotel. As instructed, she parked a couple of blocks away and walked to the hotel. Shouldn't be seen in the van by anyone at the hotel. As she walked through the lobby she felt good about herself. A good purchase. She always did like to shop.

"Ms. Falscape?"

She was at the foot of the stairs. Hearing her name startled her. She turned and saw the stranger.

Forbes had been tempted to simply enter Room 112 and confront Dave Dickson. It would be a simple matter to tell the chambermaid he had forgotten his key and ask her to open the door. But he knew better. Dickson might not remember him. It had been two and a half years after all. And if he was wounded, hiding out from those who had killed his partner, he might shoot first and ask questions later. *Approach with caution.* Yes.

There was no doubt in Forbes's mind that the woman he followed was Fern Falscape and that she was protecting Dickson. He had watched her leave Room 112, carefully checking the hall before emerging. Once, when returning and seeing a chambermaid in the hall, she passed the room and stood before another door, coming back to 112 when the chambermaid was gone. Dave Dickson was in 112. She was helping him. He must trust her. The way to enter the room and catch Dickson off guard was through her.

Forbes followed her for a day and a half. He watched her buy men's clothing, a bag of food from a deli, surreptitiously carry trash and dirty linen from the room, snitch clean ones. No blood stains on the sheets, but a distinct odor, male, a little chemical like a hospital. The trash left no doubt. Bloody bandages.

The next morning she went to the bank. She was nervous, scared, furtive. Fern Falscape wasn't in the business. She was being made to do something she didn't want to do. She returned to the room. When she left again she took a cab to American Express. He watched her buy a van. They were leaving, going camping. It was now or never.

"I'd like to speak to you a moment. It's important." He saw surprise in her eyes, fright, too. It was momentary but there.

"How do you know my name?"

Now he was surprised. He had expected her to say he had the wrong person. He was prepared for that. This was easier. "It wasn't difficult." He smiled. "The traveler's check at the drug store."

"I see." She studied him a moment: twenties, tall, brown hair, bluish-green eyes. A soft look about him, a little pudgy. She flashed a smile, more brilliant than his. "I'm complimented. You went to a lot of trouble, Mr.—"

Very good, clever. She was treating it as a casual pickup. He would, too. "Arthur, Bob Arthur. May I buy you a drink?"

"I'm afraid not. I was just on my way to my room."

"To tell about your purchase of the VW camper?"

Her eyes narrowed. "You've been following me? I don't think I like that."

He grinned, hoping to disarm her, and his gaze passed quickly down her figure and back to her face. "I assure you it was a most pleasant task."

"I'm glad you enjoyed it. Now, if you'll excuse me." She turned, and headed up the stairs.

"I'm here to help Dave."

She should have ignored it, kept on going, but this man's knowing her name had so unnerved her she couldn't think straight. Stopping, turning, staring at him was the absolutely wrong thing to do. Too late now. She would have to make the best of it. "I beg your pardon."

"I said I'm here to help Dave Dickson."

"I don't know anyone named Dickson." Somehow uttering the truth, however tenuous, helped her aplomb.

"Then Lionel Twilley—William Hatch. I knew him as Dave Dickson. We roomed together once. We were pals."

She detected a hint of pleading in his voice. He was trying to convince her, maybe himself. He wasn't sure. She smiled. "I'm sorry. I don't know what you're talking about." She turned, started up the steps, one, two, a third. He was going to let her go. Then his hand was on her wrist, stopping her.

"I know he's in Room 112. He's badly wounded and you're helping him. I want to, too. I was sent here to find him, get him medical care, and bring him in—safely."

Her whole body was rigid with fear. She had to get away from this man, warn David. "If you don't let go of my arm, Mr. Arthur, I'll scream. I don't believe you'll like that." Her voice was cold, full of warning.

He obeyed. "If you're helping Dave, you must care about him. So do I. I told you we're old friends, roomed together at Pensacola. All I want you to do is take me to him. He'll recognize me and know I'm there to help him."

She knew only that she had to get back to the room. "I really don't know what you're talking about." She started up the steps again.

"All right. You leave me no choice but to confront him directly. I'll get a key and let myself in."

A horrid image flickered across her mind, freezing her step in mid-stride. Dave had found the gun under the mattress. It was now in his sling. If someone entered the room without her identifying knock, the gun would be in his hand. If it were this man he would use it. She could see the muzzle flash, falling body, blood. She turned. "Please, don't do that."

"Then help me. Take me to him."

She stared at him unblinking, mouth open a little, very dry. "I think I would like that drink now."

Freddie believed Bob Arthur. Dave said he worked alone. No one knew of his mission. He had to find his own way back to the States. But that couldn't be. Someone in Washington had to read the newspapers, know he was wounded. Of course they would send someone to help him, someone he knew and trusted.

"I just want to talk to him a minute. Then I'll make a phone call. Doctors will be here in an hour. He'll be on his way home soon after."

"He needs a hospital. I just stopped the bleeding. He has an infection. There's a bullet inside him still."

"Then he'll get a hospital, whatever he needs. He'll be taken care of."

Thank God! To think she had almost turned this man away. Now she began to worry about Bob Arthur. If she spoke to David about him, he'd never listen. He'd never believe someone was here to help him.

"Are you sure he'll remember you, trust you?"

"Yes, I'm certain."

"He's terribly frightened, on guard constantly. I'm afraid he'll—"

"It'll be all right. Just take me to him."

This was the second intelligence agent she knew, and both spent a lot of time reassuring her everything was going to be just dandy. No problem, stop worrying. She wondered if they all did that. Was it just confidence—or a means to get people to do things they'd never consider if they were in their right minds? "All right. I'll go first. We have to surprise him."

EIGHT

An ordered universe was David Sloane's survival kit. Everything had a certain arrangement, the sights, sounds, smells, even feel of things was prescribed in his mind. He did not consciously catalogue the arrangement, committing it to memory, but from long experience he simply relied upon his unconscious mind to know when something was missing, didn't belong, or was out of order. He trusted his unconscious implicitly. It had saved his life many times.

He had been exercising, forcing himself to walk between the far wall and the bed. He had to get his strength back, walk out of this room, move either toward Parsley or escape. Now he sat on the edge of the bed, resting. His conscious mind heard the gentle tap of a fingernail against the door, one-three-two. She was back. Had she gotten a vehicle? His conscious mind also heard the key in the lock, the latch, oiled hinges, three high-heeled steps, saw her, heard, "I'm back." His unconscious mind *knew*. By the time his conscious mind realized the door hadn't closed behind her, he already had the Walther in hand.

"*No!*" She threw herself at him, knocking him backward across the bed, grabbing his arm, clutching at his fingers on the gun. "It's a friend. He wants to help you." He struggled against her weight, but it was hopeless. The bullet would come now. "Please, David. He only wants to help." He heard her words, but they were meaningless to him. Only the absence of the bullets had meaning.

He shoved her aside, at least enough to look over her shoulder. Bob Arthur. Proof of flawless memory. He was unzipping his windbreaker, pulling it open. Now the shots would come.

"I've no weapon, Dave."

Sloane studied him, then watched as he pulled up his pants legs.

"Still no weapon." He smiled. "I'd ask how you are, except I gather you've been better."

Freddie felt him relaxing. "Please, David. I had to do it. He wants to help you. I know he does."

"You can get off me now."

"Are you sure? Let me have the gun."

"No."

"You won't kill him?"

"No."

"I don't believe you. Let me have the gun."

Sloane searched his unconscious. Yes, the door had closed. Arthur had come alone.

"I won't let you shoot him."

"It'll be okay. Just get off me." His brain registered his own words, was aware of her rolling off him although still holding on to his gun hand with both of hers, but his mind leaped ahead to Arthur and what his coming meant. "Who sent you?"

"You know I don't know that. Just Mother."

"Who talked to you? A briefer?"

"Yes."

"Where?"

"Pensacola." Forbes grinned. "As a matter of fact the old cryptography lab at Corry Field."

It figured. As far as he knew Arthur had never been cleared to even know about Brandywine, let alone enter it. "Describe the briefer." He listened, bland, nondescript. Could be anyone—or Parsley himself. "I thought you retired."

"I did. They called me back. Seems they wanted someone you knew."

Yes, that's the way they'd do it. The computer had spewed out every association he'd ever had. They wanted someone he knew, someone who knew about the Agency, yet someone who didn't know much about Wolf and what he had been doing. Bob Arthur, his old roomie and drinking buddy. Then Sloane was aware of Freddie. "Let go of me and help me up."

"Not till you give me the gun."

He swore. "Why do you trust him more than me? Ever occur to you he could take the gun from you and shoot the both of us?" It was nonsense, but she bought it, rising from the bed, pulling him to a sitting position.

"Please, David. No more killing. I can't stand it."

He studied Forbes intently, as though he were somehow a different person when seen from this angle, then carefully inserted the Walther inside his sling. The grip protruded. He had easy access. His eyes never left Forbes. "How did you find me?" He listened as Forbes told the whole tale, taking great pride in his detective work. When he told of the traveler's check, Sloane looked sharply at Freddie. "You never told me you cashed a check."

"It didn't seem important."

"I asked you to tell me *everything* you did."

He had raised his voice. She didn't like being confronted. "So I forgot. What's it matter?"

"He's standing in this room, isn't he?" His annoyance at her was almost at the point of anger.

She stood up to him. "And a damn good thing.

He's here to help you—for reasons I'll never understand."

Stupid female! "Did it ever occur to you that what one person can find others can, too?" He turned to Forbes. "Now that you've found me, what are you supposed to do?"

"Phone a number. They'll come for you."

"I'll bet."

"It'll mean doctors, a hospital, David. You'll get well." Freddie was virtually pleading with him.

"What's the number?" Sloane listened. An answering service. He knew the drill. "What's your message?" He heard that. Still the drill. The message could mean anything and lead to anyone—including Parsley.

"I'm supposed to use a pay phone. If you'll let me go, I'll make the call."

"Who's with you?"

"Nobody, Dave, I swear." There was earnestness in his voice. "You know I lost my partner. I've been a civilian for over two years."

"Where?"

"Cleveland area, Elyria actually."

"What do you do?"

"Sell insurance. It's a living."

Yes. Mother liked inactive people to be insurance men, stock brokers, salesmen. They can move around, be gone a few days. Nobody pays any attention. Meanwhile the Agency uses them for little dumb, dull jobs, mostly surveillance as a sort of secret police auxiliary. Harry and he wouldn't retire because they wanted no part of that.

"Do you have a family?"

It was Freddie's question, and Sloane saw Arthur brighten. Wife Addie, a kid, another on the way. He actually got out pictures to show her. My God!

It gave him time to think. Bob Arthur. Started

the training but couldn't make it. Left after cryptography school. Code Word One. Philippines. Fucked up. His partner was killed.

Sloane watched him with Freddie. Just two old pals exclaiming over photos. Such a lovely baby. What's her name? Damn clever to send Arthur. He was so obviously unprofessional. Too obvious. Had Parsley sent him? Just dial this number. We'll take care of the rest. Sure.

"You do believe he wants to help you, don't you, David?"

He looked at Freddie. She hadn't known. Arthur had used her like a two-dollar hooker. "Sure." He smiled. "But there's no rush." He motioned to the chair. "Take your coat off and stay awhile. How about a drink?"

Freddie leaped. "I'll get it." She felt relieved.

"No, I need to move around." He hobbled to the dresser, poured a couple of fingers of whiskey into a glass, handed it to Arthur. "So how do you like retirement? I guess I'll be doing that myself now." He leaned against the dresser, his back to it.

"It's okay, Dave. Takes a little getting used to at first—you know, unwinding, getting with the pace of things."

"Dull?"

"I suppose. What isn't after Mother? But it's sort of nice—ball games, television, regular hours, neighbors, kids, the little woman." He laughed at what that implied.

He and Harry had wanted that, talked about it. Forget it. Never happen now. "No looking over your shoulder all the time?"

"That's the best part. After what happened to my partner, I'll take dull anytime."

Sloane's searching fingers found the remaining syringe, silently unscrewed the cap from the needle. "Why don't you take Bob's jacket, Freddie? It's stuffy in here."

She jumped to do it, helping strip it from the visiting agent. It was to her a symbol that everything was all right. Dave wasn't going to kill him. He was going to go away with him, to the hospital, to safety. Yes. He was talking to him, about retirement, home, kids, ball games. She had asked him once what he wanted out of life. That's what he had said: home, kids, job, a normal life away from all *this*. She had believed him then. She believed him now. Or did she? He seemed so strange—smiling, talking, yet so on guard.

"Have another belt, Bob?" He came for his glass.

"Naw, I'd better not."

"Hell, that's not the guy I knew at Pensacola." He was laughing even as he plunged the needle deep into his arm.

Freddie gasped. "What did you *do*?"

"Nothing."

"You did, too. I saw you inject him with something." She looked at Arthur's still form. "You *killed* him, didn't you?"

He looked at her in disgust. "I didn't kill him—at least I don't think I did."

"What is it?" Her voice remained high-pitched, strident.

"It'll make him tell the truth, if I didn't inject too much."

"But he did tell the truth."

Sloane glared at her. "You are the most naive person. Do you believe everything anybody tells you? How do you know he's not KGB?"

She stared at him in shock, mouth open. "But he's your friend. You *know* him."

"I also know lots of KGB. They're real friendly sometimes."

Her dismay at Sloane gave way to fascination as Arthur began to answer Sloane's questions in a dull, monotonous voice. His answers were much the same as he gave before, except that he said his real name was Duane Forbes. He also added more details about his meeting with the man at Pensacola. "What is it? Some kind of truth serum?"

Annoyed at her for interrupting, Sloane said, "I guess you can call it that."

She didn't care how annoyed he was. "You mean to say you can just inject something and make a person tell the truth?"

"Bleed his brains out—if it doesn't kill him."

"Wonderful choice!" She was aghast. "Do you know what this means? The human brain, that which differentiates us from other animals is now a—I don't know what—a *plaything* for people like you."

"This is nothing. They got stuff now that will make you tell all you know, then forget it. Then they replace it with another story."

"*My God!*"

"Only one thing wrong. If you interrupt the guy while he's telling the implanted story, he has to start over again at the beginning. It's easy to spot."

"Do you know how *terrible* this is? Do you have any idea what this means?"

"Be still, dammit." He asked a few more questions, then turned away from Arthur.

"Well, Dr. Strangelove, what'd you find out?"

"That he was telling the truth. He doesn't know anything."

"I told you that." She looked at Arthur. "What happens to the poor man now? Does he turn into a broccoli or does he just sit there and croak?"

"He'll come out of it in a minute. He won't remember anything about this. Don't you tell him."

She watched in apprehension, then relief as Arthur—really Forbes—rubbed his eyes, then seemed to snap awake a minute later. Sloane handed him a drink. "So you're a Cleveland

Indians fan," he said. Forbes began to talk about the fortunes of his favorite baseball team. Uncanny.

Sloane appeared to listen, asking questions about the Detroit Tigers, his favorite team, but his mind had leaped ahead. Finally he said, "It's almost dark. I guess we'd better make your phone call."

"Good, I'll go right now." He jumped out of the chair.

"I said *we*. I want to go with you."

"But you can't."

Sloane turned to her. "If I made it up those stairs, I ought to be able to make it down."

She shook her head. "I thought you didn't want anyone to see you."

"I don't. You're going to bring the car around to the back. We'll leave the way we came."

"Go where?"

He had expected these questions from Forbes, not from her. But it didn't matter. "To make the phone call."

"Oh, no. *He's* making the phone call. You're staying here to rest until your people come for you."

Not on her life he wasn't. He turned to Forbes. "I'm concerned about Freddie. She only did me a favor, and I don't want her involved in all this. Okay?"

"Sure. I don't see why anyone needs to know about her."

She stared at Sloane. She had just seen the handy-dandy needle at work. There were no secrets anymore. "But—"

"Pack your bag, Freddie. The three of us are going out. You're going to drop us off, then you're driving away into the sunset."

"But where are you going?"

"Somewhere I know. He can make his phone call. I'll be safe until help comes." He shoved her toward the closet. "Now do as I say. Pack."

She lifted her suitcase from the closet and began to throw her things into it. She guessed it made sense. No, it didn't. "Why don't you want to wait here?"

"Because you've been walking in and out of this hotel for days. People'll remember you. And, face it, if Arthur can find you and learn your name, lots of other people far more dangerous than this guy can, too. Pack. We haven't time to waste."

"Then you're doing this for me?"

"I owe you something, don't you think?"

She stared at him. His words were right. He did owe her. He should try to keep her out of all this. But something was wrong. She could feel it. "What about the van I just bought?"

"It's yours. Turn in your rent-a-car, drive the van back to London. Or sell it. Whatever you want."

She couldn't take her eyes from him. Something was wrong.

"Will you *pack*?" There was just a hint of irritation in his voice. "Time is important just now."

She obeyed, throwing her things into the suitcase and travel bag. The activity helped her. So did Sloane. He and Forbes were having a good ol' chat about beer parties and buddies from school. Lotsa laughs. It was okay, but somehow it wasn't. She couldn't shake her feeling that something was wrong. "David, what about your things?"

His hesitation was brief. "I'll put on a shirt and windbreaker. You can have the rest. Toss 'em in your suitcase."

"What do I want with men's clothes?"

He grinned. "Never know who you'll run into."

Okay. The grin helped. He seemed relaxed. Maybe that was it—too relaxed, too gabby. But why not? He was going to get help now, safety.

What's the expression? Yeah, he was coming in from the cold.

Sloane let Forbes help him on with his shirt, buttoning it over the sling, then the windbreaker, zipping it up partway. "Not bad for a one-armed man, eh?" He heard Forbes agree. At the dresser he began restoring his belongings to his pockets. Pen, cigarettes, and lighter went into his shirt pocket. The envelope with the passports, tickets, and IDs was folded and inserted in his right rear pocket where he normally carried a handkerchief. Picklock, money clip, and change went into his right thigh pocket for easy access, along with his wallet bearing his identification as Lionel Twilley. Finally he placed the extra clip of 9mm bullets in the right pocket of his windbreaker. The careful man in him longed to check the Walther in his sling, but he didn't want to call attention to it. The holster. Couldn't carry it and couldn't leave it. He smiled at Forbes. "Get my holster from under the pillow, will you? Government issue and Mother'll want it back." He watched Forbes pick it up. "You might as well put it on. You're going to need three hands as it is, carrying the suitcase and getting me down the stairs."

He watched Forbes begin the process, then turned to Freddie. She was staring at him, a troubled expression on her face. "All set?"

"I guess so—yes."

She seemed all eyes and very troubled. "What's the matter, Freddie?"

She shook her head. "I don't know. You seem—strange, somehow."

He grinned. "I know what your problem is. You didn't think it would end this way. You've been all pumped up playing spy. God knows what has gone on in that pretty head of yours. Having it end like this, your just driving away—well, it's deflating. You're feeling let down. That's the way most missions end, isn't it, Bob?"

She only half heard the agreement. Why did he call him Bob? His name was Duane.

"Go get the car, Freddie, drive it around in back. We'll meet you there. Take your flight bag and purse."

She didn't want to go. Something was wrong. She knew it.

"Time's a-wasting, Freddie. I don't know how much longer I can stay on my feet."

Freddie's legs seemed wooden as she walked down the stairs, through the lobby, out to the parking lot. He was strange, foreign, smiling too much, making small talk. He never made small talk. He was acting, playing a role. He was—yes, conning her, conning Forbes.

At the door to the car, key already in hand, realization came to her, fully, horribly. *He's going to kill Forbes.*

No, God, no. He mustn't!

She started to run back, then stopped. No time. Quicker to drive. Hand shaking, she fumbled with the door lock, then the ignition. *Please, God, don't let him do it.* The engine roared to life. She sped backward, almost hitting a car, shifted into low, and raced through the parking lot, tires squealing. *He's a friend, trying to help. He's innocent. Don't let him die.* Heart pounding, her ears roaring, she accelerated up the service drive, almost scraped the side of the car turning around the building. *She had to stop him.* She screeched the car to a stop at the loading dock, jumped out.

They were standing on the platform, her bag beside Forbes.

"What the hell's the hurry, Freddie? We don't need cops right now."

She gaped at him. "I thought . . . I thought you—"

"Never mind what you thought. Let's get going."

Her suitcase went in the back seat, Sloane in

after it. Forbes sat in front. She was behind the wheel.

"See if you can drive away from here so half of Munich isn't on our tail."

"Where?"

"Just drive. I'll tell you where to go."

As she moved the car forward her pulse still raced, but breathing came easier. She left the service drive, turned into the street. Part of her felt foolish. There really was no earthly reason for him to kill Forbes. He had told the truth about being sent to help him. That crazy injection proved that beyond doubt. Why kill a man who was only helping him, who only meant life and safety? There wasn't any and she was a sap for being so suspicious. Still . . .

"What's the matter with you, Freddie? You're driving like a—"

"I'm sorry. I just need to relax." She made a conscious effort to. "It's just I keep remembering the last time you sat in the back seat."

"That was different."

She could see his face in the rear-view mirror. It was largely in shadows, but his teeth were visible. He was smiling at her.

"Turn left at the next corner."

She made the turn.

"Ever been to Munich before, Bob?"

"No. Wanted to, but they sent me to Manila."

"I remember. Great town, Munich. The beer's fabulous and they don't care how much of it you drink. Right after this block."

She slowed, signaled, made the turn.

"I remember one time Harry and I were in Munich and . . ."

She tuned out the story. Why was he telling it now? In all the time she'd spent with him he hadn't related a single event that had ever happened to him.

"Right next, Freddie. Well, the bartender said . . ."

She was aware of the river off to her right. They must have crossed it.

"Well, Harry knew the guy was full of shit. He said . . ."

It was a stupid story, endless, meandering like he was making it up. "Excuse me, David, but where are we going?"

"I was wondering that myself," Forbes asked.

"We're almost there. It's a safe house. I couldn't go there the other night, but with you along it's okay."

"We need a phone booth, remember?"

"There's a secure line in the safe house. Do you want to hear the rest of my story or not?" He didn't wait for concurrence but plunged ahead. In truth he was making it up, hoping to distract them while his eyes, independent of his voice, searched the street. He was on the right one. But which alley? There. That must be it.

"Here we are. Right into the alley, Freddie. Go slow. Douse the lights."

She obeyed his commands, sliding the car into enveloping darkness.

"Stop and turn off the motor."

As she did so she heard Forbes ask, "What the hell's this place?"

"Back entrance to the safe house. Nobody'll see us go in. Stay in the car, Freddie. Bob'll help me out."

She nodded, then blinked as the dome light illuminated the interior. She watched Forbes climb out, then glanced at the rear-view mirror. She gasped. Sloane's eyes were cold and hard, like ice.

"I'll be back in a minute, Freddie."

Eyes wide with fright, she turned from the mirror, looked in back, saw him extend a hand to Forbes at the open door, being pulled out.

"No!" Her hand frantically scratched for the door handle. *"God, please, no!"* Her feet felt pavement, her body thrust upward, twisted, brushed against the side of the car.

Spit. Spit. Two flashes. A groan. A sigh. Thud of a falling body. She screamed, then screamed again.

His arm was around her, her body pressed hard against his. His hand sought her head, then clamped over her open mouth. "Be quiet or I'll knock you silly." Her whole body convulsed, lungs heaving to expel air, but little sound came out. "I'll break your neck, Freddie—right now if I have to." She felt her head being twisted. Pain intruded. Fear replaced horror. "I mean it, Freddie. You know I do."

She swallowed, then nodded. The pain let up.

"It's almost over, Freddie. Are you going to stop screaming?"

The voice was calmer, its anger diminished. Again she swallowed, nodded. Slowly the grip on her mouth relaxed.

"I'm going to release you, Freddie. But I swear to God if you make one sound I'll use the gun on you. It has splatter bullets. At this range it'll blow a three-inch hole in you."

His hand momentarily tightened on her jaw, then gradually loosened, left her, but hovered close. From somewhere came a voice. "Oh God, what have you ... *done?*"

"Had to be, Freddie. I had no choice."

"Oh, God, it's so—"

"Just stand here. And don't scream or we're both finished."

He left her and she turned, staring ahead into the darkness. By the dim light from the dome light she saw Forbes's body in front of the bumper, Sloane bending over it. A new scream welled inside her, but she thrust both fists against her mouth, reducing it to a high-pitched squeal.

"Don't watch. Look away."

She obeyed, staring into the darkness. She began to tremble, then shake uncontrollably. She closed her eyes, then leaned heavily against the car.

"It's finished. Let's go."

She forced her eyes open, shaking her head, as much from her trembling as from her negative answer. She looked away from him. From somewhere words came. "I—I know this . . . place, don't I?"

"Yes, it's where you told me you washed the car. I figured it was a good place for my body to be found."

She gaped at his shadowy form. "Yours?"

"I put my identification on him. It may gain us some time to get away." He clasped her arm near the shoulder. "I hated to put you through this, Freddie, but it was the only way." He closed the door to the driver's side, then led her around the back of the car to the passenger side. "Stop shaking. You'll see worse before you die."

Again the activity of simply being forced to walk helped her. "No, never."

"Okay, this is the worst that'll ever happen to you. But it's over now. Get in, slide behind the wheel, start the engine."

Mechanically, like a robot, she obeyed. Somehow he had climbed in beside her.

"Now put the clutch in."

As she did, his hand moved the gear to first.

"No!" The word welled out of her.

"Yes. It'll hinder identification."

"No!"

"Do it. He's dead anyway."

"No!" She reached for the door handle, then at once felt his foot shoving hard against hers. The car lurched forward. She screamed at the sickening crunch beneath the wheels.

"Back out and it's over."

She sat there, shaking all over, hands white-knuckled as they clutched the steering wheel.

"Back up, Freddie. Do it—*now*."

She couldn't control her shaking. It was like a spasm. She felt his hand cupping her chin.

"C'mon."

"I—I'm"—she sucked in air—"gonna be . . . sick." She managed to just open the door to retch outside, repeatedly, painfully. In a moment she felt his hand on her arm, pulling her back inside.

"I don't want to hurt you, Freddie, but we've got to get out of here. Now back this thing up!"

"I—I . . ."

He realized she was nearly catatonic. Damn female! "Put your foot on the clutch, Freddie." He watched her do it. "Push down. Your other foot on the gas." Slowly, one step at a time, he got her to back the car into the street, turn, drive away.

He just let her drive anywhere, but he watched her, prepared to grab the wheel, pull on the emergency brake. But he heard her weeping and knew she was coming around.

Finally when he had her back near where the van was parked, he said, "Are you all right now?"

"No. I'll never . . . be all right."

He grinned. "Good."

NINE

Freddie drove mindlessly, her universe shrunk to a ribbon of asphalt, the occasional headlights of an approaching vehicle, and the steering wheel under her hands. She didn't know what country she was in, even what planet. Her tears had stopped, replaced by a mental and emotional numbness.

"I can't sit up any longer. Pull in here."

She made the turn off the highway into a blacktop drive. Grass, trees flashed under her headlights, then some parked cars, the entrance to an inn.

"The campsite must be in back. Over there."

She shifted down, turned the wheel and drove slowly around the building, down a short lane. More trees.

"On the right. It looks level."

She obeyed.

"Turn everything off. Get some sleep."

She climbed between the seats into the back, then up to a bunk, lying on her back staring into the darkness. As from a great distance she heard grunts and groans as he followed her, felt the swinging of the VW when he crawled in the bunk below her, but it had no meaning for her. Only the darkness and emptiness did. She had a sense of falling into it.

Freddie awoke freezing and disoriented. She was in the fetal position, but it did nothing to relieve the cold. She was shaking, her teeth chattering.

"Start the damn ... engine. Get some ... heat ... in here."

The voice startled her and she opened her eyes. Shadowy light, a little brighter around the edges of the curtains. Where was she? How did—then she remembered. The van they had bought. Vaguely she recalled parking, transferring to the VW, driving off.

"Do as ... I say. Start the engine, turn ... the heater on ... full. It's ... freezing in here."

She heard the chattering of his teeth. It was too cold to talk. "All . . . r-right." Anything to get warm. She climbed down, parted the curtains that concealed the front seats and climbed behind the wheel. Hands shaking almost uncontrollably, she managed to start the engine, put the gear in neutral. The heater was a puzzle, but in a moment she had it adjusted.

"Gun the motor. Got to ... h-have some h-heat."

She stepped on the accelerator. In the rear the engine stopped. She started it again, then sat there hunched over, shaking while it roared. She tried to see where she was, but windows had iced over, creating a silvery world. She rubbed at the frost on a side window, making a peephole, grass, trees, spots of gravel. Another van or two in the distance.

"Too damn c-cold ... to c-camp. Got to get ... b-blankets ... b-butane."

He had crawled up to the passenger seat and sat shivering and shaking. She couldn't look at him. Memory had returned.

"Is that a ... little h-heat?"

What did it matter? Nothing mattered. Yes it did. "Where are we?"

"Near G-Garmisch ... I think. G-got to get ...

out of these m-mountains . . . go south . . . where it's warm."

The full name came to her. Garmisch-Partenkirchen, a ski resort up in the mountains, one of the places she had intended to visit. She had looked forward to it. Not now, not with him.

They sat there, the building heat gradually warming them, although both continued to shiver for a long time. She watched the ice on the windshield gradually soften, melt, begin to form rivulets, opening up the view. She saw sunlight filter through the pines.

"Are you going to run out of gas?"

She looked at the gauge, but it didn't register on her mind. "I'm going to leave you now."

"And do what?"

"Find my way back to Munich—home."

"Turn me in?"

"If I said I was you'd kill me."

"No. I left my weapon on Forbes's body. They have to think it was me. Finding my weapon may help. They have to figure I'd never give it up."

"He doesn't have his gun—and he's in no shape to attack me. My oh my, sometimes I can't believe my good fortune. He can't kill me."

"There are seven places where you can strike a person and kill him. It only takes one hand."

"Golly gee, you're a regular killing machine, aren't you?"

He heard her sarcasm, tried to ignore it. "I just stated it as a fact. I thought it might interest you."

For the first time she looked at him, his eyes mostly. They were a penetrating blue, but soft. The coldness she had seen before was not there. He wasn't going to kill her. "I hate killing."

"I know you do."

"I hate all forms of killing. There is never any justification for it—anywhere, anytime—on the battlefield, in self-defense, nowhere. I regularly sign petitions to outlaw the death penalty. But here I sit beside a man who has just killed in cold blood. I mean cold cold—real cold, freezing. Duane Forbes was a decent human being, a husband and father, a friend of yours. He had come to help you. Yet you shot him down like he was ... I don't know, vermin or something."

"A fly. Like swatting a fly."

She stared at him. "Wow!" Her breath was exhaled sharply. "I guess I shouldn't let this opportunity go by. It has to be educational. Tell me, Mr. Sloane, what did you feel when you killed him?"

"Nothing."

She shook her head at him in disbelief. "And what do you feel now?"

"Nothing. I told you he was a fly. I swatted it. Do you feel sorry when you swat a fly? The fly wants to live, too."

"*My God!* What sort of creature are you? Don't answer. I already know. You're a psychopath—or whatever they call them nowadays. Oh, yes, a sociopath."

"Freddie, I've killed lots of men. Most I didn't know. A couple I did. I just don't think about it."

She sat there, gripping the steering wheel, breathing heavily. "Ask a question, you get an answer. Now I know. Oh, no, I don't. How on earth did you get to be this way?"

His anger flared. "Goddammit, you have to be the stupidest female on earth. Do you really teach? In college? They actually pay you to pass on your idiocy to the next generation?"

"You're *not* going to talk to me that way." Her voice rose almost to a scream.

"Oh, but I am. You're so goddamn dumb. I'm a dead man. You're a dead woman. And here you sit wondering whether I'm a psychopath or a sociopath—arguing the niceties of the fucking death penalty."

"I'll not *listen* to you." She reached for the door handle.

He grabbed her wrist. "Can't you get it through your thick skull? Our lives are played out to the last frayed wisp of string. It doesn't matter whether you like me. It doesn't matter how dumb I think you are. All that matters is living—*survival, fucking goddamn survival.*"

His vehemence stunned her, and she sat there shaking all over—and not from the cold.

"Freddie, this is not an intellectual exercise." His voice was calmer now, more reasonable. "This is not theory in a classroom. This is real life—the last, hard, hopeless nubbin of it, and we're holding on by our grubby fingernails."

She continued to tremble for a time, then inhaled deeply, letting it out in a long sigh. "At least tell me why you killed him. He was a nice man. He didn't deserve to die."

"I know he didn't. No one ever does—including you and me. I killed him because I didn't know who sent him."

"You can't think he was KGB?"

"No, at least not directly. But Parsley could have sent him. When I gave Forbes the needle I hoped he might be able to identify Parsley. But I figured he couldn't—and he didn't. I had to kill him."

"He only wanted to help you."

"So he said—and maybe he did. But if I'd gone with him, Parsley would have been there, sooner or later. I had to kill him, don't you understand?"

"No, you're talking gibberish. What's parsley got to do with anything?"

"Parsley's not a what but a who. It's the Soviet code name for their mole high in US intelligence."

She shook her head. "What's a mole?"

"It's what it sounds like. Intelligence jargon is mostly apt. I'm a spook. A shade is someone who peeks at things and tells what he saw. A mole is someone who buries underground, gets inside, and undermines an intelligence agency."

She blinked long lashes. "I get it. The Russians have placed one of their people inside American intelligence. This Parsley person is really working for them, against us."

"The three so-called Israelis who killed Harry and Khruchenko and shot me were Americans. CSA agents. Parsley sent them."

"How do you know that?"

"I talked to one. He was definitely American. It figures the others were, too."

"But why? If you were an American, why kill you?"

"I don't know exactly what was done, but it figures Parsley told them Harry and I were going over to the KGB—meeting a Russian to defect. They were to do their patriotic duty and kill us."

"Parsley could do that?"

"Oh my, yes, very easily."

"And you think Forbes—"

"Yes, you got it." He smiled. "Maybe you're not so dumb after all."

Her eyes glinted a little at his condescension. "You can let go of my wrist now."

He was unaware he still held it. Releasing her, he said, "Did I hurt you?"

"Would you care if you did?"

"Yes, Freddie, I'd care."

She heard him, saw it in his eyes. "You have a fine way of showing it. How'd you learn about this Parsley person?"

"Harry and I suspected a mole. We got very defensive about the Agency, trusting no one, holding back information. Then a year ago we met Khruchenko in Prague. What happened at the dry-cleaning shop happened there first: gunshots aimed at the three of us. Though we all escaped—barely. Another setup. I thought Khruchenko had done it and almost killed him on the spot. But he said Parsley had done it. That was the first time I heard the name. The other night we met Khruchenko again. I gave him the needle. He told us all he knew about Parsley. But it was another setup. I guess you know the rest."

She nodded. "If you know who Parsley is, why don't you—"

"I don't know *who*. Khruchenko had no name other than Parsley. All I know is that he exists and is very dangerous."

"Why?"

"He's on The Committee."

"Why do you always make me feel like a dunce? What's The Committee?"

"It controls US intelligence activities worldwide. No one knows for certain whether The Committee exists, but we all figure it must. Somebody has to make decisions."

"Who's on it?"

"No one knows. Everyone in the field thinks The Committee has five members because the CSA divides the world into five intelligence zones. The person who heads each zone sits on The Committee—or so we believe."

"Wonderful! This Parsley creature is one of five people whom nobody knows and who sits on a committee no one is sure exists."

"That's about it, Freddie."

"No, it's not. Somebody has to know who heads a zone."

"Sure, but not his name, who he really is. I'm sure he uses a code name. Mine is Wolf. Navy records list me as Lt. David Sloane. But I've used scores of other names—and none of them is the one I was born with."

"What is it?"

"It doesn't matter. I've almost forgotten it."

"Do you have a family?"

"Yes. They think I'm dead."

"That's awful."

"No, it's not. Freddie, you're getting off the subject. Do you have to be so damnably female?"

"Damn you, you're a chauvinist pig. But you're also right. Can't you warn somebody about this Parsley?"

"Like who?"

"I don't know. The other four members of The Committee?"

"Use your head. I don't know who's on The Committee. And if I did, any one of them could be Parsley. I'd be dead on the spot."

"Okay, we'll go over The Committee's head. We'll go to the White House, the President if we have to. I'm sure he'll be very interested to know he has a traitor high in American intelligence." She saw him shaking his head in despair or maybe disbelief. "What's the matter?"

"Freddie, there is no one higher than The Committee."

She heard the exasperation in his voice. He was treating her like an ignorant child. "Damn you, Dave, I have a Ph.D. in political science. I'm *Dr.* Falscape, *Assistant Professor* Falscape. Don't you patronize me. I *know* American government."

"No, you don't. 'We'll go to the White House,' she says, 'the President if we have to.' *My God!* Freddie, the President of the United States knows precisely what The Committee lets him know, and he does exactly what The Committee wants him to."

"You're *awful*, unbelievable. You not only kill people on sight, you—"

"I thought we settled why I had to kill Forbes."

"That doesn't mean I have to like it. And I don't have to like your *stupid* lectures on American government. I know what I know."

He smiled. "Freddie, you're wonderful. The Agency must love you. It's people like you who are so easy to manipulate. You're intelligent. You're informed. You know what you know, indeed you do. You're very concerned about the problems of the world. You want to do something to make the world a better place. It's the dumb, uncaring ones who are hard to manipulate."

"*What* are you talking about?"

"Mother works on a principle called—"

"What's your mother got to do with it? She thinks you're dead."

"Oh, shit. 'Mother' is what field ops call the Agency. It is short for 'motherfucker'—another apt word."

"Okay, okay, I get it."

"Mother works on a system called Need to Know. A person is told only what he has Need to Know to think a certain way and thereby act a certain way. That applies to the President, his advisors, the Cabinet, the Joint Chiefs of Staff, anybody you can think of. They only know what the CSA allows them to know."

"Nonsense. The President gets information from—"

"Okay. I'm not talking about the price of soy beans and how many illegitimate kids were born yesterday. I'm talking about national security, what's going on in the world, where to send the troops, when to drop the bomb. Oh, the jerks in the White House *think* they make these decisions, only they don't. They think, decide, act on information supplied by Mother. It's the real world, Freddie. It's how things really work."

"I don't believe you."

"You want an example? The other day in the hotel room, I needed you. I was desperate—still am. I can't make it without you. How do I get you to help me? By all logic you should run from me like I had the plague. Do you remember calling me a psychiatrist? Answer a question with a question? I kept asking you what you thought and telling you to figure it out. That's Need to Know. I was finding out what you already knew about the dry-cleaning shop, then giving you just enough information to get you to help me. When you figured out the KGB was after me—and it is, I'm sure—I didn't tell you the real danger was Parsley. You had no Need to Know about Parsley. Forbes changed all that. Now you have Need to Know about Parsley and you do. I manipulated you, Freddie."

She stared at him. Part of her sensed she should be angry at him, but she was too fascinated to bother with it.

"It's no different in the White House or Pentagon. The generals, admirals, cabinet secretaries, aides, advisors and Presidents—all of them, ever since 1952—are manipulated. They know what they know, indeed they do. They have titles on the door that tell them they command armies, head departments, lead nations. They are *very* important. They make *fateful* decisions. Only they don't. Don't you see, Freddie? Mother already knows what they know, what they believe, what's in their heads. It is ridiculously easy to feed them a little more information to make them think differently, or maybe continue to think the same way or more so, to believe some uprising in the Caribbean or Africa or God knows where poses some greater risk to national security than it did yesterday or the day before, that we need to send arms, advisors, troops—or maybe take them out. Whatever these people do, they are manipulated into doing it."

"It can't be so. You have to be wrong."

"What do you know about the CSA, Freddie?"

"What's it matter? You'll tell me I'm wrong anyway."

"Are you going to be serious, or are you coming down with terminal petulance? The world's greatest authority on American government just might learn something new, you know."

"*Damn you!*" She saw him grin at her. It didn't

help. "Okay, the Central Security Agency is—" She tried to remember. "It has to do with communications, codes. Oh, yes, it advises the President on national security matters." Her eyes widened at her own words. "Wasn't it created by Executive Order of Harry Truman—1952, I think?"

"Very good, Freddie. You probably already know more about the CSA than most Ph.D.'s in American government. Truman was forced to create the CSA at the end of his term. He was the last President to make decisions involving national security—and he made such an ungodly mess of things no President has been given the opportunity since."

She stared at him. "I remember. Eisenhower was very upset at the CIA over the U-2 incident, swore he'd never meet alone with the head of the CIA again. J.F.K. was fit to be tied about the CIA after the Bay of Pigs fiasco, put his brother Bobby in charge of all US intelligence agencies." Her mouth came open. "Are you saying—"

"I'm not saying anything. I can't get a word in edgewise."

"But—"

"Whatever might or might not have happened twenty years ago is not important, Freddie. I'm talking right now. I'm talking Parsley."

"Let me ask a question, dammit. I'm confused about the CIA and the CSA. What's the difference?"

He consciously restrained his impatience. "And so is everyone else, Freddie. That's the way they want it. The CSA is the parent organization of the CIA. The CIA is mostly a front. It is famous—or maybe infamous—the world over. It gets all the blame—or maybe the credit. But it's really—"

"The CSA actually controls the CIA?"

"Yes—and the DIA—Defense Intelligence Agency—and the tactical intelligence branches of the armed forces. The Committee controls all US intelligence activities worldwide. Believe me, I mean *controls*. When the director of the CIA or DIA goes over to the White House, where did he get his information? Who told him what to tell the President?"

"Okay, I get it. I'm listening."

"The CSA has three main functions. It—"

"I remember now. Truman's order creating the CSA was highly classified. Nobody's seen it to this day."

"Will you stop interrupting?"

"I'm sorry. Go on."

"You don't learn anything because you don't listen. The CSA literally eavesdrops on the planet. It has set up satellites, ground stations, ships, planes, and a whole lot more so it can intercept any message sent through space, the atmosphere or under the ocean. It can intercept most telephone calls, certainly any it wants to. Believe me, I know what I'm talking about. I've been on the ships, the planes, and at most of the ground stations."

"I believe you. How about the mails?"

"It hardly reads a billion letters every day, but, yes, if it wants to read a letter or open a package, it can. Can I go on now?" He saw her nod. "Most of the messages it intercepts are in code. The CSA's job is to break those codes. I know this for a fact, too. I'm classified Cryptographic Code Word Three. It's my job to break codes. It's the Agency's biggest job."

"I remember reading somewhere that the CSA is the largest buyer of computers in the world. It measures them in acres, not in numbers. Its needs really dictate the development of computer science in America."

He nodded. "Very good, Freddie. You're getting an *A*. Name another function of the CSA." He could almost see her mind working through her eyes. "C'mon, you can do it. If the CSA breaks codes it also must—"

"Make codes."

"Yes, it makes all the codes for use by all agencies and departments of the US government, including the White House, Pentagon, State Department—and itself. Therefore—"

"Wait a minute. Let me do it. If the CSA develops the codes used by the Pentagon, State Department and all the rest, it is easily aware of what information they have."

"Duck soup, in fact. What else can you figure out?"

Her mind was alive, flying in fact. She opened her mouth to answer, then stopped. "No, you tell me. I don't want to be manipulated by you."

"Very good. You're learning. Take the three functions of the CSA and put them together—intercepting messages, breaking codes, and making codes. A message is sent—by the Russians, say. The CSA is the only one in the US who knows it was sent, the only one capable of intercepting it, the only one capable of decoding it so the message can be read. They can tell the President and the generals, admirals and diplomats, members of Congress, pet reporters, and thus the public about the message, or they can tell some of them and not others. They can tell them part of the message—"

"Or they can tell none of them. *My God!*"

"Or they can report an entirely erroneous message, keeping the original concealed within a code the CSA developed for its own use. Who is ever to know?" He saw both her hands come to her mouth, covering it. He recognized it as a female gesture of shock. "Because of the CSA's code-making function, it already knows what the President and all the rest know. It is simple to feed them a little additional information, which will induce them to think and therefore act in a desired way."

Her hands came away from her mouth and she uttered a single word: *"Parsley!"*

"He is one of five men who control all this. Khruchenko wanted to defect because he feared Parsley. For years Parsley has been feeding them information, fouling us up, helping the KGB. They trust him. He is the only one they permit to work independently. That's why he could send Americans to kill Khruchenko—and Harry and me along with him. But Khruchenko knew that one day Parsley would give the KGB some erroneous information, play both sides against the middle. He's a most dangerous man. That is almost an exact quote from Khruchenko."

"We have to stop him, David."

He saw her shock and smiled. "Got any ideas?"

She swallowed. "I don't know. We have to tell somebody—somebody in Congress, the White House. Maybe my father knows—"

"Back at that, are you? Freddie, by a 1959 Act of Congress it is illegal to identify anyone who works for the CSA other than the Director and Deputy Director—and they are figureheads precisely because they are identified. They know only what The Committee allows them to know."

"How about the press? It's a good story. Some reporter—"

"No reporter would believe you, Freddie. It would be an admission they are manipulated the same way as everyone else. Besides, there is no proof for a syllable of it. And if you tried you would be hanging a sign around your neck—"

"I know, KILL ME. God, David, what are we going to do?"

"Put the car in gear and drive the hell out of here."

She started to, then stopped. "Then what?"

"I don't know. Go where it's warmer. We need food, water, butane, blankets. We aren't set up for camping."

"Be serious. How're we going to stop Parsley?"

"We aren't."

"We have to."

"No, we don't. Freddie, when Harry and I went to that dry-cleaning shop, we were going to talk to Khruchenko, kill him, then walk away, disappear, stick our feet in the sand, and enjoy life. We knew just how to do it. We even had the tickets, as you know. Harry's dead. You want to go with me?"

She gaped at him. "You're not serious!"

"I'm dead serious. Freddie, it's your only chance. You can't go back to your job, your family, friends, anything you've known. All will be watched now. That traveler's check—and probably the rent-a-car—did you in. Fern L. Falscape is on everybody's list right now. Come with me. It'll mean a new identity, leaving everything you've known, but it's your only chance. You and I don't have to live together or anything. I'm not talking sex, but—"

"My God! I can't *believe* you."

He swore under his breath. "What're you carrying on about now?"

"Parsley, that's what. Aren't you going to do anything about him? Don't you care about your country, the world, other people?"

"I don't give a shit about any of 'em. What have they done for me lately?" He saw the stunned expression in her eyes. "The only thing or person I ever cared about in my life was Harry Rogers. The last time I saw him he was flying through the air with a three-inch hole in his chest."

"And by Parsley's command. Your partner, your *friend*, is dead and you're not going to do a damn thing about it?"

He was angry and didn't know why. "What do you want from me? Vengeance?"

She was shaking and near tears. "No, I

want— Oh, God!" She swallowed. "I want you to stop a man who's a threat to my country—the world."

"*Bullshit!*" He hurled the word.

"All right," she screamed. "Kill him if you must. You killed Forbes. Kill—"

"I don't want to hear another word about that fucking Forbes!"

For the first time she was frightened of him. He could harm her. Suddenly she smiled. "What happened to that cold-eyed, dispassionate killer?"

His rage dwelled within him a moment longer, then left as quickly as it came. He grinned. "I think he met a girl named Freddie. Lord, what you do to me. Harry and I worked together for three years and I don't think either of us got mad once."

"And they call us the weaker sex. David, I— Do you want me to call you David or Dave?"

"Doesn't matter." And it didn't. He liked the sound of both, the movement of her lips as she said either name.

"I don't care—oh, I really do, but I'll take vengeance as a motive, if I can't have patriotism. We have to stop Parsley."

He sighed, letting out his breath in a long "whew" sound. "Do you have any idea of the power Parsley wields? He's a fleet of ships and we're rub-a-dub-dub in a tub. He's a battery of artillery and we're a pea-shooter."

She smiled at him. It was her most dazzling. "But you know a way, don't you?"

"No. But I can think of a single, microscopically slim, virtually hopeless chance."

"Can you give me a hint?"

"He has to think I'm dead—and I will be if I don't lie down."

She reached over and felt his forehead. Fever up. "Okay, dead man." She put the van in gear. "You did say south, didn't you?"

*   *   *

The words had not come easy to Adams. "We have positive ID on the body found in Munich. It has been run over by a car twice and was considerably disfigured, but there were enough prints and dentures to make a positive. Wolf."

Gray: "There is no doubt in your mind?"

"None. The body bore the identification Wolf was using—and the weapon which had been Bear's."

Brown: "That episode is ended, at least. We are finished with Wolf and Bear. That is hardly cause for bereavement."

Sitting at his desk now, Adams pondered his situation. Sloane was not dead. He had shot Forbes, put his wallet and weapon on the body, then run over it to hinder ID. There could be only one reason—delay pursuit. Adams felt he had no choice but to help him. If he declared Sloane dead, maybe the mole and the KGB would buy it.

Adams shook his head. He had lied to The Committee. His only justification was his belief one of the members was a mole. If that wasn't true, or he was unable to prove it, then he was in terrible trouble. He would be dead within hours. His life was right now in the hands of David Sloane—and that was a slender reed. No way to predict what he might do. In his rage over the death of Rogers, he could be suicidal or do something entirely foolish. And another thing: Sloane may have learned nothing from Khruchenko that would identify the mole. Sloane may have killed Forbes just to save his own skin and escape the Agency as he and Rogers had planned to do. Adams swore; he couldn't help it.

Then he abruptly cast all these thoughts aside to concentrate on Sloane. He was alive, well enough to move around. And he had help. Adams picked up the photo from his desk. Fern L. Falscape. He had obtained the name from a rent-a-car found abandoned near the Hotel Columbia. No factual connection to Sloane, still he had a hunch. Pretty, taught at Calvert College, on sabbatical, visiting Munich. He had already ordered a complete workup on her, everybody she'd ever known, anything she'd ever done. Waste of time, maybe, but it wouldn't be the first time a pretty girl helped a wounded man. Sloane could pull that off.

Adams knew he could find this girl—and Sloane if he was with her. But, no. Sloane obviously wanted time. He'd even surrendered his weapon to gain it. The thing to do was give it to him. Besides, Sloane would kill anyone who approached him, and no more deaths were needed right now. Forbes had been difficult enough to account for. Fortunately there was a small private plane crash in Virginia. No one was sure how many were aboard, so Forbes was declared one of them and his wife was told. She had taken it hard—so hard she hadn't asked too many questions.

Nothing to do but wait until Sloane surfaced and made contact—if he made contact. To help this along Adams ordered a direct line of communications from Sloane to himself. Any 752 messages were to bypass all other hands and come directly to him—immediately, regardless of the time of day. It was all he could think of to do for Sloane at the moment. Had to hope it helped.

Parsley read the item in "Washington Off Guard": "Watch the headlines for a very big financial scandal involving an important Congressman from a Southern state." Parsley frowned. Cushman-Eustace had added the word "Southern." Couldn't be helped. There was always some garbling of these plants. No problem. The message had gotten through: MISSION ENDED.

The real question was whether he should have sent it. He had to let Dzerzhinsky Square know there had been a positive ID and Wolf was dead. But was he? Absolutely no reason to suspect he wasn't—except for his own lingering suspicion of Green. He had withheld information once. Could he be lying now? Unthinkable really. No reason for him to take such a risk, unless . . .

One way to find out. He drafted and encoded a message for Quigley: IS WOLF DEAD?

Beneath Dzerzhinsky Square, Dimitri Galenkov reread the message sent by Parsley. *Mission ended* could only mean the dead body found in the Munich alley had been positively identified as the wounded US operative Wolf. Very good. Any link between Yuri Khruchenko and Parsley was now severed. In a manner of speaking the death of his brother-in-law had been avenged. There was a nice feel to that. All was ordered in the universe.

Only not quite. To the Russian mind the intelligence game was not a quick, brilliant success. The Americans liked that and worked hard to achieve it. That was their weakness and one day their maneuvering toward instant achievement would be their undoing—if not the whole world's because of a miscalculation. Mother Russia was a bear, patient, plodding, always wary. But if pushed too far toward her lair, she would strike back, even if it meant her own death.

Galenkov forced these philosophical thoughts from his mind. The universe was not quite in order because one American agent was out of place. He had himself set up a system for identifying all American agents. A file was maintained on every person, man or woman, who attended the CSA facility at Pensacola, State of Florida. Sometimes it took a while to identify them all, but he himself believed there were few gaps in the files. Then the problem was to follow the movements of all these men. Quite often, he had found, simply knowing where a person had been and where he was going revealed a great deal about field operations in progress. It was not always possible to know the location of all US field agents with precision. There were decoy movements, blind alleys. The CSA people were not without cleverness. But eventually—the bear is a patient animal—the whereabouts of most US field agents were known with considerable clarity, if only sometimes long after the fact.

To wit, one Tokyo-based agent named Fox. Most interesting. Fox's partner, Terrier, had left Tokyo alone. His movements had been traced to Munich. There was no doubt Terrier was killed in the dry-cleaning shop. *Parsley will act.* Yes, he had used Terrier. Strike Terrier from the files. Then Fox had left Tokyo, also bound for Munich. Doubtlessly Parsley had sent Fox, partner to the dead Terrier, to find the wounded American agent Wolf. He must have done so. *Mission ended.* Wolf was dead. Fine. There was no reason to distrust Parsley's information—except where was Fox? He had not gone back to Tokyo, nor had he headed for America. And he should. What was keeping him in Munich—if that was indeed where he was.

Strange. Disorder in the universe. It was probably not important where Fox was. A dozen reasons could exist for his not surfacing. But a prudent man would wish that he did. Then there would be perfect order and the mission would be truly ended. Find not the Wolf but the Fox.

Disappointment had taken Quigley to the Munich morgue. He had wanted to kill Wolf himself and felt cheated that someone else had done it. KGB most likely. Dead bodies, particularly mutilated ones, held no charms for him. Ghoulish he was not. But he wanted to look upon the face of a man he had long admired before he turned and went over.

There was no face. The car wheels had run over it. But there was something else. Fresh wounds. Munich police observed that, but argued the man had been shot before he was killed. Through Interpol they had obtained a positive ID from his fingerprints. Lionel Twilley. Case closed.

No way. Where were the old wounds? The man laid out in the morgue was not Wolf; yet Brandywine, which should know, had stated that it was. Very strange. Even stranger was the message from Mother asking if Wolf was dead. Why declare a man dead, then ask if he really was? What was going on? He had messaged back: NO. Now he held a new message. He was to find Wolf and kill him. Good. It was what he'd wanted to do all along.

Quigley again became the hunter. Wolf was not dead. Someone else had been shot and run over. The body had Wolf's identification, even his weapon on it. This had two meanings. Wolf had to want the body identified as his very badly if he gave up his weapon, *and* Wolf had killed whoever was in the morgue. Yes.

What else? The body was found in an alley behind an empty warehouse near the river. All evidence indicated that's where the killing occurred. Wolf had to have gone there deliberately—an isolated, quiet area—and taken whoever he killed with him. Yes. Wolf knew the person. That person trusted him. No, Wolf could have forced him to go at gunpoint. Was it his accomplice, the person who had shielded him for almost a week? Could be and most likely was. Wolf would kill anyone who could possibly identify him. Quigley nodded. Learn the identity of the body in the morgue and he might have a clue to Wolf and his whereabouts. The dead man had to be somebody with a name. Somebody had to know him and miss him.

At police headquarters Quigley studied the files

of persons declared missing in the last week. He jotted down a few names, but none were really intriguing. He sensed a dead end. Police had probably been all over this ground. Yet there just had to be some clue somewhere to the identity of a dead man. He tried everything, no matter how remote, and thus came to a list of vehicles towed away by Munich police. One interested him. Hertz Rent-a-car. Abandoned near Hotel Columbia. He phoned Hertz. Fern L. Falscape, Maryland driver's license, American Express charge. They had no idea why she had abandoned the car.

For just a moment Quigley wondered if he was pursuing this matter simply because she was female. Probably—and probably a dead end. He decided to make two more phone calls and by midafternoon he was elated. American Express reported a Fern L. Falscape had cashed a twenty-dollar traveler's check at a drug store. Posing as an Interpol agent, Quigley quickly learned Fern L. Falscape had bought adhesive, gauze, etc., on Saturday night—and that he was the second person to inquire about the check. No name. Tall, dark-haired, in his twenties. The man in the morgue? Couldn't be sure.

The other phone call was to the US Embassy in Bonn. He now held in his hand wired copies of her photo and passport application. He was absolutely certain Wolf was with Fern L. Falscape, American, brown hair and eyes, tall, twenty-nine, college professor, pretty. Why: Wolf could be forcing her. Not important why. She just was.

Think, dammit. Think like Wolf. Okay, I'm Wolf. I'm wounded—bad. Can't walk any farther and get in a car to lie down, a car leased by one Fern L. Falscape. I force her to drive me to my rented Audi in the next block. I get out, but I can't drive. I force this Fern L. Falscape to drive me someplace where I can hide. I also force her to stay with me for a week. Impossible. Nobody'd do that. He must have known her. It isn't important. The simple fact is she did stay with him.

Think, you bastard. Okay. She rented a car then abandoned it. Why do that? Why not turn it in and stop the charges? There wasn't time. Quigley smiled. Yes, the rent-a-car had been used to run over a body in an alley beside the river. He was willing to bet a proper examination would turn up blood and tissue on the tires. Again, why abandon the rented car? Why not use it to drive off into the sunset? He smiled. Simple. They had another one.

He was rolling now. Why get another vehicle? Because Wolf was badly wounded and needed to lie down. They were going camping. Shouldn't be hard to find.

He messaged Brandywine in the code used to summon him from Tokyo: WOLF WITH FERN L. FALSCAPE.

Quigley had always considered himself lucky, but even he was surprised at how easily he picked up their trail. That they would go south was little more than a hunch, then to be right about Garmisch and find their campsite so quickly was—hell, he should be at a casino. Even better luck in Innsbruck. The *Fräulein* made an impression. Very friendly. Large purchase, sleeping bags, blankets, cooler, butane, food. Was there a man with her? Yes, possibly. What did he look like? A vigorous shrug. Quigley understood. Field ops were supposed to make no impression, be hard to describe. If necessary plastic surgery was performed to make them that way. Name? No. Camping guests were not required to register, but he did keep a record of vehicles. White VW van. Dutch plates XN6817. Quigley was elated. Did he see them leave? Indeed. They headed west.

In his rented car, Quigley raced west through the Austrian Tyrol all the way to Switzerland. Surely they would have gone that far in a day. He spent a whole day checking campsites. No, no, no, nothing. He retraced his tracks, going east, hoping they had not taken a road into the mountains. Luck again. They had stopped at a different campsite near Innsbruck. Must have headed west and doubled back. He continued east. Nothing, nothing, nothing, then—my God, Salzburg! Two days later he picked up their trail in Italy, the Dolomite mountains. In another two days back in Austria, not too far from Innsbruck. He waited for them at the Brenner Pass into Italy. They either didn't come that way or had already been there.

Even in his frustration Quigley had grudging admiration. Wolf was being damned smart, using the terrain. Most campsites didn't keep a record. You just drove in, paid, and left. A few wanted names, but they'd accept any. They didn't look at passports. And there were a zillion campsites. No way to find him, especially because he wasn't *going* anywhere. Clearly, he was just *moving*. He was meandering, utterly at random. There was no predicting where he'd go next. Quigley knew when to give up. He was under orders to work alone, not involve other CSA personnel because he was out of his zone. Fine, only he didn't have a prayer of finding Wolf without a lot more help, a huge net.

He returned to Munich and in his special code informed Brandywine that he needed help, lots of it.

Parsley hated to bring in the KGB, but he had no choice. He couldn't send more personnel to Green's zone without attracting attention, and he was already on thin ice about Fern L. Falscape. His men had bumped into the fact somebody else— probably Green—had ordered a workup on her. The phones of her parents and friends were already tapped.

Parsley knew he had to be extremely careful. This was no time for pride. If he had to ask the KGB for help, he had to do it and that was all there was to it. He swore. What he hated the most was using the letterdrop. There was no assurance it was entirely safe. But he had to. The message was too complicated to send by any other means.

Dimitri Galenkov was both pleased and disturbed. Parsley needed assistance. That in itself was an affirmation of cooperation in a common endeavor. As far as he knew it was the first time the highly independent Parsley had ever needed help. It also meant Parsley was in some kind of trouble. He would bear watching—a great deal of watching.

Galenkov studied the message. White VW camper, Dutch plates XN6817, traveling in northern Italy, Austria, maybe Switzerland, France. A large area, many campsites, but eminently possible to locate. DO NOT INTERDICT. REPORT LICENSE NUMBER BY PHONE TO MUNICH. REPEAT: DO NOT INTERDICT. Galenkov leaned back in his chair and smiled. It all had meaning. The phone was an answering service and linked to a post office box. The CSA method. One of their operatives—doubtlessly the missing Fox—would pick up the information, then act upon it. Parsley would maintain his cherished independence.

Again Galenkov smiled. Dzerzhinsky Square was not an errand boy for Parsley, the CSA, or anyone else. White VW camper, Dutch plates XN6817. Who was in it? The answer was obvious. He picked up another piece of paper. IS WOLF DEAD? The CSA cyphers and codes were good, but not impossible to break given time. Obviously Wolf was not dead. He was camping with one Fern L. Falscape.

All right. Parsley would have the help he desired. Fox would be informed in Munich. But Parsley did not issue orders to Dzerzhinsky Square. He had to learn his place.

In Cyrillic letters he wrote an order and signed his name. FIND AND DESTROY.

TEN

They had a routine, sort of—breakfast, change his bandages, showers, sometimes a little laundry, shopping, lunch. In the afternoon they packed up the van and drove, not far, maybe a hundred miles or so along any road that looked attractive, stopping by a lake, stream, field of wildflowers, a churchyard in some village, a rock, a tree, just about anything that interested one of them. Somewhere along the way she'd buy a piece of meat, some vegetables, a loaf of fresh bread, *real* honest-to-goodness bread, then they'd do the dishes, take a walk, go to bed—sometimes under the stars in their sleeping bags. It had been going on for over two weeks.

Freddie was ecstatically happy. Time was a friend she embraced, then surrendered to. Seconds ticked, minutes idled, hours passed, none lamented. Day bequeathed a new equally unremarkable day, and the calendar ceased to exist. Space was their ally. They had no map and she didn't know where she'd been, where she was or or where they were going. The word serendipity kept popping into her mind. She was on a serendipity tour, driving roads built only for her, viewing panoramas never before seen, discovering villages no one had ever visited.

She felt free, untethered, in rhythm with the universe, doing simple, life-sustaining things which God and Nature had intended, rested, utterly healthy and strangely worry-free. Oh, she knew danger lurked out there somewhere and all this had to end sometime, but she was immersed in the moment, a succession of moments, each precious, fulfilling and somehow ordained.

"Take the road to the left."

She was driving, he riding beside her. "Any idea where it goes?"

"Nope."

She slowed, geared down, made the turn. "I do." She sang, " 'Somewhere over the rainbow . . .' " Then she laughed. "I don't know whether you're the Tin Man, Lion, or Scarecrow."

"I think I'm the Wizard."

She glanced at him. "Maybe. You could be." She stayed in third gear until the van made it up a small hill, then shifted into fourth. "I love this. Just drive—doesn't matter where. Do you think it's working?"

"It has so far. I'm sure we're making it hard to find us—if anyone's looking."

"I notice you're more relaxed."

He looked at her, something he did often. She had to have the most gorgeous profile he had ever seen. "Maybe you have something to do with that. Hard to be uptight around someone who laughs all the time."

She tried to suppress a new laugh, but couldn't. "I guess I do laugh a lot. I wish you would. Sometimes I feel like I have to teach you how to."

"Maybe you do."

She drove in silence a while, then to pass the time asked him his real name. He wouldn't tell her and she teased him, thinking of every absurd name she could. Finally he laughed and contributed a couple of other weird names. He told her. David Pritchard. She pretended not to believe him, then told him she was disappointed. She liked Schuyler van Rensselaer better.

"Well?"

"Well what?"

"I want to know some more about David Pritchard."

"What's to know? I was born in a small town in Indiana. My father was a pentecostal preacher. I hated it. Church all the time—nutty stuff. No friends. Always alone. Anything I could think of to do was a sin. I ran away. My grandmother mostly raised me. I loved her. She died. Had to go back home. Hated it more. Mercifully my folks booted me out of the house when I was sixteen."

She heard the short, staccato phrases. It was as though they were being wrenched from some black hole in his mind, where he tossed all the things he didn't want to think about. "They booted you out? Why?"

"If you must know, I was caught screwing an elder's daughter behind the pulpit."

She could visualize it, the rigid, self-righteous, Bible-thumping father catching his wayward son with his pants down—literally. She had to laugh.

He didn't. "I never went back. They think I'm dead. It's better that way."

"You said that before. What d'you mean dead?"

"Dead as in dead. Some time after I joined the Navy—Harry, too—we were reported as 'missing in action.' Happens all the time. You don't really believe all the MIAs are unknown, do you? Most of them really are dead, but nobody wants to admit where, how, and what they were doing at the time. But some, like Harry and me and other field ops, rise like the phoenix from the ashes to fly away—and die someplace else."

"Haven't you contacted your folks?"

"Why should I?"

"Your mother must be—"

"All my mother cares about is the God Almighty Lord and getting her fat ass into heaven."

His vehemence stung her, and she saw the anger rising in his eyes like a cold mist. So he hated his parents. Lots of people do. Or did he? Could he care about his family more than he knew? Could he be protecting himself from hurt by convincing himself he didn't care? Or maybe protecting them from harm by being dead and out of their lives?

"How'd you get into this spy racket—forgive the word?"

"I didn't volunteer. That's for sure. Never would have. I was eighteen when I joined the Navy and went to Great Lakes Naval Training Center. Almost right away I met Harry Rogers. We've been together more or less ever since—or were. He was a runaway, too. Amazingly similar background. His mother was a religious nut. He hated it. Want to know a funny thing?"

"Sure. Haven't had a laugh in a couple of minutes."

"A couple of years ago Harry and I got together with six other Code Word Three agents. Weren't supposed to, but we did it anyway. It's hard to believe, but five of the eight were sons of ministers and the sixth, Harry, came from an extremely religious home."

"That's not funny."

"But it's strange, don't you think? There's something about being a preacher's kid that makes you different, a little out of step, a loner."

"And you rebel, if only to prove you're—"

"Yes, that's what they're looking for."

"Who's they?"

"The Agency—CSA. At boot camp Harry and I were selected for training as field ops—although we didn't know it at the time. I think we were picked because we were loners, runaways with no close family ties, and in a state of rebellion.

Harry and I didn't give a shit about anybody or anything—Mom, flag, country, apple pie, or Popsicles. We still don't—or didn't."

"You miss him, don't you?"

"Yeah. Part of me died with him. I'll never be whole again."

It was too much of a revelation. She sensed him clamming up and sought a digression. "Why no close family ties?"

"Field work requires total concentration. If you're thinking about Mom or Pop, sis or girlfriend—anything but the operation you're on—then you're dead." He hesitated. "You're dangerous, Freddie. I'm starting to think about you, worry about you."

She stole a quick look at him and smiled. "Always wanted to be dangerous." Her gaze returned to the road. She negotiated a curve.

"Another thing. The moment you care about anyone or anything, you are compromised. Mom, Pop, wife, girlfriend may have no idea what you really do, but they can be taken—killed. They are a way to get to you. Understand?"

"Yes." And she did, but not what he thought. He *did* care about his family. He was protecting them. "So you were selected because you were a loner, no close family ties and rebellious."

"And something else. They were looking for what they called 'highly intelligent problem solvers.' We didn't know it at the time but Harry and I were tested for such things as imagination, innovation, ability to analyze and—I can't think of the term they use—oh, yes, sensitivity. Harry and I have radar for danger, when something isn't right, when—"

"Nuances. You pick up expressions, flickers of an eye, body language nobody notices. It tells you things and you react immediately. It's right-brain function. Yours is highly developed. You trust it. At the same time you're highly analytical, which comes from the cortex of the left side of the brain. Most unusual."

"You know all that?"

She smiled. "You're not the only one who pays attention to other people—dangerously so. Are you really a problem solver?"

"Yes—dammit. Harry'd be alive today if I hadn't wanted to solve the problem of Parsley."

She asked how so, learning about his hesitation when Harry wanted to kill Khruchenko. If he'd let Harry kill when he wanted to, they would have been gone when the three assassins came. She didn't know what to say. He felt guilty about the death of his friend. Was that a good thing? She didn't know. She changed the subject. "So the Agency selected you. Then what?"

"We were sent to OCS"—he saw the query in her eyes—"Officer Candidate School. Okay with us. Better to be an officer than a swab jockey. It seemed like ordinary OCS training to us, but I learned later it wasn't. We received lots of extra training—history of the Cold War, psychology, politics, stuff like that. After OCS, Harry and I were separated for sea duty. I went on a destroyer as communications officer. Again I thought it was normal duty, but it wasn't. I not only learned more about communications than most ensigns, I learned all phases of ship-handling and command procedures. Whatever else I might be, Freddie, I'm a damn good naval officer."

"I believe you. Go on."

"After a year of sea duty, Harry and I were reunited at Pensacola for seven months of intensive training. God, it was hard—cryptography, electronics, computer programming, all kinds of communications, four languages, psychology, weapons, hand-to-hand combat—much more. Always there was drill in deductive reasoning. If this happens what do you do? If a person does this, what does he know and what is he thinking? It went on all the time, day and night."

"They were training you to be a field op?"

"Only we didn't know it. We had no clear idea what we were going to do—and neither did the instructors who were training us."

"But you found out?"

"Sure did. You have to understand Harry and I would never have volunteered. Get our asses killed? Not on your life. All we wanted was to be left alone and have a good time."

"So how'd they get you into it?"

"One day at Pensacola they took us into a Space Three." He described it to her. "A man sat at a small table. Didn't know him; haven't seen him since. He had three stacks of papers. Harry and I read them, initialing each page, handing it back to him. The first stack was interesting, the second startling. By the time we finished the third we knew we were had. We were trapped."

"What d'you mean, trapped?"

"We had just read the most sensitive, never-to-be-revealed national secrets, all the stuff the Agency had done over the years—and had had done to it, all the lies, all the cover-ups. If we ever breathed one syllable of it, we were dead. And the human brain being what it is, there is no way to forget it. Don't you see? There was nothing we could do but go on, do what we were told, and hope somehow to survive. We were trapped. We had just volunteered."

She looked at him so sharply she almost ran off the road. "What a dirty trick!"

"Wasn't it?"

"Instant cynicism."

"Not quite. It was heady stuff at first. We were Navy lieutenants, possessed of the highest security classification in the field, Top Secret Three, Cryptographic Code Word Three. We had the red card. With it we could open any door, obtain any information, requisition any equipment, issue any order with absolute assurance it would be obeyed. We had tremendous power."

"Hard to believe. You were what then, twenty-two?"

"Yes. Look at it this way. Our clearance made us the equivalent of a GS-18, the highest rank in the Federal Service. A four-star admiral or general is only a GS-16, and the President is only considered a GS-12. Believe me, Freddie, you aren't going to understand this country, the world, until you realize that rank, title on the door, money, power, popularity, good looks, family, connections, old school ties, intelligence, ability, experience, whatever you can think of doesn't mean a thing. What counts is security classification."

She thought of asking him to explain, challenging him, then decided against it. That wasn't what she wanted to hear. "So you were classified all those threes. You were proud of yourselves?"

"Yes—for a while, a few months, less than half a year. Then we realized that Mother didn't give a shit about us. She wanted us dead. That was the whole point of everything. Field ops discover one thing very quickly: they're going to die. They expect to die. And they don't care. They take incredible risks just to bring it on. That's what Mother wants."

"*God!* That's awful, suicidal. You're not that way."

"No. Harry and I wanted to live, and we did whatever was required. We took no chances. We developed our own code—the Agency computers never could break it—and withheld information. We knew more about some things than The Committee. We looked behind every operation, what was really going down, what they really wanted to have happen. And we did our own number. Survival. It was all that mattered. When in doubt we killed—then asked questions. Sometimes it was our own people, a couple of times utterly innocent persons. We didn't care. Survival, protecting our cover, coming back alive—it was *everything*."

She couldn't speak. His ferociousness was there now. The coldness was in his eyes, and he was the predator. He began to tell of his missions, one, another, a dozen, places she'd never heard of. He left out facts and her understanding was incomplete, but she did not interrupt to question him, knew she should not, for this was catharsis for him. He wasn't just *telling*, but reliving botched missions, double-crosses, stupidities, follies, mistakes, senseless brutalities, and useless murder. But more than that she heard his fear, frustration, cynicism, appalling bitterness. There was a common theme: he and Harry against a world gone senseless with meaningless machinations, the end of which was invariable death. He spoke again and again of the game, played ceaselessly by both sides to no conceivable purpose other than to play again. He saw himself as a killer, cold, remorseless—and he was—but was he not also victim, dying a little with each squeeze of the trigger? She felt utterly inconsequential. *Good morning, class. Today we are going to study the Federal Revenue Sharing Act.*

"Let's stop and have a beer."

She pulled off the road near a gas station, crawled in back, then returned with a beer from the cooler. "I don't care for one."

"Why did I tell you all that?"

"I guess you needed to. Maybe it has to do with getting well."

"Do you think I'm sick?"

She saw hurt, maybe anger rise in his eyes. "Killing people is hardly preferred conduct. Oh, hell, David, I'm not saying what I mean. A terrible thing was done to you. You were taken as a teenager and trained to be a killer—deliberately.

In the process you left family, friends—everything and everybody. David, they took away your *humanity*."

He stared at her a moment, then looked down at the beer bottle in his hand, raised it, swallowed. "Harry and I talked a lot about getting out. We wanted to be normal. We wanted jobs, regular jobs, a house, kids. We wanted to be like everyone else." He swallowed again. "Most of all I guess we hoped to meet a girl like you."

She smiled. " 'Girl' is a no-no, remember? We're women these days."

And he grinned. "You're that, all right. Better drive. It'll be dark before long."

She found a nice campsite, by a lake under pine trees. She had no idea where they were, other than somewhere in northern Italy. After eating and doing the dishes, they took a walk. The moon freed itself from behind the mountains, and they watched in silence as it spread upon the waters.

He kissed her. She did not characterize it or measure, only accepted it because it belonged. She took his hand and slowly accompanied him back to their van. She left him, went inside, zipped their sleeping bags together, and returned. They made love under the stars, slowly, inexorably, silently, she in the female superior position so as not to hurt his leg, two strangers inhabiting very private but shrinking spaces, each meeting highly personal needs, which they could not do alone. Afterward they slept, under the stars, in each other's arms. Neither uttered a word.

The silence was finally broken the next morning while she was changing his bandages. "If you'd said one word last night, I wouldn't have been able to do it," she said.

"A masterpiece is its own commentary."

She grinned. "Wow! That's pretty good." She unwound the bandage that bound his shoulder to his chest. "I'm ridiculously happy, David. I feel like an onion, as though layers and layers of tension and worry—utterly stupid worries, incredible follies—are being peeled away to reveal the real me, the very core of me."

"And what are you finding?"

"Just a seed, so tiny you can hardly see it—and even that may yet have a useless layer or two. Do I make any sense?"

"A great deal, only I'd put it differently. I feel hatched. I've been living in a shell for twenty-five years, not knowing what was outside, afraid to find out and enjoy it."

"Are you enjoying the outside?"

He nodded. "Only I feel cheated—a whole lot cheated. What a waste of good years."

"Don't think of them. Your shell is broken now."

She pulled the gauze from his shoulder. He was healing—and he wasn't. His wounds were getting better. Each morning they were less angry. New tissue was forming. Bandages became smaller, less of an effort to make. His leg was best, probably because he insisted on using it. He could walk unsupported, although with a distinct limp. His shoulder, bound to his chest because of the broken clavicle, did less well. But it was his fever that worried her the most. It simply would not go away, rising each afternoon and some days threatening to rage out of control. Then it would be down the next. The interior bullet. It had to come out. The infection sapped his strength at best. At worst it would kill him.

"You've got to have some antibiotics, David. Suppose I could fake a cold or something? Maybe a doctor would give me some penicillin pills. Then you could take them."

"Might work—if he didn't give you a shot in the ass."

"It's worth a try, isn't it?"

He sat in a chair, making it easier for her to wind the bandage around his sling. She finished that, then put her hand to his forehead. Warm, not too high. His hand covered hers. In his eyes she saw a blue mist of desire. She pursed her lips, slowly nodded, then opened her robe and bent over him.

Later when she was alone, she considered it all. Her orgasms had been truly shattering. All this, no doubt: camping, the sky and earth, her sense of inner peace and belonging. Maybe his fever. His hot body was a tremendous turn-on. She had felt plumbed by a flaming sword.

It was all right. Spontaneity made it so. She wouldn't have been able to if he'd said he loved her, wanted her, told her she was beautiful. His silence meant an absence of calculation. There was no deceit. Everything was body language. And she hadn't played a role, no coquettishness, flashes of skin, admiring glances, protests, seduction, surrender. Neither had made a commitment. Just need—encountered, recognized, met. Yes, it was all right; casual sex between consenting adults. Only it wasn't casual, was it? He was still here and so was she. Both had to remain. Okay, it would make dressing and undressing easier. Doing it in her sleeping bag was a pain.

Face it! Yes, big trouble. He was already in love with her and she was falling in love with him. Wonderful! The woman who loved him—wow! It would be like injecting herself with psychological leprosy. A childhood filled with preaching, prayers, and purgatory. Lonely, rebellious, emotionally stunted, he is taken by his government—*my government*—and turned into a suicidal killer. Great marriage material! Right up there with ambulance chasers, back- and right-leg-pain men, defense contractors, and home computer salesmen as candidates for husband, father, and picket fence. Any woman with half a brain would run, not walk, away from him and ever after embrace the joys of old-maidenhood. *I haven't met a man I liked, Mother.*

No, not so, not quite anyway. The government had done its best to ruin a pretty good man. He was intelligent, courageous, a resourceful problem solver. And he was at base a caring, sensitive, extraordinarily empathetic man. She could tell by the way he made love. He was patient, he savored, searched out nuances, cared about her, and ultimately shared. Take Harry. As near as she could figure they were like twins, more than twins, virtually able to read each other's minds. The government had done that, taken two young men, same age, same background, gave them the same training, information and dangers, same goals—survival. Them against the world. Yet, for the relationship to work they had to have a totally honest relationship, entirely open to develop the complete trust in each other. Great! *I know he's a remorseless killer, Mother, but once you get to know him ...*

"Freddie, are you enjoying this as much as I am?"

They were on the road again that afternoon. "I don't know precisely what you're talking about, but the answer is yes."

"All this, driving, being lost, camping—"

She interrupted him, for she wasn't entirely sure she wanted to discuss what he was going to say next. "Our serendipity tour. Never know what's over the next hill. Yes, I love it. You make it fun. Have I told you I like your curiosity? You're interested in everything, how it got there, what purpose it serves. I thought you were going to take the motor apart one-handed just to see how it operates."

He said nothing for a time, then spoke, his voice soft. "Let's not stop."

She glanced at him. "I wasn't for a while."

"I mean never, Freddie. Let's just keep on going. We're lost. I don't think anyone knows where we are. Let's keep it that way. We're halfway to—"

"Wherever—or nowhere." She concentrated on driving for a moment, gearing down for a long hill. The VW was terribly underpowered. "Leave family, home, career, everything I've wanted and worked for? I can't, David."

"I've thought about that. I think it might be possible for you to contact your parents, even see them occasionally."

She pursed her lips. "I understand why you want it, David—a new start in life. But it would never work for me."

"Why not?"

"I have nothing to run from. I like my start." She had reached the top of the hill and shifted gears. "Then there's Parsley."

"Fuck Parsley."

"He's a traitor. He must be exposed, stopped."

"The odds are impossible."

"I still have to try."

He sighed, long and deeply. "I'm so weary of the game, Freddie."

"I know you are and why. But for me—"

"Look. If by some miracle we do find Parsley and stop him, it won't make a particle of difference. All it'll do is save the lives of a few field ops and maybe halt one or two of the Agency's more harebrained schemes."

"You're wrong. Stopping Parsley will return control of government to our elected President, where it belongs."

He made a snortlike sound. "No, it won't, and you won't want it to. You don't really think the President runs the country, do you?"

"Now that you ask, yes, I do—or he should." She felt defensive and didn't like it.

"Don't be a sap. We could have Bonzo for

President and it wouldn't make a particle of difference. Look what we've had—a Georgia peanut farmer followed by a two-bit Hollywood actor. My God, you don't think either man was qualified, do you? You can't believe the security of the nation is going to be entrusted to men whose only qualifications are lots of orthodontia, a gift for pious platitudes, and a photogenic kisser on the boob tube."

"That's obscene. You're too cynical for me."

"They're only elected for four years. It takes them three and a half to find where the washroom is."

"Now you've gone too far."

"Not really that much. In four years there is no possible way any person can learn all that's happened around the world in the last fifty years, what it means, how it influences what's going on today. He simply doesn't know and there is no way for him to learn."

"Of course not. But he has aides, advisors, people to help him."

"Nonsense, Freddie. The President is surrounded by sycophants, yes men, and political hacks who are at best fools and at worst serious security risks. The White House is a seive of leaks. There is no way any one of them, including the President, is going to be entrusted with one syllable of information vital to national security. Most of them wouldn't recognize it if they heard it—and all of them would blab everything they know to grab a campaign contribution, make a buck on the stock market, or get a cushy job after the President's term is up. They are motivated entirely by self-interest, getting the President's ear, keeping him in office another four years. The security of this nation will not be turned over to people like that. It is not going to be determined on the basis of political expediency—and you don't want it to be."

He was so angry, so vehement. She was having trouble not responding in kind. "I certainly don't want the country run by a group of nameless, faceless men on some secret committee."

"Well, it is. It always will be. It's the same the world over. You don't think it's any different in Britain or France, do you? You can't believe Khrushchev, Brezhnev, Andropov, Gorbachev, or whoever really runs the Soviet Union, can you? They know only what the KGB allows them to know. And if push comes to shove, they'll do what the KGB tells them or they're out and probably in a niche in the Kremlin wall. Believe me, Freddie, it isn't an iota different in the US."

Freddie was appalled by the depth of his cynicism. She hated him for it. But she also understood he very well might be expressing the prevailing attitude of the CSA and The Committee.

"Do you understand? Eliminating Parsley isn't going to change a blessed thing."

"So we just give up, run, hide, and make whoopee in the sack. No thank you, buster."

He laughed. "You're angry."

"You're damn right I am. You spout the most cockeyed bullshit—and make me feel like the village idiot while doing it."

"Well, you're not the village idiot. You're just typically uninformed, that's all."

"Thanks."

"Be sarcastic, if you want. But the fact is you're being played for a sap. You teach political science—in college, yet. You have the title on the door, Assistant Professor Falscape. The little girls at Calvert College turn their shell-like ears to fall upon your every word and another generation rides off into the sunset having learned about the powers of the President, Congress and Supreme Court. They are expert on the Constitution. They are overjoyed to know about Liberty and Democracy and the privilege of electing our Chief Executive who runs the country."

"Stop it!"

"No, you stop it, Freddie. Wake up. The Committee runs the country, and as long as you don't know it they'll continue to."

Her sense of outrage was at full tide. She wanted to scream at him. Instead, she burst out laughing. "What did you say I suffered from? Terminal petulance?"

"I don't know. I don't remember."

"Can't say we don't have fascinating discussions."

"I imagine."

She heard the terse bitterness in his voice and glanced at him. "Why are you upset?"

"I just realized how very much I hate all this. It infects everything. Even when I'm talking to you, it creeps in. Will I ever escape?"

She heard the despair in his voice and didn't know what to say. She sought to distract him. "David, if I'm teaching the wrong thing, what is right? What would you have me teach?"

"That real power in this country—every country—comes from security classification. It determines what information you have, who you know, where you go and what you do. A person can be a common seaman, a floor sweeper, a garbage collector, but if he has a high security classification he holds the power. The person with high rank, the title on the door, may also have a high security classification. But if he doesn't, he's a figurehead and doesn't know it."

"You're talking about secret, top secret?"

"That and a whole lot more. There are gradations of all those. A man says he's cleared for Top Secret. He thinks he's hot stuff, really vital to national security. What he doesn't know is that's he's pretty far down the totem pole and mostly a flunky. He doesn't realize there are a lot higher classifications. There are three grades of Top

Secret, one, two, and three, with three being highest. Above those are cryptographic clearances, again one, two, and three, with three being the highest."

"I don't understand. What's a cryptographic clearance?"

"It has to do with what code you send and receive messages in. The higher the classification the more secure the code. A message sent in a code classified some grade of Secret will probably be broken by the Russians in five or ten minutes, if that long. My code, cryptographic three, might take them days, even weeks—if ever."

"I see. The more important the message the higher the code."

"No, you don't see. Information can be locked up in codes and known by very few people, maybe only two, the sender and receiver. Very few people ever have access to that information—basically only The Committee. Lacking that information, which they haven't a prayer of ever obtaining unless The Committee wants them to know it, everyone else is in a state of unblissful ignorance. They are manipulated. They are told only what they need to know to think a certain way and act a desired way."

"I get it. What a person thinks, believes, is certain he knows, isn't—"

"Exactly. He sees something with his own eyes. A truck pulls into the neighbor's drive. A couple of men in uniform get out. Aha, the Joneses are getting their TV repaired. Only maybe they aren't—the place is being bugged, the Joneses are getting shot—whatever. Appearances. When we believe, when we are absolutely certain, that's when we are in trouble."

"Magic, sleight of hand. What we see isn't what really happened."

"It's the stock in trade of The Committee,

Freddie. They are past masters. The White House, Congress, the generals and admirals are told of some great menace somewhere in the world. They believe it and act upon it. But where did the information come from? Do they have all the facts? Or is this supposed menace only part of some larger scheme they know nothing about? Because the true information is locked up in codes known by only a handful of people, they haven't a prayer of ever finding out."

"We have to stop Parsley."

"Dammit, Freddie, you're not dumb. Getting Parsley, replacing the whole damn Committee won't make a particle of difference. It will still go on. It always has and always will. Whoever controls information controls the world."

She said no more, just drove in silence. He had to be wrong. What he said was too deeply cynical, too foreign to everything she had ever known, believed, or taught. He was suggesting a profound alteration in the democratic form of government, a group of men in control of information manipulating the visible leaders, circumventing the Constitution. It couldn't be true. And yet ... yet, what? *You're faculty, Freddie. You're supposed to be an intellectual, a scholar.* Yes. The very least she should do was not dismiss what he said as the rantings of a madman. She ought to see if she could find evidence to either support or deny what he said. Yes, that's what she'd do.

She turned to him to say all this and saw he was asleep, head against the back of the seat. She reached over and touched his forehead. Burning up.

She decided her performance was worthy of an Academy Award—a nomination surely—as best supporting actress: supporting David, who was back in the camper; his fever had gone up and stayed there, leaving her no choice. He either got some antibiotics or he died.

She chose a less than prosperous-looking town northeast of Milan, and then a doctor with a very Italian name, and got ready. She began by chain-smoking most of a pack of filterless cigarettes, then puffed on a cigar for good measure. She had never smoked in her life; her head reeled and she threw up. Her throat was on fire and her lungs felt so congested she feared she was permanently damaging herself.

"You actually smoke—*for pleasure?*"

Sloane, who had suggested the smoking, comforted her with a laugh.

Before she entered the doctor's office she had smeared rouge on her nose and under her eyes, then sniffed black pepper so she was legitimately sneezing and coughing. The waiting room was jammed. It looked like the black hole of Calcutta, and her hopes sank. All her "symptoms" would wear off by the time her turn came.

She took a seat and began the performance of her life. She sneezed and sneezed, had a lung-bursting fit of coughing, then blew her nose repeatedly into a handkerchief, which she waved like a flag. Mothers squealed and covered their babies' faces. Old people looked at her in horror and pondered their Maker. The hubbub in Italian was meaningless to her, but she hoped it meant....

It did. She was ushered into the doctor's office. He was in his sixties, portly, sweaty, ripe with garlic and extremely harassed. He neither spoke nor understood English, but she had to hope he understood the one word she kept repeating: *penicillin*.

He took her pulse, temperature, listened to her chest. He spoke to her in Italian. She explained that penicillin was discovered by Sir Alexander Fleming and was a guaranteed cure for absolutely everything. In America they give it for acne, hangovers, female complaints, and bad grades. He shook his head. He shrugged. Then he sat at his desk and scribbled. She could make out one word: *Penicillin*. She gave half the pills to Sloane that evening, the other half the next day. It worked. His temperature came down, 98.6 and holding. She felt like weeping. He was going to get well.

They drove into Milan, which surprised her. They had avoided cities.

"I have to buy something."

"What?"

"You'll see—I hope."

"Okay, but this city driving is no fun. What kind of a store are we looking for?"

"Not a store—an outdoor bazaar."

They found it, a fleamarket. She had fun, buying a blouse, sweater, pair of pants and a lovely shawl to take home to her mother. Sloane surprised her, for he was the most finicky shopper she'd ever seen. He'd look at something, inspect it carefully, nod, say he wanted it, even get out a fat wad of Swiss francs, then change his mind. "Not what I'm looking for."

They walked on, repeating the process. Finally a man said, "What're you looking for, *signor*?" She glanced at him, young, hard-looking—or maybe it was the scar on his cheek. His English was surprisingly good.

"What have you got?"

An elaborate shrug. "We do not put out all our stock, *signor*. If I knew what you had in mind?"

"I will know it when I see it."

Now a smile. "Come with me, please."

Sloane told her to wait. She watched him follow the man to a van, climb inside, close the door. In a short time he emerged, came to her. "Let's go."

She drove north out of Milan and they camped near Lake Como. After supper she saw him loading the weapon he had bought. To her it was an ugly intrusion, the serpent in her Garden of Eden. "Do you have to, David?"

"You know I do." He inserted the last of the 9mm shells from his old clip into the new weapon. "It's a Beretta. Not as good as my Walther PPK, but my ammo fits it."

"I hate it, David."

"I know you do." He brought it to her. "This is the safety. Flick it, then pull the trigger—press really, if you can remember that. The piece is automatic and—"

"I'll never do it, David—*never.*" She shook her head. "We've been on the road three weeks and haven't needed it. No one is coming."

"We can't be sure. Besides, you're the one who wants to go for Parsley. We can't do it unarmed." He watched her. The argument had sunk in. She was accepting the weapon. He saw the beginnings of a smile, her eyes mostly.

"And here I thought we were just driving around the Italian countryside."

"So it would seem—at least I hope so." He grinned. "Now I think we must begin to get somewhere."

"Is there a commandment that I not know?"

"Sunny Spain, the Costa del Sol. You'll love it."

"I'm sure. What'll I find there?"

"Sun, beaches, bikinis, palm trees." He grinned again. "Other things."

"Like what?"

"A set and operating US code machine."

Quigley lived for his map and the pins he stuck in it. He had a large array of them in one area. They had to have visited every scenic spot and tourist trap in the Italian Alps. He studied, but he could find no meaning. They were just—yes, dammit—wandering. It had been going on for almost three weeks. His patience was thin, but he knew he should wait. They couldn't keep this up forever. Sooner or later they had to break out and head *someplace*.

The back side of the Matterhorn. Quigley swore. They were playing this tourist bit for all it was worth. Then they were lost. His post office box produced no information for two days. He felt a sense of panic and had to talk himself into patience. Finally they showed up on the Italian Riviera, Ventimiglia. They had driven in a single day from the Italian side of the Matterhorn down the Ria Rioja, the grand canyon of Europe. Nice drive. A long drive for them in one day. They were breaking out. To where?

He waited, making several trips a day to the post office. West to Nice. That had to mean Spain. Or did it? Dammit, from Nice north all the way to Grenoble. It made no sense—unless they were just crazy about mountain driving. Lost again. Three days this time. Finally Arles, where Van Gogh had cut off his ear. They stayed in the area two days, then were gone. Quigley waited nervously. He was the hunter, yet the Wolf was making a fool of him.

Andorra. Meaning at last. They *were* going to Spain. Madrid most likely, straight across the plain through Zaragoza. Confirmation came. They camped at Lérida. Yes, Madrid. They would be there in two days—and so would he, waiting for them. He packed his bag and headed for the airport. Better check the post office one more time. The message disgusted him. Terragona, the Roman ruins. They were on the southern route along the Mediterranean coast. It was not to be Madrid. Or was this some more of the Wolf's tricks?

ELEVEN

Freddie tried hard not to have it happen, but everything changed as soon as they began to head somewhere. Directions were noted, kilometers recorded, distances calculated. She enjoyed the drive along the Ria Rioja canyon, the Riviera, Arles, the mountains of Andorra, but the serendipity was gone. All was transient, a part of her life, not the whole of it.

She knew the serpent was loose, too. She couldn't forget that damn Beretta. There was danger now, pursuit, a sense of foreboding she could not escape. She began to see things she had not before. Where they had once been invisible—or so it had seemed—people now made eye contact with her. Two men stood looking at the van. Okay, except they turned away as she approached. At a campsite near Arles she had gone into the office to buy a new tank of butane. The man behind the counter was on the phone. In his hand was a piece of paper with numbers on it—their license number.

She told herself she was being silly. Maybe she noticed eye contact because *she* made it, not them. There were a hundred reasons for looking at a van. The paper with their license number did not mean he was reporting it. He could have been holding it when the phone rang. His Aunt Stella inviting him for dinner. Yes, she was acting like a fugitive.

She reported none of it to Sloane, if only because their relationship was changing enough as it was. Probably the fact he was less dependent upon her. With his fever gone, his strength returned. He walked more and his limp all but disappeared. He gained some use of his arm and she had to nag him to keep it in the sling at least part of the time.

They were alone less. Indeed their whole pattern of camping changed. He wanted to eat out—*"Whassamatter? You don't like my cooking?"*— frequently at lunch, almost always at dinner, usually a crowded place. Afterward he wanted to drink in bars, selecting a campsite quite late.

She shouldn't complain. They were having fun. He loved Spain, saying he'd been there before. In virtually every town he claimed to know a bar he'd visited, and the hunt for it involved stopping at numerous places. She discovered a new side to him. He was easy with people, friendly, sometimes a little too friendly for her tastes, and she began to wonder if he didn't have a bit of a drinking problem. How much *vino tinto* could one man consume in an evening?

But he was attentive to her, and that was pleasing. Before he *had* to be with her. He needed her just to move around. Now he *wanted* her with him. She even suggested he go off by himself, saying she was tired from driving and just wanted to read a bit and go to bed. He would not hear of it.

Yes, with his improving health a different David Sloane was emerging, more relaxed, wanting fun. He introduced her to *tapas*, the little plates of food served in Spanish bars, and insisted she try some rather strange dishes, little fish that looked like worms, whole sardines eaten head and all, squid in its own ink. She balked at baby pigeons, and he laughed. "They're delicious, Freddie. You don't know what you're missing." *Sure!* There was a confidence to him. When she was out with him, she felt he was taking charge of her, showing her a good time, leading, not asking. It was a nice quality in a man.

Did she love him? A song lyric kept entering her mind: "If you can't be with the one you love, love the one you're with." Half true at least. She was loving David Sloane. But was it just proximity, their mutual danger, their connivance to escape it? Probably, even most likely. Love was seldom calculated, she knew, yet she was hardly a blushing schoolgirl. One by one she considered the obstacles to a lasting relationship with David Sloane. Age. He was five years younger. Not important. Besides, in terms of experience he was Methuselah. Education. She had a Ph.D. and he had a—what? All his schooling, OCS and whatnot, probably didn't add up to a bachelor's degree. Didn't matter. The man simply knew a lot. He had a first-class analytical mind. His knowledge of worldwide intelligence operations gave him a view of world affairs which—face it—appalled her. Her hang-up, the chief obstacle, was his deeply rooted cynicism, his belief in a hostile world. It was almost paranoid. That plus Duane Forbes. She could not forget how David had dispatched him like, yes, a fly. A woman was sensible to have reservations about such a man—a whole helluva lot of reservations.

They drove rapidly along the coast of Spain, a couple hundred miles a day, inland to bypass Valencia, which she wanted to see, then through Alicante, finally stopping at a campsite on the outskirts of Elche. She loved it. They were camped in the middle of a palm forest. He told her it was the largest in Europe, planted by the Moors. Fantastic!

He wanted to walk into town for dinner. She didn't. He insisted. "I liked it better when you were flat on your back and did what I told you." He grinned. She relented.

The evening was no fun. He insisted on getting drunk at a succession of bars, which hardly made for comic relief. He was too loud, too boisterous, bought the bar too many times. His stupid attempt at flamenco dancing was anything but amusing. She was reduced to being a good sport, then a long-suffering sport, finally a nag. She wanted to go back to the VW.

"Jus' one more li'l drinkey. Lossa *vino tinto* in Shpain."

She heard his slurred speech, saw him weave and stagger. She forced a smile. "I think someone may want a drop left for tomorrow."

"C'mon, ol' Fred. Be a s-s-ort." He belched. It probably awoke Madrid.

She hated him. He was just a drunken American—a most ugly American in her eyes—buying drinks in Spanish bars, loud, foolish, being taken advantage of. She saw him in a new and most disturbing light. She told herself she was relieved. Public drunkenness was a far more viable excuse for dumping him than a disagreement about the role of the Presidency in US government.

Shortly before midnight he mercifully declared he was ready to go. They headed for the campsite. He leaned on her, lurching worse than he did when first wounded. Lord save us, he even began to sing—"Roll Me Over in the Clover" yet. People laughed at them. And what was really only a short distance to the campsite became a marathon—uphill on an icy pavement, although it was summer. The drunken bum even fell down—into a ditch. How tempted she was to leave him there.

At the entrance he insisted on "greeting" the manager, leaning on the long-suffering man, his arm around him, exhaling boozy breath into his face as he said over and over in a loud voice how much he liked Spain, *vino tinto, señoritas, vino tinto*, King Juan Carlos, the Elche *fútbol* team, *vino tinto* and Queen Sophia. *Bellissima.*

She dragged him away. "God, David, you're *awful!*"

"Jus' havin' a li'l fun, thassall."

"You're the only one."

They lurched toward the van. A couple of times she was sure he'd fall down, never to get up. He tried to enter the wrong van, and she had to pull him away. He began to sing again. She was ready to kill him. The last straw came at the van. After fumbling with the keys, he managed to unlock the side door. Then he took her in his arms. After all this he wanted to be amorous. No way! He smelled like a distillery. She twisted her mouth away. He was at her ear.

"I'm not drunk, Freddie. Do exactly as I say. Drop down and crawl to the front of the van. Don't make a sound."

"But—" His hand clamped over her mouth.

"If you want to live, do it, dammit."

His voice, more air than sound, was frightening. She stared at him wide-eyed, but it was so dark she more sensed than saw him. She nodded. His hand came away, then his arm. She felt him pushing her down. She crawled past the wheel, crouched in front of the grill. The sliding door opened—quite loudly. Pause. The door slammed shut. The interior light came on. He had gone inside. What was going on?

She felt a tug at her arm. He was beside her. Couldn't be. Crawling away. She followed. Past a van, a second. He got to his feet, pulled her up, led her away rapidly. She was aware of campers, tents. Once they nearly bumped into a palm tree in the darkness. Finally he stopped. His arm went around her.

"What's going on, David?"

"You'll see."

She was confused. "I don't understand. You went inside, closed the door, the—"

"Obviously I didn't."

"But the lights came on."

"Timing switch. Bought it the other day. Installed it while you were in the shower this morning."

She shook her head. "I don't—"

"I know you don't. Couldn't tell you. I had to be a very bad drunk coming home to sleep it off and you had to be— You were perfect."

"But—"

"Just watch." He moved a little. "Here."

She stood in front of him. Yes, she could see their van, at least the light shining through the chintz curtains. Then she couldn't.

"I set the timer for fifteen minutes. Figured that was long enough for a drunk to pass out and you to get to bed."

"What's going on?"

"You'll see. They won't wait long."

She blinked, for her eyes felt strained in the darkness. His arms pulled her back against him. It felt good. "You were an awful drunk."

"Wasn't I?"

"But you drank so much. How did you—"

"I keep telling you—appearance. I was in a bar, I had wine, I acted drunk, therefore I— Watch."

The flash came first, nearly blinding her, then streaks, a hideous ball rising skyward, flames, finally the thunder of the explosion and the hot wind. *"God, our van!"* She tried to run forward. He held her. She screamed and he made no effort to stop her, for her screams were only those of many. She shuddered and his hands felt the spasms of her stomach as she retched. Finally she turned within his arms and buried her face against his shoulder, the wounded one.

"It'll be all right, Freddie." He was aware of patting her back.

Her shuddering worsened, then eased. She raised her head, looking at his face in the firelight as though searching for some meaning. "That was supposed to be *us*."

"Yes. I spotted them days ago. I tried to make it easy for them." He pushed her head back against his shoulder. "Sorry about your things. We couldn't take a suitcase without attracting attention." She felt so small to him, so vulnerable. "C'mon. A bus leaves for Malaga in a half hour."

"What do you feel?"

They sat near the rear of the bus, his arms around her, her head on his shoulder. They were whispering. "Violated—raped, my person, my privacy stolen. Someone tried to kill me. They wanted me *dead*."

"Hopefully they will think they succeeded."

"I'm so—I don't know—disappointed, I guess. People aren't this way—they *can't* be." She sighed. "But I guess they are. I saw it with my own eyes. I'm so hurt, so angry. And"—she sighed again—"depressed."

"It's the real world, Freddie. I'm sorry I got you into it. But you're still here, alive. Try to think of that."

She nodded against his shoulder. "Yes, but it's so *awful*."

"I told you—don't think about it. Just be glad you're alive."

"But how *could* they?"

"Easy. A little plastique against the side or maybe underneath. Only took a second."

"I mean—"

"I know what you mean. You didn't think we were dealing with Santa Claus and the Sugarplum Fairy, did you?"

She raised her head, smiled wanly. "We didn't do this sort of thing in PolySci 103."

"This is a graduate course."

"No, post-doctoral, I think. God! Do you know who they were?"

"Not sure. Most likely wise men from the East."

"Sent by—"

"Probably."

They rode in silence for a time, then she whispered, "You've had this happen many times, haven't you? Somebody trying to kill you, I mean." He made no reply. "Part of you dies each time, doesn't it? Your humanity. All you want to do is—"

"Yes, live. Nothing else matters."

"It's so—*hideous*." She raised her head, brought her lips near his ear. "David Sloane, or David Pritchard, whatever your name is—I love you. It's stupid, an utter folly, but I love you."

Her words, so unexpected, surprised him. "Why did you say that?"

"Someone just tried to kill me. I imagine they will again—maybe succeed. I—I want to go out ... loving, not ..."

"Freddie, I—"

"You needn't say it, David. Saying you love someone is like"—she sighed—"like crossing a bridge, one of those rickety, swaying rope bridges over a deep chasm. And you don't know what's on the other side."

"I suppose. All I know is it's—dangerous. I'll be changed. I'll care about you. I won't think straight. I'll lose you and—"

"Isn't it a little late?"

He nodded. "I do love you, Freddie."

She grinned. Such happiness. And not for herself. This troubled man had ... Lord! Her smile widened. "So how are things on the other side—

where all the people are?" She kissed him then. It was osmosis, a sinking into, a becoming part of something. She pulled away. "You're on fire. The fever's back."

"Yes—all day. I didn't want to tell you. It's a bad sign, isn't it?"

She shook her head. "I think so, maybe."

"Then, we have to move quickly."

"Where?"

"To this next town—whatever it is. I got to get some rest. Maybe I can think then."

Quigley didn't believe it. He had driven hard all day to arrive in time to see the smoking ruins of the camper. He had no doubt it was theirs. The license plate had somehow survived. But he didn't believe for a second they were in it. Wolf would never have permitted it to happen.

Quigley moved quickly then, if not easily. Van gone. They needed other transportation, either another car or— He tried the bus station. That girl, her wonderful face, was remembered. Bus to Malaga, but the coast road, mountainous, hairpin turns, stops at every town, slow, all night. He flew to Malaga, waited at the bus stop, scanning faces. No Fern L. Falscape. Bus driver. *Sí, sí, señorita bellisima.* Got off at Almuñecar.

He rented a car. An hour's drive, arrived mid-morning. Small town. If they were there he should find them. They had ridden all night. Hotels. Check them. No. Think, think like Wolf, think like the girl. Yes. Let them come to him.

Freddie awoke at mid-afternoon. She was disoriented a moment, then remembered. A rooming house—a *pension* he had called it—john down the hall. She went there, came back, felt his forehead. Burning up. No thermometer now, but at least

102, maybe 103. Damn! She sensed rather than understood she must have done something wrong with the penicillin. Maybe she should have doled it out over more days. It was too late now.

"We've got to get a car."

His voice surprised her. She thought him asleep. "How do you feel?"

"Hot—hungry."

"Let's go eat. Can you get up, walk?"

"Siesta. Have to wait till four-thirty, five o'clock."

"Then what?"

"Rent a car, get out of here."

She shook her head. "David, your fever is worse than before. I think I goofed the penicillin. You haven't much time. If your fever goes up, you're going to see little people made of cheese dancing on the bedpost. The jig'll be up then. You'll be—"

"It's only a day's drive to Cadiz."

"What's there?"

"The US Navy base at Rota. Wanna make love?"

She did a double take, then smiled. "Fever always do that to you?"

"Must."

She sensed it was the last time. The room was hot in the July sun, his body more so. She hated her sweat, then forgot it, forgot everything.

"Say it again."

She knew. "I love you."

"What an improbable world we live in."

She knew she was a squirrel, hoarding, hiding away, collecting, burying deep that which might have to last a long time.

She exhausted him. "Take a sleep, lover. I'm going out. Got to get a change of clothing. I'm too young to be a bag lady."

"Okay." He felt too tired to protest, though he

knew he needed to. "Just be careful—watch everybody."

"Why? Aren't we dead? Aren't we safe?"

"Maybe. Two men were following us. There's still an odd man out." All along he had worried about the fact three men entered the dry-cleaning shop. US agents always work in pairs. Where was the fourth man?

"No end to it, is there?" She shrugged. "Okay, I'll be careful." She slung her purse over her shoulder. "Be back in an hour—thereabouts."

"Okay. I'll take a snooze. Meet you in the first bar to the right of this place. We'll get a car together."

She made purchases she didn't want—bras at two different shops, panties at another, high-heeled shoes, sweater, slacks, a frilly dress, stockings, makeup. She dawdled long past her hour. Always he was there, at another counter, outside waiting, young, so very much like David despite his sandy hair. Were they all stamped out of the same mold?

She tried to shake him, couldn't, knew it was hopeless. She entered a department store, bought a piece of luggage, paid, put her parcels inside, went up to him. She just stared.

"Fern L. Falscape, take me to him."

"Or?"

"I dislike threats."

"You're making a terrible mistake."

"You already have."

"He's trying to stop a mole. Parsley. You should be helping him, not—"

"I will kill you where you stand if you don't take me to him."

She smiled. "Then how will you find him?"

"What will it matter to you?"

She nodded. Good point. "He'll kill you. I'd like

to prevent that if I can. Please, you must listen to me. You must—" It was no use. His eyes, hard, cold, told her.

"Take me to him."

She pursed her lips, shook her head sadly, sighed, then wheeled and walked from the store. She forgot her purchases. She did not look back; she knew he was behind her.

She had been so calm in approaching him. What did she hope to accomplish? Scare him away? Now she was in a panic. All she could think of to do was walk—anywhere, just so long as it was away from the hotel. She went around the corner, jaywalked across the street. Maybe he'd be hit by a car. Run? No. Be calm. Crowds? Yes, stay with people. She turned another corner. Mistake. Crowds thinning out.

"It won't work, Fern. Sooner or later you'll have to go to him. I'll be there."

She hadn't realized he was so close behind her. She turned. "You're making an awful mistake."

"So you said. Take me to him. I'm sure it's in the opposite direction."

She sighed. No reasoning with him. "All right." She turned, walked toward the plaza, where the people were. She looked over her shoulder. Still there. She stopped, looked unseeing at a store window. He couldn't make her lead him to David. She felt him at her side and moved on. Stay with people. A bar. Yes. He couldn't use his gun there. Her pace quickened. *El Caballo Blanco*, the White Horse. She entered. God! Nearly empty. She turned around, came out, saw him. He had all the time in the world, and there was none for her. She glanced at her watch. Six-twenty. She had been gone almost two hours. David would be—

She saw him ahead, coming toward her, obviously looking for her. *No, no please.* He was a head taller than the Spanish. Why was he so tall? Why were her legs still moving, drawing closer to him? She looked over her shoulder. Still there, a most disrespectful three paces. She quickened her step to get away from him. Why? She was only getting closer to— David was looking across the street, searching for her. She was only a dozen steps away now. *Don't turn. Don't see me—oh, please don't.* His head moved, faced her. She saw the recognition in his eyes. *Oh, God!* She looked over her shoulder. Recognition in another pair of eyes, a moving hand.

It was an entirely right-brain function, a problem of space and time, recognized, appraised, and solved in an instant, uncognitive, a task no computer will ever duplicate. She threw herself at Quigley. Her arms came around him.

"Dammit, let me go!"

She held on for dear life, dear David's life.

"Very good, Freddie. Slowly let go of him. Reach inside his jacket, take his Walther and drop it inside your purse. Try not to let it be seen."

She glanced at Sloane, grateful he was still alive.

"Do it, Freddie."

It took her a moment to figure out how to do it, for this was now a left-brain function. Finally, she unslung her purse, opened it, made room, then held it against him, dropping the weapon inside. When she had finished, the two men were smiling at each other.

"Good to see you again. *Evansville*, wasn't it?"

"I always thought you were Wolf."

" 'Fraid I've forgotten who you are."

"Fox."

"Oh, yes. New man. I thought you were good."

Quigley smiled. "But unlucky it seems, meeting you on the street, two people. I couldn't cover you both."

"You should have anticipated, been prepared. When Freddie was late, I went looking for her."

"Which is why you were cited at school. Wolf and Bear were always one step ahead, never surprised or off guard."

"Will somebody please tell me what's going on?"

Sloane spoke to her, but did not take his eyes off Quigley. "We were shipmates about a year ago. We recognized each other."

"But he was going to kill you."

"Not anymore." To Quigley: "I was just going to rent a car. Would you care to join us?"

"I already have one. Would you like to use it?"

"What is going on with you two?"

Quigley answered her. "We are both in the service of Mother. We are both professionals. We understand what must happen."

The car, parked just off the beach, was a Spanish Fiat. Freddie drove as instructed—"anywhere, out of town." They sat in back. Sloane's Beretta was visible. "Don't kill him, David—please. We can just let him off somewhere. He won't be able to—"

"You know he can't do that."

She glanced at Quigley, whom she knew only as Fox, in the rear-view mirror, then at Sloane. Both were hard-eyed, wary, ready to kill. She shook her head. "I already told him about Parsley, David—what we're trying to do. There's no need—"

"He didn't believe you, did he?"

"Maybe you could just wound him—shoot him in the foot. That would slow him up, give us time to—" The reflected faces told her she was talking to icebergs. "David, please, don't kill him. I know—tell him about Parsley. He'll listen to you, understand. We need all the help we can—"

"You can tell me if you want, Wolf, but I won't listen. Nor will I pretend to. I have too much respect for you even to try a con."

"Thank you. You're a good man, really."

She listened in utter disbelief. They were two gladiators, somehow friends, entering the arena, knowing one was to die. Or maybe they were the matador and the bull. Each respected the courage of the other, while . . . Men! She had an image of missile launches. *I did what I had to do.* Madness!

"You were badly wounded, weren't you?"

"I'm better now."

She glanced at Sloane in the mirror, saw the hot, glassy look in his eyes. Strained to the limits. Running on nerve.

"How did you find us?"

Quigley told the whole story, coming from Tokyo, wanting to avenge his partner, realizing Wolf had not died in the alley, tracing Freddie, following, getting help in finding them, still not believing they were dead at Elche.

"Don't you understand? It was Parsley who sent you." Her voice had raised in pitch and sound. She was pleading with him. "Parsley did everything. It was the KGB who tried to kill us in Elche. You're being—"

"He doesn't hear you, Freddie. He'll never believe you."

"But he *must*. This is so *stupid*."

"Stop over there by that cane field."

She saw it on the right, sugar cane. She geared down, braked. There was a place to pull over.

It was all audible at first, a thud, a sigh, a deep, elemental groan. She turned around even before the car was fully stopped. Visible now. The sharp, hatchetlike arc of the hand, the flying Beretta. Sound came again, her scream. A rising fist, another blow. Sloane sagged weakly against the seat. She screamed again. There were words amid it, "Stop, *please stop!*" He did, but only to reach for the Beretta at his feet.

She was on her knees now, reaching over the back of the seat, pushing at him, clawing. "No! No! You *mustn't!*"

"Damn bitch!"

He shoved hard at her, flinging her backward away from the seat. Her head hit hard against the top of the windshield. But she now saw the Beretta, the serpent in Eden, in another hand, being raised, turned, leveled away from her, toward . . .

She screamed, lunged over the seat, grabbed at the hand which held the serpent, screamed and screamed, couldn't stop.

"Goddamn you!"

The blow, sharp, quick, backhand, struck the right side of her face. It felt like her head was coming off, yet strangely she felt more pain in her back from hitting the gear shift and dash.

"You're gonna die now, you Commie sonofabitch. This is for Dean Schwartz."

She saw the Beretta rising, leveling, turning toward Sloane. Then it stopped, and she saw Quigley's eyes, wide, full of surprise and injured disbelief. The only sounds she heard were her own terrified screams drowning out the *spit, spit, spit, spit, spit*. Only an empty magazine made her stop pulling the trigger on the Walther.

When Sloane came to, she was leaning over the seat, the Walther clutched in both hands. Her eyes were wide, probably unseeing. She was in shock, catatonic. He glanced at Fox, saw blood oozing from a cluster of places in his chest.

Sloane pushed him to the side of the seat, against the door, then reached up slowly and took the gun away from Freddie. No reaction from her. He thought of saying something, even slapping her to snap her out of it. Instead he tenderly turned her so she sat in the passenger seat staring forward.

He looked back at Fox. Had to dump the body. He got out, walked around the car and opened the door. After removing Fox's ID and extra clip of bullets, he pulled the body to the ground and kicked it into the ditch. Because he saw a car in the distance, he quickly got behind the wheel and drove off.

He tried to keep them out, but a phalanx of thoughts warred for attention in his mind. Their very existence was proof to him just how much and how rapidly he had changed. He never used to have this trouble.

He tried to arrange and catalogue them. Guilt: he had failed to protect her. Debt: he owed his life to her. Guilt: she had done more for him than he had for Harry. His attempt at organization broke down and the thoughts welled into his brain unbidden. He loved her. Strange, foreign really, impossible to believe, somehow frightening, but he loved her. What had he done to her? Pumping bullets into a body already dead. Not her! Never! The last thing she wanted, would ever do. Hated it. Always said that. She'd never get over it. Yes, she would. A real tough lady.

Gradually from the disorganization of his mind, a single thought began to dominate. He owed her. She had given up everything for him, freedom, independence, respectability, her body, finally even her values, integrity, and principles. Yes, he owed her. Parsley. He had killed Harry and was in the process of destroying this girl. Parsley. He still had no philosophical meaning for Sloane. He was just a games player. But Freddie cared about him. He wouldn't let her down—couldn't now. Yes, finally, at last, irrevocably, he would truly go for Parsley. Barely audible, he whispered into the night, "I owe you, Freddie."

He drove through Malaga, Torremolinos, then Fuengirola and Marbella, finally pulling over into a lay-by near the water. He found a container and carried water to wash the blood off the back seat.

"Where are we?"

"On the *carretera*, the coast road. Estepona is just ahead. Do you want to stop for the night? I've about had it."

"Yes. You have to tell me what I'm to do at Rota."

TWELVE

Comdr. Lemuel Pinckney Levereaux, born and reared in Charleston, South Carolina, was a proud man. His father, grandfather and great-grandfather had all been admirals in the United States Navy. More distant forebears had served in similar capacities—with great distinction, he liked to say—in the Navy of the Confederacy. As a scion of all this, he was a shoo-in for flag rank. At thirty-three he was already a commander, proud wearer of the scrambled eggs on the visor of his hat. The destroyer USS *Everett* was his first command, and he was making a distinguished record. Twice he had bumped Soviet ships during maneuvers. His gunners had knocked targets to smithereens, and the *Everett* had dropped depth charges on no less than three decoy "Soviet nuclear subs." Positive "kills" had gone into his record, along with a congratulatory letter from the fleet admiral. The stars were practically on his shoulders. He truly believed he had a chance of exceeding his father and making admiral, not just vice admiral.

But he knew instinctively that this female standing before him was a threat to all that. "You want to do what?"

"I repeat, Captain, I want to send a message to the Central Security Agency, Fort Belvoir, Virginia."

"Ma'am, I—"

"I'm a Ms., Captain."

He swore inwardly. "So be it, *Ms.*" *Fucking female*. "I don't believe you understand. This is a United States Navy destroyer. We are a fighting ship. We are defending our country. We do not send messages for *civilians*." The way he said the word it was equated with child rapists and genocidists.

Freddie was amazed at her calmness. She remembered standing in a bank in Munich quivering with fear as she merely stole some money from the Russians. When was that? A millennium ago, lost in the gray mists of antiquity. Part of her mind registered that she was now in a far more threatening situation, yet she felt only an icy determination. *Do the best you can, Freddie. The chances of it working are remote.* "Commander, you have the capacity to send a coded message. I need to do so most urgently."

"What's your message?"

"I can't tell you that, not yet at least."

Lem Levereaux, blond, flat-tummied, ramrod straight, shook his head. A civilian, a pretty young woman no less, approaches the OOD and demands to see the captain. Won't take no for an answer. Insists on her rights. He swore inwardly. This dame was an absolute career-breaker. If he sent her message he'd be the laughingstock of the Navy. "Ms. Falscape, will you forgive me for being just a bit irritated? I had a birdie putt lined up on the sixth hole. I don't get many opportunities to make a birdie, being at sea and all. I'm sure you'll understand my—"

"I do indeed, Captain, and I'm sorry to interrupt your golf game." She gave her best smile. "But my message is urgent. I ask you to send it right away. Then you can resume your game."

He sighed. "Miss Falscape, this Navy base is located adjacent to a large Spanish city, Cadiz. It is just down the road. You will find cable services, telephones, even a post office. All will be of help to you."

Freddie bristled. Patronizing bastard. "Captain, do you have a hearing problem? I said the message must be sent in code. I understand how unusual my request is. You cannot send messages willy-nilly. You will have to ask permission of your superiors. I suggest you get at it."

This woman was an incomprehensible menace. He quivered with rage brought on by simple fright—and hoped he didn't show it. "Miss Falscape, you are a most attractive young woman. I've enjoyed meeting you. Now, if you'll excuse me, I'm going to get back to my golf game. It requires undivided attention."

"Believe me, Captain, you will be in a lot more trouble if you don't send the message than if you do."

He shook his head despairingly. "Dear lady, dear Ms., you have no idea what trouble is. Until ten minutes ago I had every expectation of making admiral. Now ..." He rendered an elaborate shrug.

"Then you are acquainted with Navy regulations."

"Goddammit, I don't need any instruction in Navy regulations from you."

"Don't you? A United States citizen has a right to come aboard this ship—or any other military facility for that matter—and send a message to a US intelligence agency, just so long as that person knows the correct address of the Agency. I do. You will send my message. You have no choice."

He eyed her a moment, then stepped from behind his desk and strode toward the door.

"Where are you going?"

"To check the damn regulations—and prove you wrong."

Alone at last, Freddie sighed deeply and slumped

into a chair. She had never felt so alone, afraid, and depressed in her life. She was— No. This wasn't her. Freddie Falscape had disappeared somewhere on Wernerstrasse in Munich after going to buy a bottle of Liebfraumilch. This was some stranger sitting here, a burglar, an international thief, fugitive, dead woman, and murderer. *Miss Falscape, when did you first realize you had an identity crisis? When did you first begin to dissociate—on a regular basis, that is?*

David was gone—probably permanently. He had left her at a hotel in Cadiz—*Did you know that Columbus sailed from Cadiz to discover the New World, that bastion of hope, liberty, democracy, and pan-fried pizzas*—and driven off into the sunset. *Nope. Yup. Go get 'em, Trigger. You've got lovely lips.* He had briefed her over and over on what to say, how to act, everything that would happen. He had rehearsed her—actually played a captain far worse than this one. *David, darling, you don't know!* She'd see him in Washington. Fat chance. A man with a fever of 103 makes only an acquaintance with God. The only thing she'd see in Washington was jail. *Miss Falscape, these bars are made of tempered steel alloyed with chromium— imported from Russia. They are trying to gain most-favored-nation status at the time. Want to pay for all that grain, you know, the poor, starving, God-defying, Marxist-Leninist, anticapitalist, imperialist mother-impregnators.* She had to laugh. *Now that is funny, Freddie. Mother indeed.*

Stop it! Her mental flights were, she knew, an aberration, a way to hide what she couldn't bear to think about, also a technique to mask fear and probably fatigue. *This is serious business. You have to concentrate.*

Levereaux returned carrying a black, heavy bound book. Navy Regulations. He was severe, frosty. "*Ms.* Falscape, to what address do you wish to send your message."

"CSA, Fort Belvoir, Virginia, Zone 752."

A bright glint came to his eyes. "Ms. Falscape, I think it is safe to say every half-informed person knows the CSA headquarters is at Fort Belvoir, Virginia. Yours is not an acceptable address."

"The correct address for the message is Zone 752."

"Those are just numbers. Anyone can make them up. I cannot— "

"They are correct, Captain." *Oh God, David, be right, please.* "If they are not, you may throw me into irons in your brig, give me forty lashes, or whatever they do in the Navy these days. Oh, yes, you may keelhaul me through the fleet, Captain Bligh."

He stared at her. "Madame, I am a United States Navy officer. I believe I have a right to a modicum of respect."

She blinked. Tears glistened in her eyes, quite unbidden. "Oh, God, yes. I'm sorry."

"Why did you come to my ship?"

She swallowed, tried to smile. "Just lucky I guess."

"Ms. Falscape, my father was an admiral, my father before him. No one can remember when there wasn't an admiral in the Levereaux family. My uncle is buried on the USS *Arizona*. Another uncle was in the first wave of torpedo bombers that attacked the Japanese fleet at Midway. There was one survivor—not my uncle. My brother was killed attacking a SAM site near Da Nang. I am the sole surviving male in my family. I would like very much to be an admiral. Your presence here means I will never be. Rather, I will be the laughingstock of the Navy."

She swallowed. "Commander Levereaux, I am a bit out of my element. It is not every day I walk onto a Navy ship to send a message I believe may save my country. I would like to think that one day you will be honored for having sent my message."

His smile was small, sardonic. "And I would like to believe the Chief of Naval Operations doesn't need a ship because he walks on water." He stared at his piece of paper. "CSA, Fort Belvoir, Virginia, Zone 752. Is that correct?"

"For my sake, I hope so."

"Are you in intelligence, Ms. Falscape?"

"Do you think I would tell you if I were?"

He shrugged. "I trust you know this will take some time."

"So I've been told." And she had. David had said her request to send a message would have to go through a succesion of commands, Mediterranean Fleet, Atlantic Fleet, Naval Operations, Naval Intelligence, before ever reaching the CSA, which would have to approve receipt of the message. It might take three to four hours.

Levereaux turned her over to Ens. Douglass under instructions to show her every courtesy—which meant he wasn't to take his eyes off her. In the wardroom she accepted coffee and a doughnut, then prepared to wait. *Time* magazine offered her no distraction. Nothing did. A once-happy, carefree person had turned into a large clump of—what? No, a blob of— See, she couldn't think of clever lines anymore. *Miss Falscape, you really shouldn't be disturbed. It is only natural that under stress the synapses of the human brain dissolve into a sort of jellylike substance. There is no cure, but in time you will come to love your frontal lobotomy—and Nurse Fletcher.*

How had it happened? She went to Munich on a holiday. A man crawls into the back of her car—*yes, Mother, I always lock my car*—and she had been transformed into ... Somewhere in her mind was an image of Fox's eyes as her bullets struck him. Couldn't think about that, not right now anyway. More to the forefront was the memory of the gun jumping in her hand each time she pulled the trigger, and the strain on her wrists each time she aimed. *Just don't think about it, dear.* Right. There was no time for the crazies just now.

A song lyric came to her. "What I did for love." Wow! It had happened to her. Couldn't have. She was smart, sensible, on top of her act. "Send in the clowns." They were already there: goblins, ghosts, and witches.

"Would you like some more coffee, miss?"

She looked at Ens. Douglass, so young, so terribly young. His eyes told her she was attractive to him. *Green is a good color on you.* Strange. What could he possibly see in a thousand-year-old woman who just accidentally, quite mistakenly, wandered out of Shangri-La? "Tell me about yourself, Lieutenant. Have you got some nice, sensible girl back home?"

"Ensign, miss—and as a matter of fact I do."

"Call me Freddie. All my friends do."

Sloane saw the sign. Breezewood, Pennsylvania. Interstate 70 coming up, then Hancock, Maryland, then Hagerstown. He should be in Washington in a couple of hours, three at the most. Had to make it. Then he could crap out for a few hours.

He glanced at the clock on the dash, computed the time difference. She was on the ship, had been for at least an hour.

Sloane had moved quickly. He wanted to be in D.C. ahead of her, and he knew his energy and stamina would last only so long. He flew Cadiz, Madrid, Copenhagen, Stockholm, Montreal, Cleveland. He had flown this or similar routes many times, for it was the way US and foreign agents entered and left the country. It took advantage of the casual Customs between US and Canada. Do you have anything to declare? No. In Cleveland he had rented a car. It was a long drive to

Washington, sure to sap the last of his energy, but he didn't want to risk another airport.

He glanced at the clock again. Damn. Only two minutes had elapsed. Had to quit worrying about her. She was smart, resourceful and should be able to pull it off. His first thought had been to walk on the ship, any ship, and send the message himself. But then he'd have hell to pay getting off the ship, moving, entering the country. Freddie had to do it. She gained him time, allowed him to move. He smiled as he imagined the repercussions. A woman walks on a destroyer and asks to send a message. The shit must be hitting the fan.

He swore, a symptom of his concern. Her message had to reach The Committee, and he was sure it would. What then? Parsley could be holding her message right now. But Parsley had no choice but to let her go. Freddie's only value was as a lead to himself. She was a decoy. He had cautioned her over and over: say as little as possible, but when you do stick as close to the truth as possible. I crawled into your car in Munich. You helped a person you believed was an American intelligence officer trying to escape the Russians. I asked you to send this message. You don't know what it means. You don't know where I am, except that I said something about seeing you in Washington. Under no circumstances let them take you into custody. Stand on your rights, your ignorance. You're just a patriotic American citizen. I don't believe they'll try to take you. They want you to lead them to me. You'll be watched every second, but you'll be all right. Then, when you get to Washington ...

The message was priority and reached his desk immediately. Dimitri Galenkov read it with a mixture of satisfaction and rage. Fern L. Falscape was asking permission to send a message to CSA,

Zone 752, from the USS *Everett* at Rota. It had been sent in US Navy tactical code, Secret one. Easy to break. They knew it, wanted the message to be known. Why?

First things first. The two operatives who insisted the woman and Wolf were dead at Elche would be severely punished. Dimitri Galenkov had not believed it for an instant. The fools in the field and those at Dzerzhinsky Square who had listened to them were through. They would count reindeer till their fingers froze off and the borscht in their heads had turned to ice. So much for his rage.

A request to send a message to Zone 752. A possibly useful address, although it probably had been changed already. She was a decoy. No doubt of that. Wolf was behind it.

Galenkov smiled. It would take hours for the girl's message to clear channels. He could visualize the consternation in the US Navy. There would be delay. The vaunted CSA communications would be stymied. Yes, and the Russian bear can sometimes move quickly. He started to pick up the phone then thought better of it. Taking the girl, discovering all she knew would do no good. Chances are she knew very little. And holding her would not bring Wolf to them. He was a professional, the best the Americans had. He would not fall in love. He would not be foolish.

He thought a moment. The girl was valuable, but subtlety was required. She must be allowed to do whatever Wolf had told her to do. And she must be given a very long tether. She would lead them to Wolf eventually. Now he picked up the phone.

Adams was at home shaving when the phone rang.

"This is on scrambler, sir."

He glanced at his wife. Sleeping. "Yes."

"We have a 752 message, sir."

"Be right there."

He carefully wiped the shaving cream from the receiver, then grinned. Sloane was alive. Dead in Munich, dead again in Elche. Now he was making contact. At last!

Adams forced himself not to vary his morning routine, arriving at his underground office at Brandywine right on schedule. He endured his normal briefing on overnight events, seeming to attach no special significance to the message from the *Everett*.

"The person requesting to send the message is named Fern L. Falscape. If you'll recall, we did a workup on her."

"Yes." He accepted the folder of information.

"I think you'll find that it includes every time she farted."

Adams saw Boggs grin, but did not honor it. "Let her message come through, but do it through channels. Don't skip one."

He hated to give that order. It would mean a delay of two to three hours while the Navy brass and Naval Intelligence did their thing. He could plug right into the *Everett* in a minute, but to do so would blow his own cover. The Agency preferred that the Navy not know just how many of its messages were intercepted and known.

There was a far bigger problem. Sloane's message had been sent from a destroyer over a tactical channel which the KGB monitored constantly. The captain of a destroyer was cleared only for Secret. That code could be broken out by the KGB in minutes. They now knew Zone 752. The 7 was Sloane, the 5 was the Europe zone, the 2 himself, although not even Sloane knew that. He only knew 2 as his contact. Damn! Sloane had not only compromised himself but the whole Agency. The entire system of addresses would have to be changed. The KGB had doubtlessly already sent a dozen phony messages to 752.

Why had Sloane done it this way? Why hadn't he simply boarded the destroyer and sent the message in his own, secure code? Maybe he physically couldn't. But almost a month had elapsed since he was shot. He was alive. Surely ... Maybe he was afraid to show himself. Yes, could be.

Then Adams smiled. He understood now. A bold stunt, having a female civilian walk on a ship to send the message. He wanted time. And he wanted her as a decoy. Fern L. Falscape's only value was as a link to Sloane. He picked up the phone. "Boggs, that woman will be allowed to leave the *Everett*. She will not be questioned or detained once the message is sent, but I want an airtight net around her. Every breath she draws will be known. I'm holding you personally responsible, Boggs. If one hair on her head is touched, I'll have your ass."

Boggs was impressed. He could not recall ever hearing Mr. Green use the expression.

"All right, Ms. Falscape. Permission has come through for you to send your message."

She was relieved and her smile reflected it. "Are you surprised?"

"Quite frankly, yes. I fully expected the Shore Patrol hours ago."

"With equal frankness, so did I. I've never done this sort of thing before—and hope never to do it again."

"Not on my ship, please. You've been a large pain in the butt, if I may say so."

"Doesn't permission to send my message ameliorate your distress, Commander? Surely you must now realize—"

"Ms. Falscape, you could be warning the CSA

that there is a ticking nuke in the White House, and it would not help my circumstance." He saw her wide, luminous eyes. "Whatever else I may do in my career, no matter how distinguished my service to my country, I will be remembered only for your presence on this ship."

She blinked, swallowed. "I'm sorry, Commander."

"I'll be certain to convey that to the vast assortment of admirals who—" He sighed. "Never mind. Let's get on with it. What's your damned message that's so important?"

She wrote it out.

He stared, utterly incredulous. "All this for that?"

"Yes. If it earns the proper reply, there will be a final message."

"I can hardly wait."

Adams stared at it, then burst out laughing.
WHAT RUNS A '55 CHEVY ON FAT TUESDAY?

Clever. Sloane wanted verification all around. He was saying the message was most definitely from him. Make no mistake. And he was reaching for the top, someone who had access to his file and knew all about him. He wanted to be certain he had the ear of The Committee.

Adams was certain he knew the answer, but he went to Sloane's file to double check. Yes. While in school in Pensacola, Sloane and Duane Forbes had bought a '55 Chevy. They obtained a pass to go to the Mardi Gras—Fat Tuesday—in New Orleans. But they were late getting back—a most serious infraction. Sloane had offered the lamest excuse anyone had ever heard. He was placed on house arrest while a complete investigation was made of their entire trip, where they went, what they did, who they talked to. If Sloane had told one lie or even omitted a single detail, he would have been thrown out of the program. Everything checked, including his excuse. On the way back from Fat Tuesday, the '55 Chevy had lost its oil. They were stuck in the middle of nowhere unable to get help for a car that wouldn't hold oil. They had come up with a most novel solution.

Freddie read the one-word message.
VASELINE.

Levereaux saw her smile. "I trust, Ms. Falscape, you're having fun at the expense of the Navy."

"I assure you this isn't fun, Commander—most definitely not for me." She smiled. "I think you'll take comfort in my next message. It will be the final one."

"I can hardly wait."

It took her a minute. David had made her write the letters and numbers so often, she was sure they were burned in her brain. But now, in the act of writing them, she hesitated over one or two, then double checked, triple checked. Yes, it was right. She handed the piece of paper to Levereaux.

He read: A9KT4 284CJ 058XK A27K9.

"What is it? Some kind of code?"

"I presume so."

He looked at it again. "Ms. Falscape, may I warn you that it is a most serious offense to have knowledge of and use United States codes for purposes of—"

"Please, Commander, no threats now." She was suddenly very tired and let down. "Just send the message, making sure there is no error in transmission."

He shook his head. "I have no choice. My orders are to send it."

She arose. "Thank you for your cooperation, Commander. I assume I am now free to leave."

"Unfathomably, yes. Actually my orders are to

see you safely off this ship, this base, and to wherever you wish to go."

"You needn't."

"I have my orders, Ms. Falscape. I've assigned Ens. Douglass to escort you."

She shrugged. "As you wish, but I only require a taxi to the airport."

"Ens. Douglass will get you a fleet of taxis, a police escort, and a jet bound for—"

She laughed. "I really can't blame you, Commander." She extended her hand. "For what it's worth, I think you'll make a wonderful admiral."

Finally he smiled. "If only you were doing my next fitness report."

It took Adams only a couple of minutes. Sloane had used his last cypher, but he had not then encoded the message.

```
A9KT4   284CJ   058XK   A27K9
PARSL   EYIHA   VEYOU   RNAME
```

Adams first reaction was elation. Khruchenko *had* identified the mole. This lasted only an instant and Adams was saying aloud, years of restraint disintegrating, *"Sloane, you fucking bastard! What have you done?"*

Adams was surprised at his language, but felt it justified. Sloane had just made the most ungodly mess of things. He just had to free-lance. Just had to do it his way. He couldn't just come in, report what he knew and allow ... Dammit!

Adams had hoped, indeed fully expected, that Sloane would message that he was coming in. He'd be cautious, maybe only signal where he was, how he might be reached. After all he'd used the damn Vaseline code, a one-time pad if there ever was one. There were lots of other ways to let it be known where he was.

But no. He'd thrown down the gauntlet. He had

turned macho. He was going to John Wayne it. PARSLEY I HAVE YOUR NAME. He'd sent it only encyphered, not encoded. It would be broken out in a matter of hours, maybe minutes. The mole, obviously code-named Parsley, would know it. The KGB would know it. The whole wide world would—

Damn! Damn! Damn! He had hoped to meet with Sloane, find out what he knew. He was even prepared to work with Sloane to trap Parsley. But now? The whole blessed operation was blown. Parsley was alerted. So was the KGB. Parsley would go so deeply underground he'd—

Hold it. Think. Yes, Sloane had to know the effect of his message. He wanted to reach The Committee, so he must know Parsley was a member.

Boggs buzzed in and Adams picked up the phone, listened.

"Sir, the Falscape woman has left Rota and is on her way to the Cadiz airport. She is booked on a flight to Madrid. She is also booked for tomorrow, Madrid-Dulles, TWA. Lands at six-twelve P.M."

"She's staying the night in Madrid?"

"It would seem so. We don't know which hotel, but she is under constant surveillance. Operatives will be on both flights with her."

"Very good."

"How often do you want reports on her?"

"I want to know anything she does that is out of the ordinary, anyone she meets, talks to, if she tries to shake a tail, changes her flight, makes any abrupt movement. Above all I want to know immediately if there is any foul-up in surveillance—and there'd better not be."

Adams hung up without waiting for Boggs's reply. So she was coming to Washington, landing at Dulles Airport tomorrow. That could only mean—yes. For a second Adams thought of alerting

Canadian intelligence to look for Sloane. He might be coming later. But, no. He would slip through—probably already had. Yes. Sloane was already in Washington. Adams could feel it.

He reread the message. PARSLEY I HAVE YOUR NAME. Sloane was here, stalking the mole, code-named Parsley. The Falscape woman was his decoy, walking on ships, sending messages the whole world could know, booking flights for the US. Everything was right out in the open. Adams understood. Sloane was using her to flush out Parsley.

When Adams swore this time, it was at least inaudible. Sloane left him no choice, no options. He had to pick up the girl as soon as she landed at Dulles. There was no possible way she could be permitted to fall into the hands of Parsley or the KGB. Again he swore. He felt like a marionette, flopping around, dancing a jig, while Sloane held the strings. Damn him!

He sat at his desk and opened the file on Fern L. Falscape. He read every word, then forced himself to read again. He began to have a feel for her. The workup done on her was the equivalent of a thorough security check. She was clear. A little liberal maybe, a bit careless in signing petitions, a trifle too liberated, especially in bed. But there was nothing in her life that suggested a security risk. College professor. *Dr.* Falscape. Remember to use that. Friendly, outgoing, witty, well-liked by all. Attracted men while keeping the friendship of women. Soft touch for a hard-luck story. Bit of a bleeding heart. Yes. She had helped Sloane, hadn't she?

Adams closed the folder. He knew how to approach her. Patriotism, duty and, yes, Sloane. She had saved his life, enabled him to escape. Make her realize how much that was appreciated. Would she go one step further, help them find Sloane, bring him in, protect him? Yes, that was the way. She'd do anything for Sloane. Hell, with what they'd been through, she was probably in love with him. Probably in bed regularly. Yes. Do it for Sloane.

Adams felt sure he could handle her. Treat her with respect and dignity, appropriate to college faculty, yet be fatherly, maybe slightly authoritative. Enlist her help—for the country, for Sloane. Under no circumstances threaten or badger her. The pickup at Dulles would be done with elaborate courtesy. She would be taken by helicopter. Had to for security reasons. Couldn't risk land transit. Taken where? Adams thought a minute. Yes, Calvert College. It would be familiar to her. Great atmosphere. He'd meet her there, suggest they go to her home to talk. It would work fine. He'd make it work.

Two hours later Adams was in the Space Three making an announcement to The Committee. "We have heard from a dead man. Wolf has messaged: 'Parsley I have your name.'" Even as he spoke, Adams scanned faces, eyes, intent on any telltale sign. There was none. The traitor among them had ice for blood. Adams knew he should have expected nothing less.

White: "What is that supposed to mean?"

"I have no idea."

Brown: "You mean to say that idiot Wolf upset the Navy, jeopardized whole systems of addresses and codes just to send a meaningless message?"

"Just because none of us understands it should not lead us to believe it is not without meaning. After all, he went to considerable pains to see the message reached us here in this room. I suggest we keep this information about Parsley to ourselves."

Brown again: "We hardly have time for bizarre riddles. Wolf is clearly beyond redemption. He should be eliminated."

"That may not be easy. We don't know where he is."

White: "But you have the girl who sent the message. Is she under surveillance?"

"Yes, constantly. She lands at Dulles tomorrow evening."

Black: "Then pick her up."

"It is arranged."

Adams swore inwardly and knew he was back into a bad habit he would have to break again. But he hated to have to tell all that to The Committee. Parsley would be after the girl, too. Adams just had to hope he got there first.

Parsley did not believe it for a second. Wolf was bluffing. He did not have his name. No one did. But just to be sure he reviewed again every syllable of his conversation with Khruchenko in Vienna. Then he nodded approval. There was absolutely no clue to his identity. Khruchenko didn't know who Parsley was. No Russian did. Not anyone.

Wolf's message was nonetheless dangerous. PARSLEY I HAVE YOUR NAME. Damn! The whole world would now know the code name Parsley. Green, that sonofabitch, would make use of it. He was probably combing the computers now looking for references to it. The man was transparent. "I have no idea." Liar! He damn well did have ideas. Green was going to have to be eliminated along with Wolf and the girl. There was no safety until that happened.

A bigger worry. The Russians. PARSLEY I HAVE YOUR NAME: that would upset Dzerzhinsky Square, just as Wolf must have figured. The Russians would think his cover was blown. They would back away from involvement. They might even overreact, try to learn Parlsey's identity and eliminate a potential embarrassment. He smiled.

There was no doubt he could embarrass the KGB by telling only a fraction of what he knew.

Using a pencil and paper he drafted a new item. "A prominent US envoy is trying to break off a very public peccadillo before it earns him expulsion from his very prestigious post—and his marriage. We wish him luck." Decoded it meant: PARSLEY SAFE—WILL ACT. He'd arranged for it to be in "Washington Off Guard" tomorrow.

It would do no harm to reassure Dzerzhinsky Square. Chances were they still would act on their own, just as they had in the bungled bombing at Elche. If they had only done as he had asked, Quigley would have handled it properly. Wolf and the girl would be dead and all this trouble ended. He shook his head. A bombing—no less. Sometimes the KGB had all the finesse of a tornado. He could visualize their actions now. They would come after Wolf and the Falscape woman to find out what they knew about Parsley. All to the good. The KGB could do the job for him. Green would take the girl. She would lead him to Wolf. Then, with a little help from Parsley, the KGB would eliminate all three—if he didn't beat them to it.

Very good. After that he would have clear sailing through untroubled waters.

Sloane used a much-practiced technique for snapping awake. He held his breath until the need for oxygen put his mind on alert. Then he got out of bed and looked at his watch. Seven-thirty. Lots to do today.

From Frederick, Maryland, he had driven south on I-270, then taken the Washington Beltway eastward through the Maryland suburbs of Washington, stopping at a motel near Upper Marlboro. What he needed would be somewhere in this area.

Again he looked at his watch and computed.

Eight hours sleep. Not enough. Tired, weak. Damn fever. But he was better than when he went to bed. Couldn't think about it. Had to keep moving.

By nine-thirty, having visited gun shops and Army-Navy stores, he had spent almost six thousand dollars of the KGB's money. He bought Army fatigues and combat boots, a Walther PPK and ammunition, hollow points. It was only 7.5mm but would do. His major expenditure—making the gun shop owner extremely happy—was an AR-15, the semiautomatic civilian equivalent of the Army M-16 rifle, with an attached nightscope. Going to hunt owls, he said.

By ten o'clock he was sitting across the desk from Donald Swerington, a realtor. "My name is Judson Browning." Sloane hoped his English accent sounded authentic. "I represent a group—mostly British, but with some French and German interest. We plan to invest in a restaurant—exclusive, very posh, only the finest clientele."

"In this area, Mr. Browning?"

Sloane saw the light of avarice in Swerington's eyes. "You don't think much of the idea I can tell."

"On the *contrary*." He was properly aghast. "The growth of this area is nothing less than phenomenal. We lie at the heart of the whole Capital region. We—"

"Yes, I know. We have *investigated*. What we are looking for is an estate, preferably older, a large house that has some . . . some *aesthetic* values, a little history, perhaps. Know what I mean?"

"I do, I do indeed. As a matter of fact we have several listings which—"

"We would like it to have some acreage, trees—gardens, as we English say. There will have to be parking, you know."

"Of course."

"One more thing. We want to move quickly.

Our plan is to open by Christmas. So the place should be unoccupied, available for immediate sale."

Sloane spent much of the day in the company of Swerington. He decided the fussy little man with the potbelly and sweaty palms had to be the most unctuous and greedy individual on earth. But he found what he was looking for: an old stone farmhouse, just out of town, fifteen rooms, terrible condition, truly a white elephant. It sat atop a small hill. Great sightlines. Couldn't enter the place without being seen. And it was quiet, isolated, lots of trees. No streetlights. The place would be dark. And there were lots of ways in and out. Damn near perfect. To Swerington he said, "Very interesting, old chap, but I think I like that other place better."

"The Arundel estate?"

"Yes, that's the one. I'll recommend to my associates that we make an offer."

"You won't be sorry, Mr. Browning." He was actually rubbing his palms together. "I think it'll be perfect for you."

Nearly ready to drop, Sloane returned to his motel, slept a few hours, ate, then drove into Washington, pulling into a parking garage on Fifteenth Street NW. From there he walked a couple of blocks and entered the offices of *The Washington Post*. A few minutes later he was sitting opposite Curtis Eustace.

"You look surprised, Mr. Browning."

Sloane wasn't, but he smiled, and again using his English accent, said, "I must confess I am. I was expecting someone more"—he laughed now—"shall I say more *masculine*."

Curtis Eustace seemed genuinely delighted to have surprised him, and her bosom jiggled with genuine mirth. "Obviously, Curtis Eustace is just a pseudonym."

"Very obviously." He let his eyes swing down

her and back. That too was obvious, but he sensed it was expected of him. No doubt she was a handsome woman dressed to the nines for the evening. Her gown was of some shiny, silvery fabric, filmy, formfitting. Silver beads accented lots of cleavage, not that it needed it. Matching beads dangled three inches below her ears. Platinum hair was flawlessly coiffed. Her makeup was both impeccable and plentiful. Sloane guessed she was in her early forties, trying to look younger. She also conveyed a blatant sexuality. Probably useful to her in gathering gossip.

"These are my working clothes, Mr. Browning. I'm off to the usual whirl of Washington parties. I should imagine I'll gather several juicy tidbits for my column." Her bright red lacquered lips arranged themselves into a pout. "It's tiresome, most boring, but one must earn one's living, mustn't one."

It was stupefying to Sloane. She had a high-pitched, girlish voice, and with it mouthed that stream of banalities as though they were original and profound. Might as well join her. "Man's work is never done—or woman's." Her responsive jiggle suggested she was greatly amused. "Perhaps I can offer something useful for your column. I represent an English group planning to open a restaurant in the Washington area." He went on to give a glowing description of the planned decor—medieval—and the cuisine. "So you see, Ms. Eustace, we think it will attract the better clientele." He smiled. "You may want to drop in from time to time. I'm sure you will find grist for your mill—so to speak."

She looked puzzled. "Isn't this sort of announcement more appropriate for the business pages, Mr. Browning?"

"Call me Judson." He smiled. "We English aren't as formal as you might think. You're right, of course, and we plan to make that announcement at the appropriate time. Quite a large advertising campaign is being prepared even as I speak. But we thought a little advance mention would sort of prepare the public, get our name before . . ." He let the words trail off. " 'Washington Off Guard' has immense influence, as you know."

Now she smiled. Stunning orthodontia, really. "You want a plug."

Sloane laughed. "I believe that is the expression."

Her smile continued. "I see no reason why I can't help you. My readers are always interested in new places to dine. What is your restaurant to be named?" She picked up a pencil.

"I took the liberty of writing it out for you." He handed her a sheet of paper with hand-printed words on it. He had no access to a typewriter.

She read. "Parsley. What a charming name."

"We think so."

"You've bought the old Hedges place on Old Fence Road, Upper Marlboro."

"Yes, an old estate. Quite grand in its day. When we refurbish, it will be grand again."

"I'm sure." She stood up. "I'll be glad to help you with a little mention, Mr. Browning—I mean Judson." She smiled. "Now I must be off or I'll miss a *very* important cabinet officer."

And he arose. "Please don't let me delay you, but there is just one more thing. Could you possibly run that in tomorrow night's column? You see my superior, the managing partner, is flying in from London tomorrow. I'd like him to see that I've been on the job—so to speak."

Laughter tinkled from her. "And so you have."

She came around the desk, picking up her silvery wrap from a chair. She handed it to him, turning for him to drape it around her shoulders, an action drenched in femininity and intimacy. Sloane felt he was about to OD on perfume. But she was good—the candle for the male moth. Why was she coming on to him?

"Would you like to come along, Judson? I can introduce you to several very *important* people. It might be useful"—she turned to face him, displaying the orthodontist's handiwork and fastening vivid blue eyes on him—"and other things."

He went along, maintaining eye contact, nodding just a trifle. "That would be appealing, but, most regrettably, I have another commitment."

"Some other time then?"

"As I say, it would be most appealing."

"Yes, English gentlemen can be so ... *appealing*." She laughed then. "Where are you staying, Judson?"

He wasn't about to tell her. "The Capital-Hilton."

"Such a coincidence. Tomorrow night there is a very *grand* ball for the Guatemalan foreign minister—or some such person. It's at your very hotel. Perhaps I can see you there?"

He grinned. "Perhaps." He accompanied her out of the building, hailed a cab for her, and helped her inside. Before closing the door, he said, "I'll be reading your column with great interest—tomorrow night, especially."

"If you remember our friend from Guatemala, perhaps we can read it together."

"I won't forget. It would be fascinating—and appealing."

THIRTEEN

Freddie sat by the window of the 747, hunched over, feeling small, staring blankly at a monotonous vista of sky, clouds, and blue sea far below. That part of her brain which monitored itself and her physical condition recognized that an inevitable reaction of fatigue, depression and loneliness had set in. She was a wounded animal, in shock, lying still, trying to repair itself. But that awareness did nothing to alleviate her bleak despair. The hobgoblins were about to get loose in her mind. They could do a lot of damage, she knew.

In time a flight attendant brought a tray of food. Freddie almost refused it. There is no dining room in the pits. But she accepted the food, discovered she was starved, and devoured every crumb. Only deeply ingrained courtesy kept her from demanding another tray of food. But the food helped and she fell asleep.

When she awoke she felt better. She realized for the first time she was on an American plane, TWA, and most of these people around her were Americans, acting American, talking American. That was nice. Suddenly she knew all she wanted to do was go home—home home, not Calvert College, but the place where she could sleep till noon and her mother fussed over her, and her father ... *Daddy, I brought you a wounded bird to fix up—me. Tell me what happened, sweetie. Well, Daddy, I was in Munich buying this bottle of Liebfraumilch, when ... You were always so independent and self-reliant, dear. I know, but that was before I ... Did you know I can pick locks, Daddy? And the safety on a Walther PPK is right there. All you do is—* Again she stared out the window. The ghosts rattled the bars of her mind.

The business of landing—buckling up, facing the inevitable apprehension of touchdown, gathering her things, leaving the plane, smiling at the flight attendant—brought reality. *Life goes on, my dear. Tomorrow and tomorrow creeps in its—you know, I never did get to Stratford-on-Avon.*

As she waited for her luggage—the suitcase Sloane had her buy in Cadiz, her second such purchase—she looked around. David had said, "Go about your business. Try to act normal. Your every move is being watched, but try not to care." She looked around. Ought to be expert in spotting them now. That fellow reading the newspaper? A little too casual, isn't he? "Don't worry about them, Freddie. They are really protecting you." Sure! Just like they protect the moose and elk by thinning the herd.

"Dr. Falscape?"

She turned, saw a young, handsome black man. "Yes."

"I am Special Agent Barrett of the FBI." He motioned to a companion, a white man, even younger, swarthy, hirsute. "This is Special Agent Donatelli. Would you come with us, please?"

So it really was happening. Welcome to the Land of Liberty. She smiled. "I haven't even retrieved my luggage, let alone gone through Customs."

"It has nothing to do with Customs, Dr. Falscape. If you'll just come with us?"

She remembered. "Do you have a badge? I'm told FBI men always carry badges."

"I do, but I thought you'd rather keep this casual so as not to—"

"Good thinking, Mr. Barrett, but I'd a whole lot rather not go off with strange men, even those as handsome and debonair as you two." She smiled. He was not amused, but produced his badge. She made a great fetish of looking at it, then with her eyes made Donatelli produce his. Another smile. "Can—I mean, *may* I wait for my luggage?"

"It's being taken care of."

"I see. Such a thoughtful government. All right, gentlemen. I'm all yours—well, not quite all."

They led her past Customs and into the airport terminal. She forced herself not to think of her pounding heart, the roiling in her stomach, her slight vertigo, but rather on the fact they walked on either side of her. Just three good friends passing through Dulles Airport. "They won't know anything except your name and that they are to pick you up. You can talk to them if you want, but it won't do any good." She knew she couldn't say a word. Just walking was a triumph.

"This way, doctor."

"Where are we going?"

"To the copter pad."

Lord! David hadn't figured on that. Her eyes scanned the terminal, not for faces but for ... He said there'd be one. There had to be. Wooden step followed wooden step. There never was one when you needed one.

Then she saw them, by the exit, a pair, man and woman, blue uniforms.

She ran.

"*Help! Police! Rape! Rape!*" Her screams were really quite good. "*Help me! Please, help me!*" She reached them, saw the startled expressions in the eyes of the security guards, a mixture of surprise and fear. Hands already reached for weapons.

"Those men grabbed me! Stop them!" She turned and pointed at the running FBI men. There was rage on their faces. They had already produced their badges.

"We're FBI, this woman is—"

Freddie bolted out the door. The hot August air of Virginia buffeted her. Her eyes searched. Cars, cabs. Which one?

They were at her side, clutching her arms. "Nice try, lady."

Oh, God!

To her left came a whole series of loud detonations—bang, bang, bang—reverberating. A huge puff of smoke. Startled, she turned toward it. Everyone did. Then she saw the yellow D.C. cab race forward, stop in the middle of the street. She twisted free and ran. The back door opened. She dove inside, head first. The forward motion of the cab slammed the door against her ankles.

"David?"

"How many D.C. cab drivers do you know?"

"None as beautiful." She squirmed, pulled her legs in, slammed the door, sat up, rubbed her sore ankle. David was driving. A figure slumped against the door beside him.

"Lie down. They'll be looking for a cab with a woman in back."

She flopped to the seat. "Oh, David, are you all right?"

"I'm fine."

"What'd you use, firecrackers?"

"Isn't it the Fourth of July?"

She felt the cab turning, slowing down, turning again. "Did you kill him?"

"The driver? No. He'll just have a bad headache." Sloane pulled into a parking area, stopped, turned off the motor. "Get out. Walk to the blue Ford two places down. Get in. I'll drive."

She sat up, got out. A Wendy's parking lot, still at the airport. She went to the car, sat in the front seat. In a moment he was beside her, backing out, driving away at normal speed.

"Are we safe?"

"I think so. They'll find the cab, but they don't know this car."

She looked at him, in profile now. "Did you know you're the most beautiful person on earth?"

He turned to her, smiled. "You didn't used to think so. How'd it go in Cadiz?"

She didn't want to talk about it. All she wanted to do was collapse into his arms and forget everything. "Could we neck? Can I be your girl?"

He turned to her, smiled again. "It would be a good cover, a guy with his arm around his girl. But my left arm isn't good enough to drive with alone."

She slid across the seat next to him and settled for a snuggle. It felt so good, so comforting. Her hand touched his thigh. Then she remembered and brought her right hand to his forehead. "You're burning up."

"I'll make it. Tell me about Cadiz."

She did then, every detail, answering many questions. And he told her all he'd done. By the time they were finished they were in D.C.

"You know what comes next?"

"Could we stop somewhere, be together a bit?"

He sighed. "We haven't a lot of time. I don't know how long I can stay on my feet."

"Can't we take a few minutes? I need it, David."

They stopped at a neighborhood bar in Georgetown, sat in a booth in back, side by side. It was dark. His arm was around her and she clutched his hot hands. She even got to neck a little.

"I keep remembering that song, 'What I Did for Love.' "

"I'm sorry."

"Why? Would you rather have died in Munich?"

"You know what I mean. You were just a nice, simple-minded girl going—"

"I'm still a nice, simple-minded girl. Hold me." She felt his arm tighten around her and the heat of him. "On the plane I regressed. All I wanted to do was go home to Mommy and Daddy, be a little girl, be taken care of. Call me Cinderella."

"It's understandable."

"Right now all I want is to be held by you. I'm so sexy. I guess I'm hoping that in the midst of orgasm lies a balm for—but it doesn't, does it? I'm forever changed, David. I can't go home to Mommy and Daddy—"

His laugh broke in. "I certainly can't go home to Mother, either."

"I'm serious. God knows if I'll ever have a chance to say all this. I don't know if I can go back to teaching. Young girls from prosperous, protected families, beating on the doors of the ivory tower. 'Let me in so I can remain prosperous and protected.'" She held his right hand, the one that came around her shoulder, in both of hers. She squeezed, pulling herself tighter within him. "I keep remembering his eyes, Fox's eyes."

"I told you. Don't think about it."

"But I have to. This may be the only chance I'll ever have. He was so startled, surprised, so terribly disbelieving. Remember nuances? Oh, God, there were a million of them—I don't know, fear, hatred, agony, desperation, yet somehow gratitude."

He felt her tremble. "You had to do it."

"Don't try to comfort me. Don't say what I want to hear."

"Freddie, very few people ever see the person they kill."

She turned her face to his, sharply. "That helps. We shoot an arrow into the air and know not where it lands. We drop a bomb, maybe a big bomb and—we don't know. We never look into the eyes of the widows and orphaned and suffering." She turned her face away, pursing her lips.

"Among the few who have ever seen the person they killed, hardly any are women."

"That's very good. And that's what's wrong. We need a regular training schedule. On Tuesdays women whose last names begin with E, F, and G kill a man, watch his eyes as he dies. Maybe then we wouldn't give toy guns to our sons, send them to John Wayne movies. We wouldn't glorify war—and death. We would know, as women and mothers, to pity the executioner. We'd understand that each time anyone pulls the trigger some of our humanity dies. And we'd stop thinking up names for what was lost. Courage is a big one. Bravery. Self-sacrifice. Crusade, Jihad, defense of Liberty. It's funny. We've hated every war, the waste, the futile casualty lists, sworn each time it would be the last. Then it quickly begins again, the patriotism, the flag-waving, the glorification of death as courage and proof of manhood, nationhood, and support for ideals. It is all just getting ready, isn't it, preparing ourselves mentally for a new war?"

"Freddie . . ."

"I know, don't think about it. You're right. I can't right now. There isn't time. But when this is over, if it ever is over, if there is an us, a you and me—oh, I don't know what I want. All I know is I love you. We belong together. Two killers. Don't fire till you see the whites of their eyes. We've seen the whites. And we are now in darkness, searching around on the floor, frantic, trying to find and put together the pieces of our humanity, our lives. And when we find them, the glue that holds them together is rationalization."

He kissed her then, tenderly, the only way he knew to comfort her. "I told you, I feel hatched. You broke the egg in Munich. I do love you."

And she smiled. "We'll make a great pair. A

grown man just beginning to live and a grown woman who has lost the meaning of her life." She kissed him. "Now you'd better brief me on what I'm to do."

He moved to the other side of the booth, wanting to see the comprehension in her eyes. For the next half hour he told her where to go, what she would see, what would happen, how she should act. Deep inside he tried to quiet his own fear. Over and over he told himself they wouldn't take her. She was of no value except as a lead to him. They held hands across the table, both of them, left-right, right-left. They leaned, kissed. She left him there, walked out of the bar, drove away. He had never felt more lonely in his life.

It was dark as Freddie parked the car, his rent-a-car—he said he already had another—turned off the motor, looked around. It was as he described, amazingly so. She got out, locked the car and began to walk. She tried to be a person with tunnel vision, concentrating wholly on the task ahead, controlling the mind, forbidding all other thoughts. David could do this. She knew it would never work for her.

A small office building resembling a post office. She opened the door, turned to her right. Yes, just as he said, a desk, a young man in a Pinkerton uniform. They made eye contact. "I have come for Parsley."

"I beg your pardon."

"I truly believe you heard me."

"Mr. Parsley?"

"Not mister anything. Just Parsley."

Marine Lance Corp. Julian Rubin was pleased in a way. His was dull duty. Civilians rarely entered, simply because none of the offices in the building dealt with the public. Oh, there were occasional shoppers wanting directions, a phone, or a john. Easily taken care of. But he'd never had anyone ask for someone not on his list. He looked at her carefully. Pretty, even beautiful, frilly green dress, high heels, nice legs, nice everything. He made a fetish of looking over a list encased in Plexiglas. "I'm sorry. We have no Mr. Parsley here. You must have the wrong—"

"Oh, but you do. I think you'd better pick up that phone and tell your watch captain or whoever your superiors are in security that Fern L. Falscape is here asking for Parsley." She watched him stare at her. "Better write the name down so you make no mistake. Fern L. Falscape." She spelled the surname for him.

Lance Corp. Rubin tried one more time. "Really, Ms. Falscape. I don't—"

"Believe me, you'll be in worse trouble if you don't report my message."

He hesitated, then picked up the phone—an unnecessary act, he knew. Her presence was already monitored on TV and her every word recorded. The blinking light on his console told him that a Yellow Alert was already flashing throughout the complex. It meant there was a threat to security and brought instant protective measures. Safes were closed, files locked, interior doors sealed and deactivated. Elevators would not run. Everyone was a prisoner, kept in place, unless they had the special emergency cypher for the locks. Few did. If the automatic fluoroscopic examination had showed Freddie carried a weapon, let alone displayed it, or if she had threatened Rubin or made an attempt to enter the interior doors, a Red Alert would have flashed, complete with sirens. Defensive measures would have been taken, including emission of debilitating gases in the exterior lobby.

All this Rubin knew. When he rendered her message into the phone, it was a perfunctory act.

In his ear he heard the voice of his watch captain. "Keep her there."

Rubin put down the phone, motioned. "Please have a seat. Someone will be with you in a moment."

She smiled. "Surprised?"

He was disarmed. Such a nice smile. "A little, yes."

Freddie went to a plastic chair across the lobby, sat, waited. She even picked up a magazine. Nonchalance was a learned art, something to be practiced.

It had been her idea, suggested long ago as they had approached Cadiz. "David, why don't I go to CSA headquarters at Fort Belvoir, knock on the door and ask for Parsley? We'll at least gain their attention. It worked for Martin Luther, didn't it?" He had opposed, saying it was too risky. She had argued there was no time for a cat-and-mouse game. He could keel over at any moment. They had to move quickly, and going straight to Parsley was the simplest, most direct route.

"It would be bold, wouldn't it, David?"

"Oh, it'd be that, all right."

She had thought he had forgotten it until today when he told her where to go, what to say.

"I thought you didn't like my idea."

"I don't, but I figure it's not too big a risk. Parsley will never be stupid enough to surface and approach you. But you may get another member of The Committee. Him we need."

"Why?"

"It's our only chance for a normal life, Freddie. If I kill Parsley, we'll be—"

"I get it. No one will know why. We'll be hunted forever." Her eyes brightened. "Maybe you wouldn't have to kill Parsley. Maybe you could turn him over to—"

"We'll see." He went over the whole plan again.

"Is Parsley at this place I'm going?"

"I honestly don't know."

"I gather it's something more than a shopping center. What place is it?"

"Don't ask. You don't ever want to know."

"All right, I don't. Tell me the plan again." He began to tell her of going to Brandywine. "I know that. I mean the whole plan, the big picture."

"You want to find flaws?"

"It can't hurt."

"Okay. I don't know who is going to leave Brandywine with you, but I'll bet the bank it's a member of The Committee. They can't risk anyone even knowing about Parsley."

"Do you think it'll be the man who knew about Vaseline?"

"752? Probably."

"Suppose it's Parsley?"

"It won't be, but if it is it won't matter. He'll come with you. I'm the one he wants, not you."

"All right. I take this guy to the abandoned place at Upper Marlboro."

"You know how to find it?"

"Yes, I'll be there."

"You leave the guy off, then drive away. I don't want you in any danger."

She nodded but knew she didn't have the slightest intention of leaving.

"I mean it, Freddie. I want you out of there. You'll just be in the way. It'll be pitch dark, but I'll have the nightscope. I'll be able to keep him in my sights at all times. I don't want to have to worry about you and what you're doing."

"Okay. You hold the man I bring until Parsley shows up."

"Yes. He'll come when he reads the newspaper. It may take a while for him to show, so don't worry."

"Me, worry? I won't give it a passing thought. How can you be sure Parsley will come?"

"He has to—because of the man you've brought.

He's either on The Committee or very close to it. The last thing Parsley can do is risk my talking to him. His cover would be blown."

"Suppose he just sends some men to—"

"He won't. It would confirm everything I'm saying."

"Sure, but suppose Parsley doesn't think that way."

"Then there'll be some bodies. I'm in a great defensive position. With the rifle and nightscope I can pick off an army. Parsley is trapped, Freddie. If he tries to fly the coop, his absence confirms his identity on The Committee. If he comes, I have him. There is no way out. Do you see any flaws?"

She hadn't and didn't—except for Murphy's Law. There were risks to everything. David had come up with as good a plan as possible. Only thing now was to carry it out, concentrate on what she had to do, keep her cool. Toward this end she actually looked at the magazine in her lap. *Sports Illustrated*. Yuk! Didn't need anything macho just now. She set it aside and picked up another.

Boggs, assistant to Mr. Green, was aghast. Fern L. Falscape, here, at Brandywine! Incomprehensible. Defied belief. He even had security flash the lobby scene on his screen. Yes, it was either her or someone who looked like her. Asking for Parsley. Who the hell was that? What was going on?

Boggs shook his head. What a royal foul-up. Heads would roll—most especially his. This was a real careerbuster. Damn! It had seemed so simple. Pick up the Falscape woman at Dulles, put her in a chopper and fly her to Calvert College where Mr. Green was waiting to talk to her. What had the lousy FBI done? Fallen for the oldest trick in the book. Cry rape and run. God Almighty! Then the FBI had compounded the error by not reporting the event for almost an hour. They had been sure she couldn't get far, certainly not out of the airport. They'd have her back in minutes. Those minutes dragged. Getaway cab spotted at Wendy's. Just hold on another minute. Just a few more minutes.

Boggs had stayed in touch with Mr. Green by radio at Calvert College. He had said very little, but his silences were highly pregnant. After nearly two hours he'd called it a wash and said he was coming in. From the copter pad he'd phoned to say he was stopping for dinner before coming in. Dinner. Boggs knew it would be a long time before he got any.

Again he looked at the lobby scene on his monitor. Just sitting there reading a magazine. Cool lady. What the hell was she up to? Goes to elaborate pains to escape the airport then shows up here at Brandywine talking in riddles about parsley. No way to figure. But Mr. Green would have to be told. Boggs was about to do so when the red phone "rang," which is to say flashed a light. Ordinarily Mr. Green would answer it at his desk. In his absence Boggs picked it up.

The voice he heard was electronically altered, unrecognizable. It rendered a few words which Boggs knew was a recognition signal. He didn't know Mr. Green's authorized reply. But it meant that higher authority was calling. He didn't know who. "This is Boggs, sir. Mr. Green is not on station."

"I wondered why the damn yellow alert was still on. I'm shutting it off. I'll take care of the lobby matter."

"Yessir."

"Are you in touch with Mr. Green?"

"Yessir, I can be."

"I have a message for him. Get it to him at once."

Boggs listened, wrote. "Yessir." There was no reply. The voice was gone. Quickly Boggs made radio contact with Mr. Green's car, waited, repeated the signal. No answer. Damn! Must be out of the car eating. Nothing to do but wait. Shouldn't be long. Wait! Boggs felt so damn futile, like a eunuch. And he was about to be one. Mr. Green would have his balls when he returned.

From the periphery of her vision, she was aware of the approach of two men, but she kept her eyes riveted to the magazine article. It was a point of pride to know what it was about: how to color-coordinate your nail polish, lipstick, rouge and eye makeup. She was badly uncoordinated.

"Ms. Falscape?"

She looked up. "Yes."

"Will you come with us, please?"

She discarded the magazine—intricacies of color coordination she'd never know—stood up and accompanied the men to the interior door. It was amazing how much those few steps helped her. Any action was better than sitting, waiting. The door opened with a buzzing sound and one of the men passed within. She paused, turned to the desk, smiled. "Thank you."

Lance Corp. Rubin smiled back, although he knew he shouldn't. "You're entirely welcome."

"I do hope so. I do indeed." She passed through the door, heard it close behind her. Again she paused, looking at her two companions. Young, very serious. Military, she figured. They led her down the hallway to her left, turned a corner, went a little farther, pausing before an unmarked door. One knocked, waited, and was rewarded with a buzzing sound.

"You may go in now, ma'am."

"Aren't you gentlemen going to join me?"

"No, ma'am. We're to remain here."

It sounded ominous, but she fought the feeling. "Too bad. You'll never know what's behind the green door."

She turned the knob, pushed, entered. It was an office of modest size, vinyl couch, table, six chairs, desk, swivel chair, all in federalese. Even the photo of the President on the wall was government issue. There was a very sick rubber plant in the corner. But Freddie's mind recorded little of this, at least at first, because of her surprise.

She had expected a single individual, a member of The Committee, 752 who knew about Vaseline. There were four men clustered around the table. At the far end was a man in Naval uniform, some kind of officer with gold oak leaves on his shoulder. She should know the rank, but couldn't think. To his right was a Marine in olive-green uniform. Two bars. Captain. To his right was a civilian in shirt sleeves, yellow with tan stripes. Across the table another civilian. Brownish plaid sports jacket. He pushed a button on a recording device. All of them were young, late twenties, early thirties, and they were very serious and, yes, hostile. She felt like a bug about to be squashed.

They did not invite her to sit. "Fern L. Falscape?"

The question came from the Navy. "Yes."

"Where do you think you are, Ms. Falscape?"

She looked around the room, saw the furnishings, noting it was outfitted as an office but not used as one. There were no papers. Ashtrays were empty. All this was an exercise in calming herself. What was going on? David had said she'd go right to someone on The Committee.

"Ms. Falscape, I asked what you think this building is."

She looked back to the table, made eye contact with the Navy man. "A public office building adjacent to a small shopping center in Brandywine, Maryland."

"Is that all?"

"My entire instructions were to come to this building, approach the man at the desk, give my name and ask for Parsley."

"Who gave you those instructions?"

"You know who."

"I'm afraid not, Ms. Falscape." It was the man with the tape recorder. "Who sent you here?"

She exhaled in a long sigh. "Please. There isn't time for this—this *game*."

The Navy: "We assure you this is not a game, Ms. Falscape. You are in very serious trouble."

"Oh, God!" She brought her right hand to her forehead, rubbed it. Greasy, unclean. "There isn't *time* for this." Her voice was raising in pitch. "Is one of you Parsley?"

The man in shirt sleeves: "Who or what is Parsley—other than a vegetable used—"

"Oh, *please*! This is just wasting time." She swallowed, then remembered. "What runs a '55 Chevy on Fat Tuesday?" She was rewarded with four pairs of blinking eyes and silence. They didn't know what she was talking about.

"On July nineteenth you boarded the USS *Everett* at the US Navy base at Rota, Spain, and demanded to send a message and, indeed, did send a message in code. Where did you obtain that code?"

"Please, I'll—" She paused, struggling to control her panic. She sighed, inhaled, swallowed, forced herself to relax. "Listen, I'll answer all your questions, every one of them—but not now. Later, after—"

"I'm afraid you'll have to answer *now*, Ms. Falscape."

"I can't. Don't you understand?" Frantically

she looked from face to face, all so stern, then shook her head. "You don't, do you?"

"We understand that it is a most serious violation of the law to steal, use, disseminate or in any way reveal United States codes." The Navy paused for effect. "You are in a great deal of trouble, Ms. Falscape."

All she could think of was David out there at the abandoned farm waiting for her to bring ... She didn't know who, but someone who would be a witness, someone who ... "Will one of you gentlemen come with me—or all four of you for that matter?"

A long pause festooned with utter disbelief. The Marine finally spoke. "None of us are going anywhere, Ms. Falscape."

"*Please!* You don't *know*. You don't *understand*." It was no use. "Then I'm going. I must." She wheeled, took two strides, grasped the doorknob, turned. Locked. She looked back at them. Her eyes were wide, she knew. She also knew she was scared to death.

The Navy man rose. "Try to calm yourself, Ms. Falscape." He motioned to the end of the table. "Have a seat."

Her mouth opened in another plea, but it was never uttered. No use. David's plan was . . . disaster. Suddenly she felt very tired, so utterly futile. All this—for what? Obediently she slumped into the chair.

"Why don't you start at the beginning, Ms. Falscape. It's often easier that way."

What worried Sloane was not that he felt physically rotten as that he was not mentally sharp. His head was fuzzy, full of cotton. He couldn't think. And that was dangerous. He had fallen back on instinct, experience, memory, reflexes, but he had no confidence in them. Be cautious, careful, leave nothing to chance. The mere fact he had to keep warning himself told him what bad shape he was in. Never had to do that before.

He had driven by the farmhouse, checking for cars, any sign of activity. There was none. About two hundred yards past the house he turned, lights out, into a farmer's lane and parked the car near a barn. This set a dog to barking, but he figured it would quiet down soon. At the worst the farmer would discover the car and wonder whose it was.

Quickly he set off through the fields. He wore the Army fatigues and combat boots. His face and hands were blackened so they would catch no light. He slung the AR-15 with nightscope over his left shoulder, but it hurt and he switched it to his right. Inside his shirt was the Walther PPK in a shoulder holster.

He wanted to approach the farmhouse from the rear, which meant a trek of maybe half a mile. There was pasture at first, then a cornfield. A barbed-wire fence. He swore when he scratched his finger, then snagged his pants. Never would have happened if he wasn't so damn weak and dizzy. High grass, then a woods. Black as sin. A branch slapped his face and he fell over a stump. After that he used the nightscope. He could see everything outlined against a green background. Easier then, except his feet got wet crossing a small stream. By the time he reached the edge of the woods he was panting, dizzy, sweating yet shivering. He rested a moment, leaning against a tree. He closed his eyes, then opened them because everything started to reel. Then he cursed his traitorous body.

He unslung the rifle and peered at the scene through the nightscope. It was as he remembered. Immediately ahead was a grassy field, once a lawn, a couple of trees. Maybe fifty yards away, up a shallow incline, was the farmhouse, three stories high, stark, abandoned against the night sky and trees that fronted it. He examined the back of the building, marveling at how the nightscope picked up every detail, cracked stone, chipped paint on a windowsill, some vines creeping up the side. Most of the windows were knocked out. No sign of life. To the left of the house—his right as he looked—was the remains of an old barn. Most of the wood was stripped away, leaving only a partial skeleton. No cover there. He moved the scope. To his left was a ramshackle shed, much of its siding gone. Probably once a garage. There. A small building, made of stone like the house. Couldn't tear it down. Milkhouse, most likely, or smokehouse. He headed for that, forcing himself to a dog trot.

The door was gone, the window knocked out, a hole in the roof. Still, he could detect the faint odor of sour milk. The window was small, high, eye level. He rested the rifle on the sill and studied the back of the house at close range through the scope. Nothing. Just an abandoned farmhouse. He even peered inside through a broken window. Still nothing. He brought the rifle and scope inside and leaned against the wall. The stone felt cool against his forehead. Lord, what he'd give for a few hours' sleep. *Don't think about it.*

He looked at the house again, this time without the scope. It really was of no use to him. His business would be out front where there were lots of trees and cover. But he really ought to check out the house just to be sure. Leave nothing to chance. He sighed. If only he weren't so tired. *You're not tired. You're in the pink.*

He left the milkhouse and stepped toward the house. Damn quiet. No wind in the leaves. No bird sounds. Not even a cricket. Then he heard something. Behind him. What? A sort of rustle.

The garage, or what had been a garage. He raised the rifle, both as a weapon and a source of vision, scanning the open doorway, spaces between the boards. Nothing. He bolted, jumped really, inside, swung the rifle. Nothing. Must've been a rat or mouse.

Sloane stood in the doorway looking out through the scope into a field of green. Level place, then the driveway, lane really, running downhill to the road. Seventy-five yards maybe. Lots of weeds and grass. Check the house, remember? Again he scanned the back of it, the side which was toward him at a sharp angle. Nothing. Take no chances. He stepped out of the shed toward the house.

He first heard the car, distant, moving slowly, then saw the headlights flash at the top of a small grade off to his left. They blinked through the foliage as they approached. Moving slowly. Couldn't be Freddie, could it? Wasn't it much too soon? He shook his head. Why couldn't he keep better track of time?

The car passed the driveway, then he couldn't see it for the house. Just a car passing by. It was a public road, after all. Maybe the farmer up the way. The distant barking of the dog, the same that had yapped at him, confirmed his guess. He waited, for he could still hear the car, if not see it. The sound changed. Backing up. Then he could see the tail lights of the car, the brighter brake lights. It came back a little farther, past the drive. Headlights. Turning, flashing brilliantly up the drive. Freddie. Things must have gone well for her.

"Let me see if I have this straight, Ms. Falscape. You were with a man you can identify only as Wolf, and he—"

"I didn't say that. I can give you his name, address, phone number. I can even tell you where he is at this moment. Is that really what you want me to do?" Freddie glared at them. Her fear, frustration, indeed desperation to end this fiasco and leave had made her angry. If she had ever been more sarcastic and sharp-tongued, she couldn't remember it.

The man to her right, the one in the sports jacket who manned the recorder, cleared his throat. "I don't believe that will be necessary, Ms. Falscape."

She looked at him. He was a trifle older, very bland behind steel-rimmed glasses. He looked government issue, as though he were stamped out, the beige model; everything about him, including hair, eyes, complexion, clothes, was some shade of tan or brown. She realized how hard he'd be to describe—maybe even recognize if she saw him in another context. "You work for Mother, don't you?" She saw the faintest flicker of reaction in his eyes. "These other three don't know—" In her anger a vulgarity formed in her mind, but she didn't utter it. "They're just military, security most likely. But you aren't. You know what I'm saying. You know who Wolf is, why he's wanted. You know who I am, why I came here." She had eye contact and wouldn't let go. She saw the first hint of coldness rise, then give way to evasiveness. He looked away, down at his recording device. "Are you Parsley?"

His eyes returned to hers. They were bland again, utterly noncommittal. "You mentioned that before. Who or what is Parsley?"

"*A bloody, goddamn traitor, that's who!*" Her eyes filled with tears, surprising her almost as much as the vehemence in her voice. But she also felt profound relief. It hadn't all just been for love, had it? "And wh-while—" She heard the break in her voice, swallowed, gulped in air. "And while you sit here playing this ... this *fucking game*, he's getting away."

His eyes, steady, unblinking, seemed to envelop her. "And who do you think this person you call Parsley is?"

"*I don't know.* No one does." Already she had a growing sense of futility. "He's a Soviet mole on The Committee."

"What committee is that?"

"*You know damn well what committee.*"

"I'm afraid I don't, Ms. Falscape. Please tell me."

"The Committee that runs Mother." She saw the look in his eyes, so bland, so noncommittal. It infuriated her.

So did his voice. "You're making very little sense, Ms. Falscape. Would you like a glass of water, a cup of coffee, perhaps?"

Patronizing bastard! She shook her head. "Never mind. Never mind anything." She exhaled in a long "whew" sound.

The Navy was heard from. "The fact remains, Ms. Falscape, that whatever you thought you were doing you did send a message in code."

She looked at him, glared really. "All right, you want to play games. I can, too. What code? I don't know anything about codes."

"Ms. Falscape, you sent four groups of five symbols."

"Oh, those. Was that a code of some kind?" She was at her sarcastic best. "Tell me, Admiral, or whatever your rank is, if it was a code, what did the message say?"

He looked hurt. "I can't tell you that."

"I can. It said tsssk, puumk, shist, and any other sound you want to make up."

The Marines landed. "It won't work, Ms. Falscape. Those symbols you sent were an official code, property of the United States government. Where did you obtain it?"

"Square one." She sighed. "I told you."

"Tell us again."

She looked from face to face, starting at the left. When she got to plaid jacket on the right she thought she saw the faintest glimmer of a smile spread his thin lips. It was to him she spoke. "Are your orders to hold me here until—I don't know—until something happens?" She glanced at her watch. "You're doing a good job. It's been nearly an hour." Tears, quite unbidden, welled into smarting eyes. "And it's a shame—a *fucking* shame." She wiped her eyes. "Please excuse my language. I don't usually talk this way."

"Ms. Falscape—" The phone rang on the desk behind. "Excuse me." Plaid jacket arose, went to the phone, held it against his ear and mouth. "Yessir, this is he." Pause. "Yessir, we do, sir." Pause. "Yessir." Pause. "Yessir." Final pause. "Yessir, right away, sir." He replaced the phone.

When he looked at her, Freddie tried to read his eyes. It was difficult. There was puzzlement there, maybe acceptance or resignation, and, yes, just a hint of respect. He came to the table, snapped off the tape recorder and picked it up. He jerked his head toward the door, a sign to the others to leave. They rose, headed for the door.

"You're going?"

"If you'll excuse us, Ms. Falscape."

She couldn't believe it. "But—but, what am I supposed to do?"

"Just remain where you are."

They trooped out. She heard the door close behind them.

As the headlights slowly ascended the drive, Sloane retreated into the garage. He stepped to the side but was still able to see through splits in the boards. The lights of the approaching car were blinding. Must be halogens. He looked away, trying to preserve his night vision. What was the matter with Freddie? He'd told her to approach with the lights out.

The car stopped at the head of the drive, motor still running, the air conditioner making a rattling sound above the engine. The headlights lit up the interior of the garage. Sloane felt frozen, then angry. *Turn off the lights, Freddie. What the hell's the matter with you?*

He waited. It seemed an agonizing time.

"Turn off the damn lights, Freddie."

They remained on.

"Turn off the fucking lights!"

Then they were, but Sloane was now blinded. He couldn't see a thing, not even the outline of the car. He stepped into the doorway and raised the rifle to use the nightscope. A man opening the car door, getting out. He swung the scope to the passenger seat. Empty.

"Where's Freddie?" The man apparently could see him. He was raising his hands.

"Don't shoot—*please*. I'm unarmed."

Sloane shook his head. *Damn dizziness.* What was going on? "Where's Freddie?"

The man closed the door so the interior light went out, then stepped forward, hands up. "You— you mean Ms. Falscape?"

Sloane was confused. He couldn't think—and he knew there was something he should figure out. *Parsley*. His finger tightened around the trigger as he viewed this man through the scope. Slender, glasses, frightened. *Parsley*. "That's it. Keep your hands up. Just step forward—very slowly. I've got a nightscope. I can see every move you make."

"Please, I'm unarmed." But he obeyed.

"Stop right there." He was in the open, halfway between the car and Sloane. "What have you done with Freddie?"

"If you m-mean Ms. F-Falscape"—the voice was

tremulous—"she's at—she's where you sent her, sir."

"*Damn you, Parsley.*" In three strides he was there. "*Where's Freddie?*"

"Sir, I—"

Sloane slammed the rifle hard against his throat, pinioning him from behind, his arms still raised. "*Tell me or I'll choke it out of you!*"

He heard only his choking, gurgling sounds—not the *spit, spit, spit* of bullets from the upstairs windows. He looked up, saw the sustained flashes of automatic firing—even as the man slumped against him and he felt the hot pains of bullets tearing into his own flesh.

Agitated, pacing the office, greatly mystified, Freddie turned at the sound of the door opening, saw a man perhaps an inch shorter than she, fiftyish, wearing an ill-fitting, light brown, summerweight suit. He was nondescript. Were they all bland? No, he wasn't. His eyes. Sharp on her, intense, very interested, even excited. There was high intelligence in those eyes. The door closed behind him.

"Dr. Falscape, I'm sorry I wasn't here when you arrived. My name is Green."

There was resonance, authority in his voice, but she did not waver from the eye contact. "Green as in Parsley?"

His gaze flitted down her figure—no reaction, just a flitter—then back. "What runs a '55 Chevy on Fat Tuesday?"

Her eyes widened in surprise. She was to ask *him* that question. "Vaseline." Her voice sounded funny. She swallowed. "What is your address?"

"752."

"What was the final message?"

"Parsley I have your name."

She stared at him, mouth open a little. "You know that?"

His smile was benevolent, even avuncular. "I've been trying to help you and David Sloane for two months. He was badly wounded, wasn't he?"

"You know that name?"

"I selected him, I trained him, I assigned him—Harry Rogers, too. They were the very best. I'll admit to special"—he hesitated over the choice of word—"special *regard* for Sloane. We have a long association. I would like to see him retire— live however he wants to live." Another smile. "I imagine you may have some role in that. I have to tell you that I fear he is in great danger."

"I know he is, but—" Her eyes widened. "What do you know?"

"Let me ask you a question." His voice was deadly serious. "Is David Sloane at the old Hedges farm on Old Fence Road in Upper Marlboro?"

She stared. Her mouth was open a little. "How do you know that?"

"I was out when you came. As a matter of fact I was waiting for you to be brought to me from the airport so we could talk. I just returned here. There was a message saying Wolf was at—"

"A message? No one knows but me. How did—"

"I don't know, Freddie. That's why I'm asking you if that is indeed where he is?"

She swallowed—hard. "Yes, I'm to take you there."

"Then we'd better go—and quick."

He moved so fast she had to run in her heels to keep up—down the hall, through the lobby, out into the street. The rear door of a long black car was open. He helped her inside and crawled in after her. The vehicle took off at high speed.

There were three men in the front seat of the wide car. One drove. The other two had weapons, rifles she guessed, held upright between their legs. She recognized the man next to the window as the guard who had been in the lobby. She turned to look out the back window. A following car full of men. There was a flashing blue light on top. Only then did she realize their car had one, too.

"I figure about ten minutes. Try to relax."

She glanced at him, saw his face in headlights from approaching cars. He seemed unperturbed. He wasn't even looking at the highway. Was he Parsley? Couldn't be. He knew—and yet. Something was wrong. She could feel it. Her mind leaped from indecision to fact. He knew where David was. David was in danger. But how? "Who left you the message?"

"I have no idea."

"Could it have been P—" His hand came sharply toward her to silence her.

"Freddie, the men in the front all have security clearances, but there are still some things even they don't want to know. Understand? We'll have a chance to talk later."

She understood. Need to Know. Just thinking with her mouth anyway. Had to be Parsley who sent the message. But how did he know? And what did it mean? David was out there waiting for her to bring this man, address 752. *Green as in Parsley?* Then the two of them were going to— She shook her head. "David had a plan, Mr. Green. He was—"

"It doesn't matter, Freddie. It's all fouled up."

"Somebody found out where he is. But how?"

"I don't know."

"Do you think they got there first and—"

"Don't think about it. We'll know soon."

Panic rose in her. "Oh, God, it's all my fault. I should have—"

"Yes. You should have come to me from the airport. You should have trusted me." He spoke to the driver. "Isn't Old Fence Road south of—"

"Yessir, we'll be there soon."

Freddie felt physically ill with worry. David had set a trap only to be trapped himself. Oh, God! How did it happen?

"Is that the road?"

"Yessir. I'm turning now."

"I think it's the third or fourth—"

"I know where it is, sir."

Freddie was forward on the edge of her seat, body rigid, staring ahead as the car turned into the lane. Her eyes scanned everything illuminated by the headlights, trees, weeds growing in the lane, bushes, the edge of a stone house.

"There, sir."

"Stop here."

She saw it, too. "Oh, God!" Her hand flew for the door handle.

"Wait, Freddie." He grabbed her right wrist. "Let the men do it."

Trembling all over, unaware of breath, she watched the three men in front get out, rifles at the ready. Other men, running past their car, headed for the house now lighted by spotlights. Then she saw other uniformed men emerge from behind the house, conferring with those from the car.

"We'll know in a second, Freddie."

Almost catatonic, she watched the three who had been in the front seat walk forward, bend over, touch the body. She saw a head shake. They moved to their left, bent over again.

One of the men, the driver, walked back toward the car. It seemed to take forever. He leaned inside. "Two dead, sir."

Oh God! Freddie tore her hand loose and bolted from the car.

"Stop her!"

A hand grabbed at her but she pushed it away and ran forward, stopped, looked down. A sob escaped her. The body lay on its back, the chest and neck a mass of blood. Hideous. "It's—" Her breath came in short gasps. "It's not . . . him."

"There's another body, Freddie."

She looked at Green, nodded. He turned her and, hand at her elbow, led her three steps to the left. A crumpled body near the side of the house.

"Turn him over, Sergeant, so we can see the face."

Freddie watched as the body was turned. An arm flopped, then a leg. It might have been a rag doll.

"Give us a little light here, please."

She watched the flashlight illuminate features. The single bullet had hit right between the eyes, passing upward through the top of the skull. The face was covered with blood. She turned away to lay her head against Green's shoulder. His arms came around her. Tears came now.

"It was an ambush, sir. Spent shells upstairs. No sign of perpetrators."

"Thank you, Lieutenant. I want to take the second car. Can all of you—"

"Yessir. We'll be here awhile."

"You know what to do. No traces. Take the bodies to—"

"I know, sir."

Freddie felt herself being led away, placed in a car. Green came around to sit behind the wheel. "Do you know where he's gone?"

She sat slumped in the seat, head down.

"Freddie, the first man you looked at was Boggs, my assistant. He received the message that Sloane was here. Since I was out of the office—waiting for you—he came here and walked into the trap. I don't know who the second man is. He obviously fell from the second-floor window when shot. By Sloane no doubt."

She raised her head, looked at him. *Green as in Parsley?*

"I told you. I selected him, trained him. It was

my special program. Only twenty men. Sloane is the sole survivor. And he is *alive*, Freddie. Boggs's car should be there. It isn't. Sloane must have gotten in it. But there was a lot of gunfire. He may be wounded. We have to hurry. What was Sloane's plan?"

She felt paralyzed by indecision. She could only look at him.

"You were to go to Brandywine and bring me, weren't you?"

No reply.

"You were to drop me off and leave. He wouldn't want you at risk. Where were you to meet?"

Only silence.

"Freddie, you have to trust somebody sometime. Do it now. His life may depend upon it. Where were you to meet Sloane?"

She sighed. His life, yes. Their life. "I have no choice, do I? Drive. I'll take you there."

FOURTEEN

Sloane was grateful for the pain. It was all that kept him going. The bullet had shattered his left forearm. It was both useless and excruciating, but it called forth the dregs of his adrenaline, overriding his vertigo and fatigue. He could think, and he knew his life and Freddie's depended on his doing that right now. Had to.

Who had come? He remembered the face through the nightscope. Didn't know it. Never saw it. *Think, dammit. Work it through.* Aloud he said, "You set a trap for Parsley, then walked into one of theirs." A sharp pain shot through him and he grimaced. "Good pain, real good. They were upstairs waiting for you. Who's they? Doesn't matter. Musta had a nightscope. Had to have seen you ... yet waited till ... the car came. Wanted both. Yes. Had to be. Who?" *Not Parsley.* "Wouldn't have walked into his own trap."

Work it through. Car came. Lights on. No Freddie. Unarmed. Hands up. Ms. Falscape. Knew her name. She's where you sent her. Called me sir. Yes. Had to have come from Brandywine. Yes. But who? Not Parsley. Who? Owed his life to him—or what was left of it. Took most of the bullets, all but one that hit his arm. Made a shield. Sloane remembered dragging the body, firing upward, wildly, one-handed, squeezing off rounds till he reached the car.

Think, dammit. Called me sir. Small fry. Nobody on The Committee or even close to it ever called a field man sir. The bastards. Square one. Parsley still alive. No contact with 752. And where was Freddie? *Fuck it.*

He pulled into a closed gas station and got out. Had to do something about the arm. As quickly as he could, he slipped out of the fatigue jacket and looked at the arm. Bleeding like a stuck pig. Couldn't take much of that. Survival training came back to him and he pulled the web belt from his pants, wrapping it snugly around his upper arm as a makeshift tourniquet. Then he found a rag under the front seat to wrap around the forearm. The fatigue jacket, buttoned up, made do as a sling. Practically like new. "Think, you shit. Think for your life." He stood there a moment, looking back up the road he'd just traveled, as though it offered answers. Then he looked the other way. Two blocks down was the main drag of Upper Marlboro. Yes. It had to work. It was his only chance.

He climbed back into the car, but left the door open for light as he rummaged in the glove compartment, discarding maps, other unwanted items. There. He opened the envelope. Registration. Darryl Boggs. Who the hell was Darryl Boggs? No matter. He searched out his ball-point pen and began to write across the face of the car registration. 752. The writing was ragged. His hand was shaking. He hesitated. "Go on." Couldn't think. "Goddamn you, remember! Harry'd never forget a thing like that." It came then. Only took a minute, then he drove off, letting the forward motion of the car shut the door. He turned right on Main Street, drove a couple of blocks till he came to a red light, stopped, put the car in park and got out. Above him he saw the light changing to green and heard the car behind him honk. Sloane waved as he walked toward the curb. Now all he needed was a cab—and a phone. He was sure he could remember the number of the Capital-Hilton.

Freddie was surprised at her own reaction. Her sense of herself said she should have been overjoyed not to find David dead. But her tears and trembling had been genuine. Relief, most likely. David alive! *Thank you, God, thank you, thank you. I'll go to church every Sunday. Won't miss one.*

"You have to give me directions."

"I know. Drive into Upper Marlboro."

She glanced at him, pursing her lips. *Green as in Parsley?* Silly, didn't mean a thing, yet she had such a sense he was Parsley. "What is David Sloane's real name?"

He sighed. "I honestly don't remember, Freddie. That information is deeply hidden. It isn't even in his working file. And you should want it that way. When this is over and he is retired, he will go back to that name. You don't want everyone knowing it—most especially the KGB."

She nodded. Made sense. Everything he said made sense. And yet ... There was something about him.

"Freddie—"

That was part of it. How easily he had slipped into the familiar. She hadn't given him permission to call her that.

"I don't know how much Sloane has told you. Not too much I hope. When your name was learned, a very thorough check was done on you. There is nothing in your life to indicate you shouldn't receive a security clearance—perhaps even a high one. But the fact remains you don't now have one, and that is a problem. What do you know about what's at Brandywine?"

"I was asked that during my interrogation. David told me to go to the building, approach the guard, ask for Parsley. He applied Need to Know. I was told only what I needed to know to—"

"Which is probably way too much. Who do you think Parsley is?"

"A Soviet mole on The Committee."

He sighed, deeply. "Clearly, I'm going to have to do something about getting you a security clearance. I have to ask. Have you told anyone about all this?"

"No."

"Your mother, father, a friend—at Calvert College perhaps?"

"How could I? I've disappeared for two months. I'm sure my folks are worried sick—and well should be."

"Have you written anything down—a diary, perhaps, a journal?"

"No. Why are you asking all these questions?"

"I think you know. All this is going to have to be hushed up. Not one syllable can ever be known."

"Most especially how The Committee uses codes to hoodwink the White House, Pentagon, Congress. Right?"

"I wish you didn't know that."

She heard the hard edge to his voice. "You have nothing to fear. As David says, no one will ever believe it. People don't want to—can't bring themselves to. Turn right here."

He did. "Whatever you might think of our methods, we are not bad people, Freddie."

"Please don't call me Freddie. I don't know you and I don't trust you."

"But you are taking me to where you are to meet Sloane?"

"I don't know. You talk so much I can't think."

It was true. She didn't know what to do. Should she just drive him around, give David a chance to—to what? If only she knew what had happened. Was he all right? He could be wounded again. Oh, Lord, he'd never survive. He could be lying somewhere right now, dying, half dead, maybe already— *Don't think about it*. They were to meet at a motel, edge of town, Room 34. But that was after he had— And none of that had happened. Parsley was alive, maybe driving this car. The witness, address 752, was—where? Maybe driving this car, maybe—

She saw blinking lights ahead in the middle of the street. They slowed to pass. Police car, tow truck.

"Do I keep on going straight?"

"Yes."

What purpose would be served by driving around? Just delay. David had wanted her to bring this man, whether he was Parsley or not. Just a different location, that's all. Same result. And if David doesn't show up. *Don't think about it. Yes, my darling, good advice.*

A few blocks later she said, "Turn into that motel." He did. The big car moved slowly past the neon vacancy sign. "Room 34. I don't know where it is." She found it, around to the back, the quiet side, away from the street, ground floor. The car pulled in front. The headlight illuminated the gold numbers on the door, then were turned off. Room 34 was dark, no sign of life. "Well, Mr. Green as in Parsley, shall we go in?" They stood before the door. "Have you got a gun or something?"

"Don't be silly."

"That's not silly. If he's in there he may well shoot you and ask questions later."

"He won't. Do you have the key?"

"Should be unlocked." Her hand found the knob. It was. She twisted, pushed, opening the door just enough for her to enter. Dark inside.

Her fingers groped for the light switch to the left of the door, found it, flicked. It was a single-occupancy room, desk and chair, lamp, nightstand, bed against the far wall. She stepped within, the knuckles of her hand white as she gripped the doorknob. David Sloane was sitting on the edge of the bed, weapon in his right hand. He used it to motion her to step aside. She obeyed, then turned toward the doorway. "You may come in now, Mr. Green as in Parsley." Without willing it, she inwardly braced for the muzzle blast.

"You're a hard man to find, Wolf. But then you may be the best there ever was."

Sloane didn't know what he expected—probably not this man, so calm, smiling, uttering those words. "Thank you."

"Oh, God, David, you look ghastly." She ran to him. His eyes were bright, glazed. She had seen it before. He was ready to pass out—might be already. She saw the empty sleeve, blood stains. "You're wounded again."

He glanced at her, sharply, briefly. So beautiful. He felt relieved. "You okay?"

"Yes, I'm fine—but you . . ." She unbuttoned his fatigue jacket. "Oh, God, your arm!"

"Nicked. Having bad luck with it."

The wound was awful. "How long has that tourniquet been on?"

"Dunno." He was glad to see her, know she was safe, but he wished she weren't there. "Take his gun, Freddie."

She reached for his arm. "Got to loosen that tourniquet. You'll lose the arm."

"*Dammit, do as I say!* Take his weapon."

She was torn a moment, then went to Green. She hesitated again. What was she supposed to do, pat him down like in the movies? He surprised her by opening his coat to reveal the weapon at his shoulder. She took it from him. "He says his name is Green."

Sloane looked at him—or tried to. His vision was fading in and out as he struggled for consciousness. No, didn't know him. "Name means nothing to me."

"I assure you I know you. David Sloane."

"You know that name?"

"He knows Harry's name, too—the messages I sent. He knows a lot, David, but I don't trust him."

"You shouldn't."

"Sloane, you're half dead. Let me use the phone, call an ambulance."

Sloane made a sharp movement with his Walther. "No. And don't move. Freddie, move away from him. Come here. Loosen the—" A sharp pain made him grimace. "Loosen the . . . damn tourniquet."

She came, fumbled with the belt. "Oh, David, what're we going to do?"

"Wait."

"Sloane, you're going to lose that arm—at the very least. You may die. Can't you accept the fact I'm trying to help you?"

"No."

"I've been trying to find you for two months, bring you in. I want Parsley as bad as you do."

"Couldn't he be telling the truth?"

"She's right, Sloane. Listen to her."

Too many voices, too much confusion. "How did—" He lost the thought. All he wanted to do was fall back against the bed, let it all go. Couldn't. Had to—

"Your arm! My God." She had unwrapped the rag, saw the terrible wound, splintered pieces of bone. Nausea rose in her. "You gotta have—" She went to the phone, snatched it up.

"No, Freddie. I'm all right."

"No, David, you're—"

"I know what I'm doing, Freddie. This won't—take long. Then you can—phone."

She sighed, replaced the receiver. "All right." She returned to him. Maybe if she tried loosening the tourniquet.

"You've been stupid all the way along, Sloane. You've violated every method there is. It's over. You're in now. Let me help you."

Sloane looked at him, blinking, trying to keep him in focus. "How'd you"—again he lost the thought, then recovered it—"know where to come?"

"What're you talking about?"

"That farm." He shook his head. "I forget . . . the name."

Freddie helped him. "The Hedges place."

"I received a message saying you were there."

"That's what he told me, David. He said he was out waiting for me to be brought from the airport. When he got back there was a message."

"Be *quiet*, Freddie. I can't think."

"Yes, I'm sorry." Slowly she released the belt, watching the flow of blood in the wound. It seeped. No major artery, thank God. She snugged the belt back against the arm, watching the blood flow. Had to let some blood into the arm, yet not have him bleed to death.

"Take his gun, Freddie. Go stand in the corner—the one to his right. Keep the weapon on him."

"But you need—"

"Stop arguing. Do as I say." He kept his concentration on Green, yet was aware she obeyed, held the gun. "She can use it."

"Yes, I killed Fox."

"It figures. Only a woman would empty a gun into a man at short range."

"Take three steps forward, Green—away from the door. Turn around to face Freddie."

"What's the point to all—"

"Do as I say." Sloane watched him move. "Who did the message come from?"

"I don't know. I told you. I was out waiting for Freddie—"

"I'm Dr. Falscape to you, dammit."

"Be quiet, Freddie. Go on. Who was the message from?"

"I don't know. I was out. Boggs took the message, acted on his own."

"I see. Higher authority. Someone on The Committee."

"I suppose. Could be."

Sloane tried to laugh, but it came out as a croaking sound, then led to a cough. "I know ... who"—another cough—"the message ... came from."

Freddie gasped. "You do?"

"Good, then who is it? Let's stop all this—"

"Yes, David, if you know, let's—"

"*Listen!*" He strained his hearing. Car engine. Door closing. Had to be him. Had to work.

Freddie gasped as the door opened, instinctively turned to it. The weapon she held in both hands followed. The man didn't see her, but registered David, then reacted sharply to Green. "So it's you, White."

"Did you come alone?"

Adams looked at Sloane. "That's what you said to do—although I feel like a damn fool."

"Who is that guy? What's he doing here."

Sloane managed a smile. "Very good, Green or White or whoever you are. But I think you know him. Three more and we can have a meeting of The Committee."

"Will you *please* tell me what's going on, David?"

"Simple, Freddie. I had Boggs's car. I knew they'd go for it to find me. I made it easy to find. I left it—"

"In the middle of Main Street. I saw it."

"He left me a note." Adams turned to Freddie. "It was in his cypher, the one you sent from Spain. It was addressed to 752 so only I could read it. It told me to come here and come alone." He turned back to Sloane. "Very good, Sloane. I'll take over now."

"*Not on your life.*"

Adams was surprised. His eyes showed it. "But—"

"That you're 752, can read my cypher doesn't mean a thing. You can be Parsley just as well as this guy here."

"And that's exactly who he is. I thank you, Sloane."

Adams glanced at White. "Very clever, Mr.—or should I say Parsley? Only trouble is Sloane and I—" He looked at David. "We've met. Do you remember?"

Sloane nodded. "Yes. The 'graduation exercises.' You were the man in the Space Three with the stacks of papers, nice little goodies that trapped Harry and me."

"Yes."

"It doesn't prove a thing." He shook his head, trying to clear it. Had to hold on—just a bit longer. "So it looks ... like we have two Parsleys, Freddie."

"But which one?"

Sloane motioned to Adams with his weapon. "Ever so slowly toss your weapon over there—on the chair. I said *slowly*. I'd happily kill you—you bastard."

Adams obeyed, shaking his head slowly. "Is there no way to convince you, Sloane?"

"I fear not."

"Yes, there is." Freddie's voice was bright, excited. She looked at Adams. "What is David's real name? No, there's a better way. A man was sent to find us in Munich. What was his name?"

Adams sighed with relief. Bright girl. "David's real name is Pritchard. The man in Munich was Bob Arthur. He and David had been classmates at Pensacola. I sent him."

"What was Arthur's real name?"

"Duane Forbes."

She stared at him. How wonderful. So simple. "This one's not Parsley, David. I knew it all along."

"Think, Freddie. The Committee has access to all information."

"You're wrong, Sloane," Adams said. "I keep my files locked, totally secure."

"You mean *my* files," White insisted. "I locked them only after you broke into the computer."

Adams glared at him. "Very clever, Mr. White."

"I know the first one's Parsley, David. I can feel it. I'm sure."

"What do you want me to do? Shoot him?"

She saw his gun barrel swinging to the left. "No, David, don't! You can—"

"I know. What time is it?"

She glanced at her watch. "Two-ten." She saw him nod approval. He looked ghastly, pale, glassy-eyed. He was weaving, barely able to sit upright. "Please, let me call an ambulance. You're—"

"Yes, do it. I've about had it."

His words surprised her and she rushed to the phone.

"Gentlemen, one of you is Parsley. I don't know which and I don't care." He stopped, panting. Just speaking took all his strength. "I should ... I know. Parsley killed Harry, so many ... good men. And ... for what? I should ... kill ... you both." He raised the Walther, moved it from one to the other. "But I'm tired ... tired of the game. I do no ... no more for ... Mother—not even ... kill." He made a motion with the gun barrel. "Go ... out the door ... both of you."

Freddie had the operator on the phone. Now she held the phone away from her face. "What're you doing, David?"

"Letting 'em go."

"You can't! One of them is Parsley."

"Then you shoot 'em."

"Sloane, listen to me." Adams made a step toward the bed but was stopped by the leveled weapon in Freddie's hand.

"He's right. Both of us have killed enough. And for what purpose? To play a game—which begets another game and another. Yes, go. One of you is Parsley. Settle it between yourselves. Kill each other. Just leave us *alone*." Tears welled into her eyes. "We love each other. All we want is to be ... be left alone. We've done enough."

Adams studied her a moment. "Yes, you're right. You've done enough. May I say what a remarkable woman you are?" He turned. "Shall we go, Mr. White—settle this between ourselves?"

Parsley was delighted. It was more than he could possibly hope for—a chance to walk out of there. The plan was already formed. Green was no match for him physically. One blow, then he could ...

To Freddie they looked like two cock roosters, sparring, looking for an opening. "Go! Just leave!" She headed for the door to open it.

"No, Freddie. Stay with me. Get the ambulance."

"Yes, we'll leave." Parsley bowed toward Adams. "After you."

Adams would have preferred the reverse order, but knew, with the guns still on them, Parsley would try nothing till they were outside. He went to the door, opened it wide, stepped out into the sultry night air. Quickly he stepped to the side to let Parsley come out. But Parsley stopped in the lighted doorway, looking straight ahead, gaping really. His mouth came open.

"No!"

Adams turned to follow Parsley's gaze, saw the car, its occupant, the bright muzzle blast, then heard Freddie scream from within the motel room as Parsley's body fell inside, spurting blood.

FIFTEEN

Sloane was in surgery almost eight hours and Freddie remained at the hospital throughout, nervously pacing the hospital corridor, drinking too many cups of very bad coffee. It was just before noon when the surgeon, still wearing his greens from the OR, came to her. He was in his early fifties, stocky, a bit rotund, and said his name was Lowenthal, orthopedics. What she really noticed about him was that he was somber, deadly serious. That scared her.

"You're a friend of Lt. Sloane?"

That surprised her. She never thought of David as being in the military. "Yes, I'm Fern Falscape. How is he?" She almost hated to ask.

Dr. Lowenthal shook his head. It seemed a ponderous act. "We got the bullet out, Ms. Falscape. Nasty. Lodged near his liver. Roaring infection. You got him here just in time."

"Will he be all right?"

He studied her. "You look exhausted."

"I'm all right. Please, tell me about David."

More hesitation. "How technical do you want me to be?"

"Not very—*please*."

"All right. He's on antibotics now. I guess you don't care which ones. It will take a few days, but we should be able to knock the infection out of him."

"Thank God! What about his arm?"

Lowenthal shook his head. "That's a problem. Did you know he was wounded twice—the shoulder and his forearm? One is an older wound."

"I know. Is he going to lose the arm?" She was almost afraid to ask.

"We had to reset the clavicle—that's his collarbone."

"I know."

"Then the scapula, the shoulder bone, was not healing properly. We had to rebreak and put that back together. He's going to have a lot of discomfort there. He'll be out of action for a while—so to speak."

"What about the forearm?" His reply was another spate of head-shaking. Freddie thought he'd make a marvelous undertaker. "Could you save it?"

"He lost a lot of bone. There was damage to blood vessels. We had to do a lot of reconstructive work. We used a technique called—"

"Please, just tell me if he's going to be all right."

"He's going to need another operation in a few weeks or months to—"

"You saved the arm?"

"The bone should mend. We patched up the blood vessels. If there isn't too much nerve damage—" Finally he smiled. "To answer your question, I think it reasonable to expect ninety percent use of the arm—with luck, maybe full recovery. We can really do a lot with these things nowadays."

Tears came to her eyes. "Can I see him?"

"He's in recovery and will be for a while."

"I'll wait."

"Ms. Falscape, he's going to be out of it, at least until tomorrow. There's nothing you can do.

I suggest you go home, get some rest. You look very tired."

Her impulse was to argue, then she wavered. "I'm sure you're right. I am tired. When will he be able to—"

"Not before tomorrow afternoon." He touched her arm. "Why don't you come back then? I'm sure he'll be glad to see you."

She thought about checking into a hotel, then decided to go home, splurging on a taxi all the way to Calvert College. Her car would be in the garage. Hopefully it would run. During the hour's drive, she had the complete, deluxe walking tour of the pits. *Over here, Miss Falscape, is the Marquis de Sade room. You'll adore it. Notice the decor. It gives the effect of dripping blood and those white specks do resemble human—* It was the letdown, she knew. David was going to be all right. She should be happy. But what fun was that? *Continue with the tour, gentlemen. I haven't seen the dungeons yet.*

She hoped entering her own house would cheer her up. It didn't. The place seemed ghostly, almost historic, a sort of Mount Vernon of her misspent youth. *In this very room Fern Falscape— her friends called her Freddie, you know—used to entertain students, fellow faculty members. They were happy, carefree times before—stop it!*

She did it in the only way she knew, throwing herself into a flurry of activity, opening up the house and attacking the accumulated dust as though it were the Polish Army and she were Erwin Rommel. Late in the afternoon—the car started, bless it—she went to the supermarket and lavishly invested the KGB's money in groceries and potables, returned home and made enough coq au vin to feed four. She ate the whole thing, topped it off with the rest of the bottle of wine—*Freddie Falscape, wino*—then slept like a baby.

When she arrived at the hospital the next day he was sitting up in a chair beside the bed, which surprised her. His left arm, shoulder, and chest were encased in a body cast and he was still hooked to the IV, but otherwise he looked not bad, more clear-eyed and with decent color. Her eyes filled with tears and she didn't know what to say.

For Sloane she was imponderably gorgeous, pale blue dress, a trifle frilly, heels. She had nice calves in heels. There was a lump in his throat and he really didn't know what to do about it.

Finally she could smile, a rather watery one. "Does it itch?"

And he could say, despite the constriction, "Not yet."

"Oh, David." She ran to him, held his head against her breast, then kissed him. His temperature was down. "I hear you may get to enter the Olympics yet."

"So it seems."

She was sitting beside him, holding his good hand, talking when Adams came in. She looked up at him, uncertain about her reaction to him.

"May I join you a moment?"

Sloane nodded and watched him sit on the edge of the bed.

"I have come to offer you a deal which hopefully you cannot refuse."

"Which is?" Sloane felt hostile, wary. Couldn't help it.

"We will of course take care of all expenses here at the hospital and any other treatment you may require. You will also receive accumulated back pay, expenses, etc. It should be a tidy sum."

"That's the deal?"

"Only part of it. You will be permitted to retire—I mean really retire—live whatever kind of life you wish." He smiled. "I should imagine Dr. Falscape may have some role in that."

Sloane was not about to be conned. "What's the catch?"

"A simple one. Silence. None of this ever happened, not last night—I mean the night before last, not anything in the last two months. You were in the Navy. You never worked for the Agency. Most importantly, you don't know me. Never saw me."

Sloane looked at him a moment, really looked, his eyes squinting in concentration. Then he said, "Is that all?"

"All—the very all. You are free as of this moment. I don't even want you debriefed."

Still Sloane eyed him. Then he nodded, just once. "Agreed."

"Well I *don't*." Freddie stood up. She was angry, defiant. "I didn't go through all this just to"—she was so angry she was flustered—"just to ... to declare it ... it *never* happened."

Sloane looked up at her. "What're you going to do? Write a book?"

"Maybe, I don't know. But I do know I'm very upset about what is going on—a US government agency covering up—you're doing it right now—concealing information, manipulating the White House, Congress, the ... the *whole* government ... the *whole* world."

Adams looked at her. "You are a free citizen, Dr. Falscape. You have a faculty position. You are free to teach whatever you wish."

She stared at him, then rendered a snorting sound. "I get it. Nobody'll believe me. Is that what you're counting on?"

"You may find difficulty in proving such allegations."

"Or proving any of this happened. *Oh, God!*" She looked at Sloane, then at Adams. Their eyes were bland, noncommittal. And she knew why. "A silly female tilting at windmills. Is that it? I can't prove anything, can I?"

"Duane Forbes died in a plane crash in Virginia. The man you knew as Fox—and what was his real name, Dr. Falscape?—was victim of a still unsolved Mafia execution. Police are hoping to identify the man found in the motel room night before last. They aren't having much luck."

She studied Adams, that damnably bland face, then slowly sat back down. "I get it." She turned to Sloane. "May I say I'm disappointed in you?"

He reached out and took her hand. "I know you are, Freddie. But I have to end the game. There's only one other way."

Tears came to her eyes. "I know." She bit at her lip. "I want an end, too. And I want you." She looked at Adams. "May I at least know what happened? Was that other man Parsley?"

"Yes. I knew him as Mr. White."

"Who killed him?"

"Haven't you figured it out, Freddie?"

"No, Just a dummy, I guess."

"Hardly." He looked at Adams. "May I tell her?" His shrug suggested he could do as he pleased. "Freddie, back in Munich in the drycleaning shop, Yuri Khruchenko told Harry and me that they contacted Parsley through news items. He particularly mentioned use of gossip columns. It was the only way I knew to reach Parsley. The best-known gossip column is "Washington Off Guard," written under the pen name Curtis Eustace."

"I know that. Curtis Eustace is a woman named Evelyn Cushman. You went to see her, planted your phony item about a restaurant named Parsley."

"Curtis Eustace—or Evelyn Cushman—all famous Virginia names—was a rather flamboyant woman, built, rather blatantly sexy. She appeared to be rather dumb, even stupid, terribly gushy, but I suspected it was an act. I've told you about appearances, Freddie."

"Did she come on to you?"

"Yes."

"Please," Adams interrupted.

Sloane looked at him, saw the expression in his eyes. "I'm sorry. I am thoughtless. Did you do what you had to?"

"It is taken care of."

Freddie shook her head. "What are you two talking about? I'm still back with the sexy columnist coming on to you."

"It made no sense, Freddie. Oh, it did—but only when I realized she was hardly hot for my society. She's really nympho if she tries to make out with every guy who walks into her office spouting an ersatz British accent." Again he looked at Adams, shaking his head to say it couldn't be helped.

Freddie gasped. "You think she knew who you were?"

"Yes. As soon as I handed her the Parsley item for the paper she had no doubt. She wanted to introduce me around—which meant *keep* me around. I got out of it, but agreed to be shown around the next night."

"I get it. She was—"

"I didn't. The fever, I guess. Jellied my brains. Never would have gone near that farmhouse if I had. But—" He rendered an elaborate shrug, a gesture indicating his folly. "Even when Boggs showed up alone I still couldn't figure it out."

Freddie shook her head. "Now I'm confused again."

"I think I can explain, Dr. Falscape."

"You may call me Freddie—I think." She gave him a quizzical look.

Adams did not react. "Parsley and I played a cat-and-mouse game. He knew I suspected a mole and was withholding information, hoping to recover Sloane—and you—to identify him. But he also knew I didn't know who he was. Therefore, all he had to do was eliminate Sloane, you and me. Then he was home free."

"I still don't understand how—"

"Parsley's mistake was the usual one, Freddie—appearances. He saw Curtis Eustace only as a dumb broad, a conduit for coded messages. It didn't occur to him that she was KGB. He thought his contact was some unknown person in the Soviet Embassy, or wherever. He simply never realized Eustace-Cushman was his contact."

"Did she know him?"

"No. He was too careful to blow his cover to anyone. His messages all reached her roundabout, though the grapevine as gossip. But she did know there was a mole named Parsley on The Committee."

"Supposing such a group does exist."

Sloane grinned at Adams. "Yes, supposing." To Freddie he said, "Got it figured out, or shall I go on?"

"Better go on."

"I laid my trap—dumb trap—at the farmhouse. You were supposed to bring someone from Brandywine. I figured it would be—" He turned to Adams. "What do I call you?"

"Mr. Green. I really am Green."

"Freddie was to bring you. I figured Parsley would read the newspaper and show up later. I'd have Parsley and a witness."

"I know that."

"But there were at least two other plans, Freddie—maybe three, if I count yours, Green. The first was Eustace-Cushman's. She had orders to eliminate Parsley. Dzerzhinsky Square now realized he was a liability, and Khruchenko was right in believing him a menace. If he were identified and shot full of chemicals, he would be at least an embarrassment and maybe blow the whistle on a lot of their operations. When I showed up, Eustace-Cushman saw her chance.

She got a message to Parsley—somehow. I don't know, maybe a letter drop."

"Yes, a letter drop. We have identified it."

"She simply told Parsley to go to the farmhouse. She had now set a trap inside my trap. She had people—KGB most likely—"

"Yes, they were."

"—on the second floor. They had to have nightscopes, which means they had to have seen me. Yet they didn't shoot. They were to wait—for Parsley—then get us both at once. Eustace-Cushman wanted both Parsley and me."

"But Parsley didn't show."

Sloane nodded at her. "You got it. Parsley survived so long by never taking chances. He did what he could within the Agency and never tried for more. More importantly, he *never* showed himself to anyone. Eustace-Cushman didn't know this and that was her mistake. Parsley used the information she gave him about the farmhouse to set his own trap—for Green and me."

"I can explain. White was head of the North Am— Let's say he was in a position to claim he had located Sloane and he was hiding out at the farmhouse. He left a message to that effect for me. I'm sure he knew I was out of the office. As a matter of fact I was sitting in a car in front of your house waiting for you to be brought from the airport."

"Yes, he knew that. He said it in the car. He almost had me convinced he was you. He seemed to know so much." She bit at her lip. "What I don't understand is what he was planning to do when he got you there, Mr. Green."

"He had time. There was no hurry. He knew it would take me a while to get to the farm. My guess is that he planned an ambush much like the one already in place—only he would use our Agency people."

"Yes. There were men already there when I arrived with Parsley."

Sloane nodded. "But Parsley's plan was fouled up when your assistant—what's his name?"

"Boggs. He couldn't raise me. I was at dinner. He took it upon himself to go talk to you."

"And the KGB saw a man and—" She grimaced. "Must have been awful."

"Yes, I was lucky. Boggs took most of the rounds, allowing me to escape."

"It was foolish of Boggs. He had no field experience." Adams shrugged. "But . . ."

"He wanted to play spy."

"I'm having a commendation put in his record."

"I'm sure he'd be pleased." Sloane's voice ladled sarcasm.

"David, you said Parsley never revealed himself. Yet he came to me at Brandywine."

"Yes, and it probably was a mistake. If he hadn't, he'd be alive and we'd all be sitting here wondering who Parsley is."

"Why did he?"

"Hard to figure. Chances are he knew about the shooting out at the farm."

"Yes," Adams said. "It was on police radio. A farmer in the neighborhood reported it."

"The man with the yapping dog. Parsley wanted to see the results of his trap, be certain Green and I were dead, then he'd dispose of you somewhere. Besides, he probably felt confident he could convince you he was Green."

"He almost did."

"Then when he got there, found the men he'd sent, saw the dead man was Boggs, not Green . . . I don't know whether he knew me or not."

"I never said it wasn't you. He seemed to know."

"Maybe guessing or bluffing. In any event he had to make a sudden switch in plans. He knew I'd have a back-up rendezvous. He got you to take him there."

"I still don't know who killed Parsley. The woman columnist? But I don't see how she knew where—"

"My busted arm seemed to knock some sense into my skull. I realized that female had to have set a trap for me—and Parsley. When you didn't show up in the car and Boggs said you were back at Brandywine, I knew the bullets had to have been intended for Parsley. There was no way to know what had really happened or what was going on, but I saw a chance and took it. It figured, Freddie, that if you possibly could you'd come to the motel, our back-up rendezvous. It also figured that somebody—I didn't know who—would go after Boggs's car. So I made it easy to find on Main Street and left a message—"

"In your private cypher telling me where to go."

"Why did you come alone?"

"Because I trusted you." Adams rendered a wan smile. "And I hardly wanted the whole world to know about this operation."

"So you knew the man I brought was Parsley, and Mr. Green here—"

"No, Freddie. I honestly didn't know who was Parsley."

"I did—and I was right."

"But you could just as easily have been wrong. There was only one way to prove it—let them walk out the door together. The timing was iffy, but I figured she had enough time to get there—or send somebody."

"You phoned her?"

"Yes, Green. She'd told me she would be at a party at the Capital-Hilton—invited me, in fact. It would have been my last party ever, I'm sure. I phoned her there. I told her my boss from England, the big wheel in the Parsley restaurant chain, wanted to meet her and where we were staying. . . ." He let his voice trail off. "Let's say she was surprised to hear from me. I was supposed to be dead, Parsley, too."

"David, you mean to say you sent Parsley out, knowing he would be killed?"

"As far as I was concerned they were both dead men. I didn't much care." He leveled hard, cold eyes on Adams.

"How did you know about Evie?"

"I didn't—or better said, I figured wrong. When I sent the message, *Parsley I have your name*, it wasn't entirely a bluff. There just had to be some connection between the gossip column and Parsley. It was too iffy an arrangement. How could anyone be sure she'd print a given item? And if you were the Russkies would you trust such an arrangement? I just had to believe she was related to or sleeping with somebody who could verify at least some of the stuff. I thought it was Parsley."

"When did you know she was my wife?"

"Not until you walked out the door."

"Your *wife*!"

"Yes, Freddie. She knew Green, knew he wasn't Parsley. She let him walk out. The man behind him had to be Parsley."

Adams looked forlorn. "I never told her anything, Sloane."

"You didn't have to. Your movements, your presence or absence, whether or not you got phone calls, dozens of little things added to what she knew from Parsley's messages and KGB orders, and gave her a virtually complete picture, didn't it? You did say you've taken care of her, didn't you?"

"Yes. It would have been nice to keep her in place, feed her misinformation, but—" He sighed. "An impossible situation, really." He looked at Freddie, then Sloane, as though seeking approval. "She's already filled up several tapes. Highly useful information, I'm sure."

"You don't know?"

"I turned it over to others on—to people I know. I've resigned."

Suddenly Freddie felt sorry for him. "You mean your wife was—"

"Yes, Dr. Falscape. Parsley was valuable, but I may have been more so—however inadvertently and unintended."

Sloane grinned. "Maybe you guys should emulate the KGB. They handpick wives from within the organization."

Adams managed a smile. "I fear it would never work in the US. But it is a weakness—obviously." He stood up. "I must be going. Lots of last-minute things to do. I wish you both"—he hesitated over the sentiment—"good lives—and long ones."

Freddie watched him head for the door. "Mr. Green, are we safe? Doesn't the KGB still want us—for what we know?"

Adams turned. "You didn't have any visitors last night, did you?"

"No, but it still seems to me that—"

"Sloane can explain it to you. I'll just add that you ought to understand why I urge silence. The KGB wants this—this *embarrassing* episode ended as much as we do. As long as it never gets out"—he shrugged—"everyone is content."

She shook her head in disbelief. "You sound like you're on the same side—putting the Agency's interests ahead of the good of the country, both countries. Is it a case of anything for the game?"

Adams looked at her, then Sloane. "You've got a very good woman there, my friend. Take care of her."